SAFE HARBOUR

Also by Janice Graham

Firebird
Sarah's Window

SAFE HARBOUR

JANICE GRAHAM

A *Time Warner* Book

First published in Great Britain in 2003
by Time Warner Books

Copyright © Janice Graham 2003

The moral right of the author has been asserted.

A CIP catalogue record for this book
is available from the British Library.

HARDBACK ISBN 0 316 72602 8
C-FORMAT ISBN 0 316 86089 1

Typeset by Palimpsest Book Production Limited,
Polmont, Stirlingshire
Printed and bound in Great Britain by
Mackays of Chatham plc, Chatham, Kent

Time Warner Books UK
Brettenham House
Lancaster Place
London WC2E 7EN

www.TimeWarnerBooks.co.uk

A Nicolas, mon cher et constant ami

AUTHOR'S NOTE

Although St John's was indeed inspired by the American Cathedral of the Holy Trinity in Paris, both St John's and the King George Hotel are entirely fictitious settings inhabited by purely fictitious characters. If anything, I hope the story and its characters reflect my deep affection for the cathedral and my many friends there. I am particularly grateful to Dean Ernie Hunt who so graciously took the time to answer my many questions; I would also like to thank Miia, Joanne Dauphin, Harriet Rivière and Sharon Gracen for sharing with me their love and knowledge of the cathedral, its operations, history and legacies. Also to be thanked is Philip Myers for his entertaining anecdotes on doing business in the new Russian economy.

Finishing this book would have been much more difficult without the incredible kindness and courtesies of my friends and neighbours who took on so many domestic responsibilities while I hobbled around on crutches with a shattered ankle: my dear Fatima Tazrout, Micheline and André Jéhan, Francine and Jean-François Mège, Kwan and Eddie Lee, Gila Mesples and Sabine Cassat.

My deepest gratitude to my editor, Barbara Boote, and my agent, Bob Tabian, for their encouragement and constant support, and to Joanne Coen for her terrific work fine-tuning the book, and her unfailing sense of humour.

1

If you are in Paris in the late autumn you will notice how a sadness settles over the city. The air turns brittle cold, and the drizzled grey sky becomes a spiritual force driving the soul inward, just as the rain drives the sodden leaves into the damp earth. Things get buried in the autumn.

Light diminishes. The clocks are rolled back and morning comes in a dull, heavy-lidded stupour, and night falls early.

It was nearly dark and the street lamps had already come up all through the city when Father Crispin Wakefield set off from the cathedral on the Avenue George V. The broad avenue was beautiful and alive and dazzled you with light from hotels with grand names like the Prince de Galles and the King George, and all the boutiques and bistros seemed to swell with radiance. It was splendid the way the city sprung up at night in defiance of the darkness.

This time of year was always difficult for Father Wakefield. He shrank inwardly with the coming winter; he felt himself to be more animal than human during those days, and when Tuesday five p.m. rolled around he dragged himself out of the warmth of his study, loaded up his motorcycle, fastened on his helmet and struck out across the city. It was easy to pick him out as he wobbled through traffic in his yellow slicker, weaving recklessly down the avenue toward the river that was now as dark as the Styx. The cathedral loomed behind him, a stationary and steadfast thing anchored in the fluid gloom of the city.

Father Wakefield varied his route, but he had his favourite places, knew always where he could find the miserable ones, especially now with winter coming on. Sometimes he made promises, and he honoured those, although often the man or woman didn't show, but the priest was always there. It was easier like this for many of them. They wouldn't ever come into a place like the cathedral. They hated those images and icons. So he took himself out to them. He was a little of everything to everyman. He carried with him a little food and medicine, toothbrushes and soap, and sometimes some of those perfume samples his wife or daughters brought back from Marionnaud when they had spent a lot of money there. He wore a black and red motorcycle helmet that might have been more suitable for a younger man with bleached or tinted hair, and he always wore his clerical collar.

There were times when he was greeted with hostility and times when they insulted him, and his French was good enough now to understand what they were saying. He was never offended, but that was his nature. They nearly always smelled of drunkenness and urine, and the stench would hit him like a sharp blow to the head, sometimes triggering a wave of nausea. But he did what he could, fed those who needed feeding, and listened to what they had to say. If someone needed medical care he would get them to a hospital. Sometimes he would shell out for a new pair of shoes; new things were always treasured. Sometimes the best thing was just a little laughter and a smile.

On this afternoon the traffic along the *quai* in front of Châtelet was so dense even motorcycles couldn't advance. No one was moving and it had started to rain. Crispin noticed a girl – not much older than his Megan – sitting on the kerb hugging her knees, her head down and face hidden, a cheap sports bag at her side. She was neat and dressed warmly and her hair was clean. She looked up and you could tell by her eyes she was in trouble.

2

Crispin was good at reading people and their language and he believed she had made herself visible for a reason. He ran his motorcycle up on the pavement and removed his helmet and knelt down beside her. The first thing you noticed about Crispin Wakefield was his eyes, and after that a sincerity that flowed from them, and there was never any judgement even if you had done very evil things. Those eyes expressed something that lay beyond the range of words or deeds. This was not enough, but it was where it began.

In great cities like this one you could always find your minority and slink away from challenge, which is the way most of the people Crispin knew lived their lives. Crispin did just the opposite, but there was still that shock, and sometimes fear, when you come up against lives being lived so differently from your own. This is why he always finished his goodwill tours with a drink – most often at Harry's Bar or The Cricketer. Harry's was a hard-drinking crowd and he didn't like the smoke, and it had a sordid feel about it like the sleazy bars in Tiajuana, but they could make a good whisky sour and in the summer it was a good place to drink margaritas. The Cricketer on the Rue des Mathurins was boisterous and inviting, and on a Friday evening if it wasn't raining the Brits took their pints out on the pavement which is something the French would never do. Tonight Crispin needed cheering, and he stood a better chance of running into a familiar face at The Cricketer, so that's where he headed.

He was glad he did, because Rhoderic was standing at the end of the bar shovelling peanuts into his mouth, and you could always count on Rhoderic for scrappy conversation. Rhoderic was a barrister and very dignified-looking – the kind of man who could wear a white wig and black robe without looking silly – but he was not the most competent of lawyers and, even worse, he would work for free for his friends. He didn't have many clients who paid him, and he'd had a rough few years along with everyone else, and now there was not much work and no staff except a ghost-like secretary. Other people would never know this to hear him talk, but he let his guard down with Crispin and the priest often caught a flicker of hopelessness in his eyes.

Crispin shook out his slicker and hung it on a prong, placed his helmet on the rack above, and looked up to see Rhoderic wave him over.

'Hey, Crispin! Good to see you.'

'What's up, friend?'

'The usual. You're out doing your thing again?'

'Yep.' Crispin wedged himself in to a little space at the bar, and Rhoderic slid the peanuts towards him, but Crispin shook his head. 'I need a drink first.'

'Tough day?'

'Sad.' Crispin looked down at his knuckles, red from the cold. 'Real sad. Found a sixteen-year-old girl who'd just tested positive for HIV.'

'Bloody hell.'

'That about sums it up.'

Rhoderic was a tall man with long arms and when he summoned a bartender they always came. Crispin ordered a Scotch on the rocks and then said, 'Poor kid just got the results back and was just wandering around.'

'No home?'

'Not around here. Some little village down near Nîmes, she said.'

'What'd you do?'

'Oh, you know. Same old thing. A little counselling. Something hot to drink and a sandwich. I got her to call her folks at least.'

'Tough,' Rhoderic said, and you knew he meant it. He had a heart, which was why Crispin could relate to the guy.

'Her folks are driving up to get her in the morning. I got her a hotel room for the night.'

Crispin reached for the Scotch as soon as it came; he took a long drink and it felt like fire but it tasted good and burned away a little of the sadness. He wished the girl could find something to make her forget.

'Crikey, if I went around paying for hotel rooms for strange women, my wife would slay me.'

Crispin shrugged. 'I just slap it on a credit card.'

'Oh, that's right. You Americans all run around with your private lines of credit.'

'Middle-class welfare.'

'Damn nuisance, all this mess.'

'Yes, it is.' Crispin wasn't quite sure what he meant, but he got the general drift.

Rhoderic said, 'We do what we have to do.'

Crispin drained the last of his Scotch. 'Dreary thought, isn't it? Always doing what's expected.'

'We might do things differently if we didn't have our families.'

Rhoderic had six children from three different wives. Crispin only had three, but they were all girls, and Paris had taught them a thing or two about spending money.

'Well, on a lighter note, I thought you might want to see this.' Rhoderic bent down to the briefcase between his feet and withdrew that day's *Herald Tribune*. He turned it over to the back page.

'Didn't you say you knew her?'

'Who?'

Rhoderic pointed to a name in bold-faced type in the 'People' column. 'JULIA KRAMER.'

Crispin took the paper from him and looked at the photograph of Julia standing between her husband and a British director who had shot one of the films that had brought her recognition. It was not one of those posed photographs but showed them with their heads together, deep in conversation, and Julia with her eyes on Jona and that limpid smile of hers. The men were in tuxedos and Julia wore earrings that looked very expensive. Jona looked like he always did in the pictures Crispin had seen of him – a bald man with a satin-smooth smile and tiny gimlet eyes obscured by thick black-rimmed glasses. They were at a gala to celebrate the sale of the King George hotel to a British chain. The caption said that Jona was the new hotel president. It also mentioned that Julia was to begin shooting a new film with the director.

'The King George's right up the street from you.'

Crispin nodded.

'Didn't you say you grew up together?'

'Yeah. They were our closest neighbours. They farmed a little land. Raised a few cattle. Like we all did.'

'You should look her up.'

Rhoderic stuffed the paper back into his briefcase and Crispin thought about it while he took another drink of his Scotch. Casting a glance at his reflection in the mirror behind the pretty bottles of rums and cognacs and gins, he wondered if there was anything in his face she might remember or even like. Once there had been a time when he had been so sure of things. Now all he felt was an extravagant sadness and a longing for infinite things the world has never seen.

'Oh, I don't know,' he answered Rhoderic. 'Been a long time,' and his eyes shifted away from himself to the reflection of a pretty woman with long dark hair and he preferred this.

Rhoderic ordered another pint but Crispin was already feeling the Scotch and didn't dare order again.

Crispin glanced at his watch. 'I've got to go. Got to find a birthday present.'

'Whose birthday?'

'Megan. My eldest.'

'How old is she?'

'Coming up to fourteen. An expensive age.'

'It only gets worse.'

The rain had stopped. Crispin unlocked the motorcycle and headed up Boulevard Haussman towards the big department stores, and along the way he looked for a kiosk where he could buy a copy of the *Herald Tribune*. He found one and folded the paper tightly and slipped it inside his jacket pocket. He parked the bike and walked down the street to the Galeries Lafayette. He liked the way the newspaper felt stiff and fresh next to his chest, and he knew now why that lost girl on the kerb had wounded him so with her look. She had Julia's eyes.

2

As canon of St John's, Crispin was given lodgings adjacent to the cathedral, as was the Dean. But the Dean's apartment was a spacious thing with its own private entrance off the Avenue George V, while the rectory where the canon resided was enclosed within the cathedral walls. This stone cottage had been built in the Gothic style of the church, with ornamented windows and pointed arched doorways that reminded Lola, Crispin's youngest daughter, of Sleeping Beauty's castle. The way it was nestled in the shadow of the imposing cathedral walls made you think you were somewhere special and nowhere near stores that sold luggage that cost as much as a their car.

The cottage had suffered waves of renovation over the century as living conditions in the city had improved, resulting in some curious fixtures that had become running jokes in the family, like the deep square tub where you had to bathe in a seated position (Crispin could only use the shower because his knees would not fit) and a toilet built into the top step of what used to be the stairway to the attic – and appropriately referred to as the throne room. There were no closets, only the massive armoires where Lola would hide to read her picture books with her Tinker Bell flashlight. Her favourite armoire was the one in her parents' room because it held Phoebe's fox coat and she loved the smell of the warm furs and her mother's perfume. Secretly she believed that one day the back would open up and she would enter Narnia.

But the only real disadvantage they found with the rectory was that their front door opened on to the courtyard just opposite the arcade that led to the offices and reception halls of the cathedral. Phoebe often complained that she could be overheard every time she raised her voice, and she was tired of jokes about her cooking ('My goodness, is Phoebe roasting lamb again?'). Crispin, however, loved the proximity, not only for the convenience of his work but because the cathedral had become his home. It was his bastion and he was its feudal lord.

Tuesday was Phoebe's night out, and Crispin always ordered pizza to be delivered to their door. Lola called it their American night, but as he glanced around the tiny kitchen for a place to set the boxes it looked like they had never left America. The worksurface was cluttered with brand names like Old El Paso salsa and open bags of Doritos and Pringles and empty Coke cans. In the sink sat a jar of Skippy peanut butter with a knife plunged into its heart. Even the bananas in the fruit bowl wore Chiquita labels.

'Who was that?' Phoebe shouted from the hallway. Her shoes made sharp clicking sounds on the hardwood floor.

'Pizza man,' he called back.

She appeared in the doorway with her earrings in her hand. Phoebe was tiny with beautifully sculpted features, but she was anything but fragile; she had been working as a personal trainer when Crispin met her.

'You called them already?'

'Lola said she was hungry.'

Crispin set down the pizzas and turned to look at his wife. She was stunning in a lizard-like jacket trimmed at the cuffs with chartreuse-tinted fur. Crispin hoped it was fake.

'You look nice.'

'Don't glare at me like that. I got it on sale.'

'I wasn't aware that I was glaring.'

She had a way of tightening her jaw when she thought she was being unfairly accused, and she looked away while she worked an earring through her ear.

He said, 'I got a birthday present for Megan today.'

She was having trouble with the earring. 'Oh Cris, I told you I'd get her something tomorrow. You don't even know what she wants.'

'I got her a silver necklace. With a little horse on it. I thought it was pretty.'

'I hope you can take it back. The French are so unreasonable about that.'

'Maybe she'll want to keep it.'

'I doubt it. She's very picky about her jewellery.'

Megan was passionate about horses and competed in shows every other Sunday. Crispin could never go, although Phoebe attended them religiously, which was just one of many reasons why his eldest daughter was estranged from him.

Phoebe turned away from him and walked towards the bedroom while she screwed the back on the other earring. You couldn't help but notice Phoebe's walk, and the high-heeled shoes with spade-like toes. She wore black fishnet stockings that were quite the rage but reminded Crispin of Halloween. Everyone admired Phoebe's style, but for Crispin it had become a burden.

He found Lola in the living room watching *The Little Mermaid* which is what she did when her sister Cat needed the room to study. There were only three bedrooms in the cottage, so Lola shared a room with Cat. There were seven years' difference between the two sisters, and Crispin thought the arrangement was unfair to Cat, but Megan would no more consent to share her room than to carry a bucket of gas into hell. It had been a workable solution because Lola was a quiet child and compliant, two character traits foreign to the rest of the family. Crispin worried more about Lola than the others, which was just one of several ironies in his life.

The five-year-old sat upright in the middle of the sofa, her thin little legs pointed at the television screen. She wore a Tigger dressing gown over her *Lion King* pyjamas, and *101 Dalmatians* slippers dangled from her toes. She reminded Crispin of the kind of elderly lady who would collect teapots.

'Hey, kiddo. Dinner's here. Where shall we eat?'

She turned her face up to him, but a response was not forthcoming. Lola weighed even the most insignificant decisions with a kind of Supreme Court deliberation.

'I thought we'd make it a picnic night. Spread out a tablecloth on the floor. That okay with you?'

She turned her attention back to Ariel, who was being chased through a sunken ship by a shark. Crispin interpreted her silence as agreement and opened the buffet to look for a tablecloth.

'Too bad we don't have one of those checkered ones like they had in *The Lady and the Tramp*,' he commented.

'Mama has one. I think she keeps it in the closet with the sheets.'

Crispin found the tablecloth and wondered how Lola knew these things since the tablecloth was old and faded and Phoebe hadn't used it since they moved to France. He spread it on the floor in front of the television.

'Shall we use a candle?'

Lola thought for a moment, then nodded her head.

'Go wash your hands,' he said, and she hit the pause button, then slid to the floor and dashed off towards the bathroom.

When she returned, the tablecloth was spread with cheese pizza and Coke and carrot sticks. Lola smiled, and Crispin imagined he saw a little of himself in her face, but he knew better. She sat cross-legged next to him and tucked the napkin into her pyjamas, then folded her hands under her chin and tilted her face upwards where she imagined God to be. She pronounced a hasty grace, and Crispin sneaked a look at her while her eyes were shut.

They were interrupted by Caitlin's voice in the hallway. 'Is the pizza here already?'

'In the oven.'

'Somebody could've told me.' She sounded miffed.

'I didn't think you'd be hungry yet.'

The oven door squeaked open, there was a rustling of boxes, then Caitlin's voice rose in an exasperated cry.

'Dad, didn't you get pepperoni?'

'Last time nobody ate it.'

'We always get pepperoni!'

Caitlin was overweight – not excessively so, but enough to make adolescence seem like a steep climb to Golgotha. Crispin had acquired a certain sensitivity to these gender issues and had learned patience.

'Sorry, Cat. I'll remember next time.'

She grumbled loudly while slamming a few kitchen cupboards and he let it pass, knowing next week she would be on a diet again and would not touch the pepperoni.

Caitlin passed Megan in the hallway on her way back to her room and Crispin noted with relief there was no exchange of words – their mutual silence signifying there were no current grievances to be aired. He did not like to deal with Megan. She had acquired a sense of empowerment no child should have, a problem that was Phoebe's doing. She was Phoebe's monster; and only Phoebe could contain her.

Megan stepped barefoot over their tablecloth, barely missing the bowl of carrot sticks, and leaned over the coffee table to rifle through a stack of magazines. Even at home when she was lounging around or doing homework Megan had an acute sense of fashion. At the moment she was wearing skimpy tartan boxer shorts slung low around her hips and Phoebe's black silk tank top. Only Megan dared enter her mother's closet and help herself to whatever took her fancy, and Megan's fancy changed several times a day. And yet, for all her vanity, there was a riveting grace about the child that turned heads in the street. Men followed her with their eyes, and Crispin watched them closely when she was around – partly out of pride, but mostly fear.

He said, 'Pizza's in the oven if you want some.'

'I'm not hungry,' she mumbled, but then she looked up and showered them with an unexpected smile. 'You two look like you're having fun.'

'Sure you don't want to join us?'

'Right, like I'm just dying to watch *The Little Mermaid*.'

Her thick honey-blonde hair hung loose around her shoulders and she smiled again in an artless way that ensnared the heart. Just then Crispin felt in the pit of his stomach that raw love of parent for child. Wholly unsentimental and instinctual. You could blindfold Crispin and he would recognize his children by the smell of their skin.

'Dad, you didn't take my magazine, did you?'

'What magazine?'

'The new *Teen People*. Mom just got it for me today.'

'Haven't seen it, honey.'

'Well I can't find it.' She straightened, her temper rising. 'Cat! Did you take my magazine?'

Lola visibly flinched at her sister's raised voice. She covered her ears with her hands.

'Cat!' screamed Megan.

'No!' came the reply from down the hall. 'Why would I read your stupid magazines?'

'Well it's not here!'

Crispin watched in awe as she vented her frustration on cover models and politicians and editorial reviews. Magazines and newspapers sailed to the floor.

'Shit,' she muttered.

'Megan!'

They were saved by the melodic jingle of Megan's mobile phone which she carried with her from room to room. She even slept with it clutched in the palm of her hand.

'Hello?' she answered sweetly, and her face became all radiance and joy. 'Hey,' she said, and hurried from the room, leaving the magazines strewn around the floor.

'Saved by the bell,' Crispin said with a nudge to Lola and she looked up at him and giggled.

They were alone again with Ariel and her underwater friends. Megan and Caitlin never ate with them. He understood they needed a break from routine, but it hurt him that their hallowed family mealtime lost its sanctity whenever Phoebe was out. Only Lola enjoyed his company. He had concluded that five was a perfect age.

Crispin was in bed but still awake when Phoebe returned. He looked up from St Thomas Aquinas and removed his glasses as she kicked off her shoes and dumped her coat onto a chair.

'Did you have a good time?'

'The restaurant was awful.'

'Where'd you go?'

'This very chic place up on top of the Pompidou Centre. Gerry recommended it.' She unbuttoned the lizard jacket revealing a beige and pink lace bra that Crispin had never seen before.

'They had these toilets with opaque walls so you could see the shadow of the person in the stall next to you. Can you imagine? And the light was so bad in there I couldn't even see to put on my lipstick. Ridiculous.'

'How was the food?'

'Very mediocre and very expensive.'

Crispin took refuge behind St Thomas. He had repeatedly asked her to be sensitive to their financial situation, but she felt a certain appearance had to be maintained as wife of the canon. The Dean's wife, Geraldine, was the self-appointed doyenne of this elite circle of churchwomen, and they were a force to be reckoned with. Among the five of them, they knew every bit of gossip worth knowing, and many things Crispin would have liked to know. At its best, he considered her dinners a necessary business expense; Phoebe was his intelligence operative, although he was not totally convinced of her loyalty.

'Did Gerry say anything about whether or not the Bishop's still coming next week?'

'No, nothing.'

She slid in next to him and clicked on her bedside lamp.

'Cris?'

'Yeah?'

'You know, at one time last year we talked about getting a horse for Megan.'

'Yes, we did.'

'Can we think about it again?'

'Sure. Thinking doesn't cost me anything.'

'Is it totally out of the question?'

'Yes.'

He did not look up from his book; he did not want to meet her gaze.

'Isn't there any money at all left from the company?'

He took a deep breath and tried to focus his attention on the words of the saint. 'There hasn't been any money left in years.' She knew this, and he wondered why she was so stubborn about it, as if she suspected him of hoarding savings in a Swiss bank.

'I just can't believe it. What happened to all of it?'

'I can give you an exact account if you want. But it'll take me a few weeks.'

She answered in a peeved voice. 'It was a rhetorical question. You don't need to get sarcastic.'

'I wasn't being sarcastic. It would honestly take me that long.'

If there was anything Phoebe hated, it was accountability, particularly where money was concerned. She was like a child, wholly unprepared to deal with the reality of numbers.

'Well, I just thought it would be a good idea. It's such a healthy sport.'

'And an expensive one.'

'They would get outdoors, Crispin. They miss the outdoors. And these schools are just hopeless when it comes to sports.'

'You're just talking about Megan, aren't you?'

'It's not just for Megan.'

'Cat doesn't ride.'

'She might want to if we had a horse.'

'She's allergic to horses.'

'That can be managed with the right medicine.'

'Anyway, Lola's too little.'

'She can start on Shetlands. They'll all want a horse in time.'

'It sounds like you already have one picked out.'

'Well, actually there's one at the stables that's up for sale. Megan's ridden her a couple of times. A beautiful *selle français*.'

'We can't afford it, Phoebe.'

He waited tensely, trying to gauge her reaction. He would have liked to turn and read the look on her face, penetrate behind her eyes. Phoebe did not dissemble well and there were always clues. He closed his book and reached to turn out his light.

Phoebe got up and threw on her robe.

'I'll read downstairs,' she announced flatly as she flipped off her reading lamp.

After she had gone, Crispin threw back the blanket and dropped to his knees beside the bed. It was an old habit, one he settled into immediately following his conversion, but

Phoebe found it annoying. She thought prayers must surely be as effective stretched out in a warm bed as on one's knees. Crispin was inclined to agree, but he did not kneel to make himself heard. He wanted to empty his mind and free his spirit, and he would have lain prostrate on the cold wood floor if it would have helped.

This night his mind did not want to settle down. It seemed to want to grasp at disturbing thoughts, and he took deep purging breaths to cleanse his brain. Moments passed and he was almost there, nearing that still place where he found his strength.

Into this vacuum swept Julia, not so much as thought but as image. He did not see her the way she appeared in the photograph in the paper, but as she was at the age of fifteen, the year she went away. The image was incomplete, eroded by time, but it left the unmistakable impression of Julia, the startling eyes and impish smile. Just as quickly as it appeared, the image faded from his mind, and he was left with an inexplicable heaviness of heart.

When Phoebe returned, he was still pondering the significance of this brief yet potent resurrection of his past. She crawled quietly into bed without turning on the light. She did not even notice he was still on his knees.

3

Sometimes in the evening before he changed for bed, Crispin would slip across the courtyard and let himself in to the cathedral. He knew the place well, and he navigated easily through the darkness, up steps and across the transept into the choir. His favourite spot was on the chancel steps below the altar where he liked to sit and meditate, but to look at him you would think him more a brooding poet than a spiritual leader. At times he would stretch out on his back on the floor behind the railing to study the vaulted ceiling; he liked the visual harmony from this angle and found it so relaxing that on occasions he had been known to fall asleep. Once Phoebe came along in her nightgown and had to wake him up and take him home to bed.

There were other times when he was too agitated to find peace, and he would sit on one of the acolyte's chairs staring bleakly at the scuffed tips of his shoes with his thoughts ricocheting from one petty problem to another.

But much of the time he came here just to feel the cold draughts of her breath and listen to her silence. The cathedral changed when empty like this, without the crowds of people. On rare cloudless nights, pale traces of moonlight filtered through her darkened glass windows and infused the air with opaque light and Crispin imagined she was somehow impregnated with everything she had ever witnessed and heard, with all the vanity and prejudice and loneliness and hope that humanity had silently laid at her door.

On this Friday evening Crispin had come in to rehearse a sermon he was to give the following Sunday — a privilege Dean Noonan allowed his canons only when he was out of town. Public speaking still terrified Crispin; it sent his bowels into spasms and made his palms sweat. Back at his old church in Chicago he had taken to drinking a beer before the service each Sunday to steady his nerves, and here in Paris he kept a small reserve of Beaujolais in his study for such occasions. His phobia was aggravated by the fact that Dean Noonan's oratorical skills were far superior to his own. It was a fact of life that pride and ambition ran rampant through the ranks of the clergy just as in secular sectors of society, and someone had to be Bishop he conceded, but he was vexed by the hubris of some of his brethren. It was during his initial interview four years ago that Crispin sized up his superior as a man of such ilk, a graduate of Princeton's school of theology who prided himself on his reputation as an intellectual powerhouse. That afternoon Dean Noonan had made it clear that all he really wanted was a self-effacing canon to perform weddings and carry the burden of pastoral care. It would fall to Crispin — were he to be so called — to oversee what the Dean privately felt to be the dullest work in his parish: ministering to the sick, the grieving, the troubled, the dying.

Crispin's role was greatly enhanced when his entrepreneurial experience became known and he was put in charge of the cathedral renovation project, but he still looked forward to those rare Sundays when he could stand at the pulpit and address his parish. Since these opportunities were so infrequent, he chose his topic with care. He had spent two weeks writing what he hoped would be an enlightening sermon on the manifestation of the Holy Spirit, and he had not finished memorizing the end. After running through it once from the pulpit he stepped down into the choir and stretched out on his back on a pew and recited it in his head.

It was six o'clock in the evening and the Dean's secretary was just leaving; she always closed up shop and left like clockwork because she had a train to catch. You always knew it was her because of the sharp clicking sound her heels made on the marble walk. When she had gone, Crispin felt a deep silence settle over the cathedral. The typed manuscript slid to the floor and he folded his hands over his chest and closed his eyes.

It wasn't always easy to recognize Julia Kramer, even if you knew her name and had seen her films. Julia's face was not memorable in itself; it had a mysterious way of transforming itself which was one of the things directors found so intriguing. It changed dramatically when captured under a certain light or at a certain angle, or depending on how her hair was styled, if she wore it wild and loose or pulled back so you noticed the wide forehead and slender arched brows and dreamy eyes. Sometimes she appeared so different that when she walked onto a set you wouldn't recognize her until she spoke to you or smiled.

This is why the church secretary didn't recognize her when she passed her on the steps. Julia stopped her and asked for Father Wakefield and the secretary said he was probably in the chancel.

Julia was not at home in churches, not anymore, and she stood far at the back near the entrance. The cathedral was cold and eerily silent, and she was afraid to make the slightest sound. She took a few steps forward and the echo of her footsteps in the great emptiness made her feel very small.

She had been trying to reconcile the image of a priest with her memories of Crispin Wakefield, and now she tried to imagine him behind the towering pulpit, hands gripping the lectern, looking down on the congregation. Strangely, she could picture him up there, the boy whose strength of character had remained so vividly in her memory long after everyone else had been forgotten.

At the same time she felt a little sad about it, the way you feel about traitors or defectors, people who break the commonplace rules of life. Becoming a priest was not like becoming a dentist or a car dealer. Priests are celibate men, she thought. They do not marry and produce offspring and fight with their wives. She had always imagined Crispin would go on to live a conventional life, and for some reason this image of Crispin the conformist had comforted her, perhaps because she had always confused conformity with happiness.

She felt uncomfortable standing there with his note in her hand, the one he had left at the hotel just this morning. She wondered what reason there would be for them to meet again. She could not imagine what they would have in common. It had been so long ago, and for so many years, even into adulthood, she had clung to the image of Crispin as her saviour. Then Jona had come along and there was no need to cling to memories any longer.

She smiled to herself and stuffed the note into the pocket of her coat. Now here he was again, right down the street. In this dense city of millions, here was Crispin.

She approached the altar down the long central aisle, and as she glanced up into the vaulted ceiling she suddenly recalled how as a little girl she had sat in the balcony of the Methodist church in Cottonwood Falls on Sunday mornings and imagined herself a ballerina in pink net and satin shoes twirling on her toes around the railing, defying gravity while she spun gracefully and ghost-like through the air. She smiled at the memory, something so innocent, so impossibly absurd.

The chancel was roped off with a scarlet cordon, and after a moment's hesitation she unhooked it and went up the stairs past the choir and stopped in front of the altar; what a strange thing it would be to choose this way of life, she thought.

She did not see Crispin, but she heard him, a faint rumbling snore that startled her. She gasped and whirled around just in time to see an equally startled priest rise from the pew where he had been sleeping and scurry to his feet. He was standing on his sermon, and he bent to retrieve the scattered mess of papers while mumbling an apology.

It was his appearance that confused her; he seemed so very ordinary, a man of average height and build with longish hair greying at the temples, and a kind of eccentric disregard for appearance that you sense in people who have serious things to do in the world and who cannot be bothered with matching socks. His sweater was buttoned unevenly, and the pockets sagged with the weight of their contents (the cathedral keys and Megan's mobile phone which he had confiscated in a rare act of parental discipline).

'Oh,' she said with her hands crossed over her chest and her eyes wide. 'I really wasn't going to steal anything, I promise!'

He was standing very still. 'Oh, my goodness,' he whispered, fixing her with a long steady look.

'Cris!'

She approached the choir and gazed up at him with her mouth open to form some kind of exclamation but she could only shake her head in astonishment.

'Julia,' he pronounced in a low voice. 'I never imagined . . .'

'So you're a priest.'

'I'm a priest,' he nodded. 'I can't get over you. Standing here. All grown up.'

'And growing old.'

'Oh no. You're in your prime.'

'Hollywood doesn't seem to think so.'

'So you got my message.'

She smiled and waved the note at him. 'Read it about a dozen times since this morning.'

He climbed down to where she stood and when he reached her the smile faded and she said in a voice that ached with tenderness, 'I always hoped I'd see you again.'

'Hey,' he smiled, and he wanted to give her a hug but she was a woman now, not a girl, and so he took her hands in his and squeezed them. 'I'm glad to see you.'

They were interrupted by the sound of a girl's voice behind them.

'Dad?'

Crispin turned and smiled at Cat standing below the chancel steps. She wore an oversized sweatshirt and jeans and looked very American. 'Come here, honey,' he motioned. 'I want you to meet somebody very special.'

Cat was unsettled by the sight of her father and this woman she had never seen before, the way they stepped back from one another when she approached.

'Julia, this is my daughter, Caitlin.'

'Hello, Caitlin.'

'This is Julia Kramer.' But Cat showed no recognition, only wary scrutiny.

'Hello,' said Cat.

Julia picked up on Crispin's embarrassment, and she touched his hand which was a mistake, then crinkled up her nose with a smile and said to him in a low voice, 'Not the same generation, Cris. Different references.'

'Hey, Cat's my film buff,' he defended.

But then Caitlin's eyes grew wide. 'Oh, you're Julia!' She smiled, and the tension ebbed. 'Dad's got all your films.'

Julia looked pleased and said to him, 'Do you really?'

Cat interrupted to say, 'Hey, Mrs Fleming called.'

'What'd she say?'

'You have to call her back right away. It's urgent, she said.'

'Oh no,' he muttered. 'It's probably her husband. He's been sick.'

He thanked Cat, which was intended to dismiss her, but she remained there watching them. They stared uneasily back at her, waiting for her to leave. Finally, Crispin said, 'Tell your mom I'll be right up.'

'Okay.'

Unwillingly, she turned and left.

Julia whispered, 'You have a child?'

'Sure.'

'So you're not Catholic?'

'Good grief, no. Episcopalian.'

'So you're a priest, but not a celibate one.'

'That's right.'

She looked genuinely relieved, and he laughed.

'I was trying to imagine you like that . . .'

'You were?'

'Well, yes, and I just couldn't.'

'Good grief, neither could I. I have three daughters.'

'Three?'

'And a wife.'

She smiled, genuinely pleased. 'Then you must be very, very happy.'

It seemed like such a strange assumption, that she should equate the two.

'Well, I came to all this . . .' he said, gesturing to the altar, '. . . after my first two were born. It was what you might call an early mid-life crisis.'

'But you're happy,' she repeated. She seemed to want to believe this.

'I made the right choice. I have no doubts about that. None whatsoever.' But then he added in a low, somewhat drier voice, 'But I'm sure Phoebe does.'

'Phoebe? Is that her name?'

'My wife.'

'What a delightful name. I'll bet she's beautiful.'

'I hope you'll meet them.'

'I'd love to.'

'Can you come for lunch on Sunday? With Jona of course.'

'Jona's away. He's in New York.'

'Then come on your own. Come to the service. I'm giving the sermon.'

The smile froze on her face. Crispin added quickly and with a grin, 'It's not a long sermon. I try not to bore.'

'Oh, it's not that.' She reached out and touched his arm in a reassuring manner. 'I just haven't been to church for so long.' She glanced behind Crispin, and her eyes swept across the high altar to the triptych painting. 'I never knew this place was here. I mean, I didn't know it was an American cathedral.'

'We're a very friendly bunch.'

She seemed to relax a little then, and said, 'Of course I'll come.'

'Eleven o'clock.'

She leaned forward and gave him a light kiss on the cheek, and he caught the sweet scent of her perfume. 'I look forward to it.'

He watched from the chancel as she descended the stairs and disappeared into the shadows and the heavy door closed behind her. Then he re-attached the scarlet cordon and gathered up the pages of his sermon and exited through the back, throwing the light switch on the wall and sending the cathedral into darkness.

He went home and straight to the kitchen, where he found Phoebe and Megan putting away groceries. The way both of them fell silent and turned their backs to him meant that Cat had told them. He drew a deep breath and then told Phoebe he had invited Julia Kramer to lunch on Sunday. It took Phoebe a moment to recover because she had not expected him to be so forthright. Phoebe had a suspicious mind but this had everything to do with her nature and nothing to do with Crispin's.

Megan asked, 'Is this that actress? The one you grew up with?'

'Yep.'

'Cool.'

'Well, we'll go out,' Phoebe said. 'I don't want to cook.' You could tell she was grumpy, but also secretly flattered.

'I'd rather entertain here,' Crispin said.

'Cris, you know how I hate cooking Sunday lunch. There is absolutely no privacy here on Sunday – the kitchen window looks straight out on to the cloister and I feel like I'm on display. And you're giving the sermon so I know you'll be a nervous wreck. Let's just go out.'

'Eating out's expensive.'

'We can leave the girls at home.'

Megan cried, 'No! I want to go!'

'That sort of defeats the whole purpose,' Crispin replied.

'I do not want to cook Sunday lunch.'

But Crispin wouldn't argue with her and Phoebe had learned that after a certain point it was useless so she just set her jaw and started thinking about the menu.

'We'll have lamb.' She said it like a threat.

'Lamb's fine. You do good lamb.'

'Lamb is not fine. Lamb is what we always have when we invite guests for Sunday. I'm tired of lamb.'

'Then do something else.'

'Anything else is too much work.'

'Do roast beef.'

'I won't eat roast beef,' Megan cried. 'We'll get mad cow disease.'

At that moment Megan's mobile phone rang. Crispin sighed and handed her back her phone and she fled to her room.

'Crispin, the girls won't eat rare roast beef and that's the only way you can eat French beef. You cook the stuff and it's like rubber.'

'Lamb is fine, Phoebe.'

He kissed her gently on the cheek and left the kitchen to call Mrs Fleming and that was the end of the discussion. Crispin often managed to disagree without arguing much and yet in the end he got his way. At least that's how Phoebe saw it. What Phoebe didn't see was the turmoil in his chest and how badly he felt about not being able to afford to take them all out to dinner. In the end it was all about money.

4

Crispin was a quiet sort of man but could be stubborn, and he had a way of getting under your skin and nettling you with his stubbornness. He never seemed to take offence at even the most offensive behaviour directed towards him, and in the end he earned your respect even if you were the kind of person who generally showed little respect for others. Dean Noonan was one of those people and perhaps this was why they worked well together although they didn't really like one another. Thomas Noonan wielded his authority like a tyrant and treated insubordination like sacrilege, and had he not become such a star in the social and theo-political firmament of Paris, he would long ago have fallen to insurrection within the ranks. He had that unmistakable aura exuded by men of ambition, and his wife had once confided to Phoebe, 'If Tom had been English and Anglican instead of American and Episcopalian, we'd be living in a bishop's palace by now and he'd have a seat in the House of Lords and invitations to Windsor Castle.'

Still, Paris was not a bad spot for ambitious priests, and although Dean Noonan's French was not as good as it should have been, he was certainly fluent enough to sparkle in interviews with radio and television stations whenever they needed a spokesperson from the Anglican or American community. He was very dapper and his black hair and china-blue eyes looked very good on television even when his messages missed the mark or he failed to sound convincingly Christian.

'A perfect example of how bullshit baffles brains,' Crispin

had grumbled to Phoebe one evening as he sat on the edge of the bed and stripped off his socks.

'But Tom's brilliant!' Phoebe had countered from the armoire where she was searching for a hanger. She was wearing a long transparent nightgown and you could see between her legs and it distracted Crispin so it took him a moment to reply.

'That remark refers to other people's brains. Not his.'

'Oh,' she said and turned away, and had Crispin been a jealous man his pride would have been injured, because you could see how Phoebe thought Tom Noonan was the cat's pyjamas and wished Crispin had a few of his qualities.

Dean Noonan taught a class in theology at the American University and wrote scholarly papers that were published in journals no one ever read, and he travelled a lot. He never seemed to be around when you needed a definitive answer or some emergency erupted, like the time they took old Bishop Whitley out to lunch on the Champs-Elysées. On the way back to the cathedral he wandered off in the crowd and got lost and it took several police units two hours to find him. After a while everyone began to notice how Crispin could handle crises in a decisive and reassuring manner, so it was only a matter of time before the staff began to look to Crispin as the man who got things done.

For years there had been a high staff turnover and hiring was something Tom Noonan insisted on doing personally. He would charm people into the job and then they'd be miserable and leave, but after Crispin arrived people tended to stay on a little longer, and although you quickly learned never to badmouth the Dean to Father Wakefield, you knew he would listen to legitimate complaints and try to handle them as best he could.

It was a huge cathedral in terms of service programmes and activities, and there were scores of people involved in day-to-day operations – docents, front desk volunteers, Sunday

lectors, the AA programme, the Choral Society and the counselling centre, and Crispin always knew who was doing what
and when. But unless you were one of the inner sanctum you
would never guess how well he knew the cathedral's finances.
Crispin kept all kinds of figures in his head, like how much
was in the Endowment fund or how much had been contributed to the Moscow Children's Hospital or the flood victims
in Mozambique. He never tried to impress you with these
things, it's just that he seemed to care a lot. You became aware
of his value slowly when you got to know him. And then
sometimes it was like an epiphany and you suddenly realized
that the man you thought was so ordinary was really someone
quite special.

It's hard to say when Dean Noonan began to feel the change
but it's sure he felt it. Increasingly people left him to his scholarly pursuits, and questions and problems got rerouted to
Crispin's desk. At first Noonan was only too happy to pass
off all these annoying details but then he noticed the change.

When Crispin arrived at the cathedral four years before,
they were in the early stages of a government mandated
restoration and cleaning of the cathedral's facade and tower.
They had already gathered estimates, obtained bids and managed a successful campaign to help cover the costs estimated
at over four million francs. Tom Noonan was good at the
fundraising and you could count on him to come back from
Dallas and Washington DC with his pockets full of pledges
from American Friends of St John's. He liked to talk about
the receptions and the dinners they gave for him, and even if
you didn't recognize the names he flung about, you could be
sure they were wealthy and influential patrons and Tom would
squeeze them for every penny they had.

The actual restoration and cleaning was a mammoth undertaking, and there wasn't really any one person overseeing it
all, but committees, and within the committees were factions

and some powerful personalities. After Crispin arrived they began coming to him to sort out their differences. He was always calm and level-headed and for some reason he didn't inspire jealousy, but most of all they saw how much he loved the cathedral. The first time he climbed up on the roof with the architect and the senior warden, and got down on his hands and knees and saw for himself the holes, crumbled the rotting wood between his fingers and caressed the broken stones the way a man would caress the woman he loved, you knew how he felt about it.

The ravalement was a massive undertaking, and the firm that had done the restoration of the Eiffel Tower was commissioned to do the job. Once the scaffolding went up and they had built a steel cocoon around the north facade and the tower, you could take the elevator up and walk along steel-girded corridors in the sky and look out at the city spread below. Crispin couldn't get over the romance of it all, and he would go up whenever he could to watch the sculptors and masons as they worked. There were stones to be polished and stones to be sanded down to remove the calcite deposited by decades of heavy rains. There were stained glass windows to be cleaned and grills to be repaired and ironwork to be regilded. On the street below passers-by thought only of the dust and noise and the inconvenience of having to use the pavement on the other side of the street. They walked by and thought of something solid and massive and indestructible up above; they never thought of it as something alive.

When the team cleaning the north facade discovered the problems with the tower, Crispin made an initial inspection to see firsthand the disaster, and when he came to Tom Noonan with his file bulging with notes from his meetings with the *maitre d'oeuvre* and architect and engineer, the Dean tried to weasel out of the meeting pleading that he was to leave the next morning for Washington DC and had much to do. But

Crispin cornered him just before noon, backed him into his office and closed the door. Then Tom Noonan said the only way he could handle bad news was over a rib steak and a bottle of good Bordeaux and so they went out to lunch together to a place in the Rue Marbeuf. Crispin didn't like lunching with Tom Noonan because he ordered pricey wine and things like *foie gras*, and they would end up going halves on the bill even though Crispin only had roast chicken and chips.

They had a good table near the window and Tom was studying the menu with his reading glasses perched on the end of his nose; he looked over the top of his menu at Crispin and said, 'You're not going to order *poulet frites* again I hope.'

'I sure am.' Crispin had laid aside the menu and was going over the notes he had taken during the inspection. 'You know what they're going to have to do, don't you?'

'Who?'

Crispin glanced up. He thought Tom was kidding but then he saw he wasn't. 'The cleaning crew.'

'Oh.' Noonan hid behind his menu again.

'Well, one of the pinnacles will have to be dismantled and repaired and remounted. That means we'll need another level of scaffolding and we'll have to hire a crane. But the pinnacle at the far right corner—'

Tom interrupted him to catch the waiter and they ordered. When the waiter had gone Tom took off his reading glasses, slid them into his breast pocket and fixed Crispin with an attentive look.

'Go on.'

'The one at the far right corner is so badly rotted they'll have to rebuild it. We're lucky the whole thing hasn't fallen down and killed someone.'

'How much is this going to cost?'

'I'm not finished.' Crispin closed the file and leaned back. 'The tower's leaning.'

'Aha.'

'Probably because of the weight of the iron cross. We're going to have to call in an expert on this.'

'They said to expect surprises.'

'Yeah, but we didn't expect half a million francs worth.'

'Half a million?'

'About that.'

Tom let out a low whistle.

'I don't think we can get any more out of the Ministry of Culture,' Crispin said. 'We'll just have to raise it ourselves.'

'I don't know where.'

'We'll have to go back to our parishioners. Friends of the Cathedral. Everyone. Tell them what we've found and ask for their help. We can do it.'

The waiter came over with their wine. He opened the bottle and Tom tasted it and declared it acceptable.

'You'll have a glass, won't you?'

'No, thanks.'

'Oh, you have to. It's a very nice Meursault,' he said and motioned for the waiter to pour Crispin a glass.

Tom was finding all this talk about leaning towers a little tedious, so he took advantage of the interruption to switch to one of his favourite topics of conversation – the reprobation of his brethren. A parishioner had once noted that Dean Noonan's favourite sport was sitting on moral high ground fishing the waters of human frailty. His latest grievance was an Episcopalian rector in Rome who had been too lax on a priest tainted by scandalous rumours of homosexuality.

'The priest should have been fired,' the Dean said.

'Could they prove anything?' Crispin asked.

'Oh, I don't know. In some of these cases there's no way of proving a thing unless you want to have the guy trailed by a private eye. The priest denied everything. But even so,

33

he should have been given his marching orders.'

'And if he was innocent?'

'Where there's smoke there's fire.'

'Not necessarily,' Crispin said and helped himself to another glass of wine. He figured if he was going to pay for half the bottle he'd darn well drink his fair share. 'It's pretty easy for false rumours to get started. You know that as well as I do. Just listen to our wives.'

'Still, we must be above reproach.'

'You leave early tomorrow morning, right?' Crispin said, thinking it best to veer off in another direction.

'Flight's at eight a.m. You'll have to do morning prayer service.'

'I was planning on it.'

The wine was beginning to have an effect on Crispin and it loosened his tongue a little and he said all of a sudden, 'You'd make a damn good bishop, Tom.'

Tom's eyes had that look of someone taken off guard, and right away Crispin knew he had hit upon a truth.

'What makes you say that?' Tom replied.

'You like being on the go, don't you?'

'Yes. I do. Bishops must be peripatetic creatures. They must go out. Out to the world.'

'Yes, yes, they must,' Crispin nodded. The wine had made him enthusiastic and Tom Noonan was seeming like a pleasant fellow.

'You see, Crispin,' and he threw back his shoulders and his chest swelled the way it did when he was pronouncing his truths from the pulpit, 'the bishop's mission is universal. He has his cathedra but you seldom see him there. His ministry embodies the unity of the church.'

'Absolutely,' Crispin cried, and he raised his glass in a toast. 'Here's to peripatetic bishops. Should you ever become one, may you serve your mission well.'

'Well, thank you,' Tom nodded with studied humility.

The waiter brought Crispin's roast chicken and Tom's steak and they smiled congenially at one another and fell to eating. After a moment, Tom wiped his mouth with his napkin and cleared his throat. 'Well, I guess I might as well tell you. I'm one of three finalists being considered for the bishopry at the National Cathedral in Washington.'

Crispin's head cleared all of a sudden and he looked up.

'Tom! That's tremendous! Congratulations.'

'I wasn't planning on telling anyone.'

'I'm honoured.'

'Actually my trip tomorrow is for the final interview. Of course you'll keep this under your hat, won't you?'

'If you want it that way.'

'Although I think maybe it wouldn't be a bad idea to get a search committee going to find a replacement. Discreetly, of course – until the decision is final.'

It was like announcing he knew he had the job. Washington DC was the most powerful and influential diocese in the country, and Crispin could only guess how many applicants he had been up against. Probably hundreds. And they had narrowed it down to Thomas Noonan and two others.

Tom laid down his knife and fork and declared himself a contented man. 'You should try their mushroom steak some-time,' Tom said. It was almost conspiratorial in tone, the advice of a good friend.

Crispin shook his head. 'I'd just be disappointed.'

'Oh, yes. I keep forgetting. You were raised on good ole' corn-fed beef.'

'Yep.'

'A farm boy.'

Even with his head mellowed by wine Crispin didn't like the way he said it.

Tom lifted the empty bottle of Meursault.

'Well, we sure went through that, didn't we?'

'Indeed we did.'

You could tell he was disappointed; the way a man gets when he feels he's not had his fair share. Crispin still had half a glass of wine left and the look on Noonan's face reminded him of Caitlin coveting Lola's ice cream.

'You're leaving us a bit in the lurch, aren't you?' Crispin said.

'I admit the timing's bad.'

Crispin's eyes fell on the file he had brought along. Noonan could read his thoughts.

'I've brought in a lot of money for the cathedral,' Tom said. He folded his hands under his chin with a contemplative air, a pompous mannerism that never failed to irritate Crispin. 'But someone else is going to have to carry on. I think the search committee will see the necessity of bringing in someone with qualities similar to mine.'

'Assuming you are called to the bishopry, how much can we depend on you to help us raise these additional funds?'

'I can't answer that. I'll be in a delicate situation. I can't very well return to DC, to what will be my new diocese and ask them to cough up more money for you.'

'What about Atlanta? And Dallas? They have some deep pockets there.'

'I won't have the time to make many more trips.'

'When will you know for sure – if you have the seat?'

'Oh, it could take several months.'

'And then?'

'I'd have to be in DC on the first of June.' He folded his napkin and waved for the bill.

Crispin said, 'I wish you luck, Tom. You'll make one darn good bishop.'

He meant it sincerely. That's the kind of man he was. But Tom Noonan lacked the fundamental purity of heart to recognize this rare quality in others, so he only smiled that smug smile of his and saw envy where there was none, and contention where there was an honest desire for peace.

5

For a while he lay there like he often did, guessing the time, but finally he groped for the alarm clock and pressed the button to light up the face. It was only 3:46 a.m., and he rolled over and sighed a great tedious sigh and at that point Phoebe mumbled, 'Please stop thrashing around.'

'I'm sorry. I didn't know I was thrashing.'

She batted at her pillow. 'If you can't sleep then get up and at least let me sleep.'

'All right.' He let out another deep sigh and flung back his blanket but did not move.

She rolled over and through the darkness he could feel her eyes on him. 'Crispin, you've given hundreds of sermons over the years.'

'Not here.'

'Well, here is no different from anywhere else.'

'I'm out of practice.'

'You do a wedding almost every week.'

'That's not the same thing.'

He sat up on the edge of the bed and felt with his feet for his slippers. 'I'll get up so you can sleep.'

'You'll do fine,' she said and reached out and patted him on the back. Then she rolled away from him and nestled down in the bed.

The rectory had been built in good English tradition and the stairs were hardwood like the floors and they creaked all the way down. It was very cold downstairs and he thought about building a fire, but then there would not be enough wood to make a fire this afternoon when Julia came to visit, so he pulled the tartan blanket from the sofa, wrapped himself in it and sat in the dark, staring at the soot-blackened fireplace where the fire would have been. He was trying to sort out whatever it was that was worrying him. Partly it was the sermon and his fear of public speaking, but partly it was Julia. He didn't want to admit Julia made a difference and so he tried to tell himself she didn't, but in the end he knew she was part of his need to make an impression. He was having doubts about the sermon and thought it was all wrong. He rose and padded into his study with the blanket trailing on the floor behind, and he sat down behind his desk, flipped on his computer, and began writing from the heart.

Just before dawn he completed an entirely new sermon. He was afraid it might be a little too evangelical for his parishioners but he would take that risk. He printed it off and then lay down on the sofa in the living room and slept. He awoke when he felt Lola standing over his head. He opened his eyes and saw her bending over him with her alert dark eyes on his face and her soft hair rumpled as if she had just come in from a Kansas windstorm.

'Hi muffin,' he mumbled.

'Will you make me some cinnamon toast?'

'Sure, sweetie.'

He rolled over to look at his watch but his arm was asleep, and he waved it around to get the blood circulating.

'Is your mother up yet?'

'No.'

He looked at his watch and for a moment he thought he wasn't seeing clearly.

'Oh good Lord!'

He flung off the blanket and stumbled towards the bathroom crying Phoebe's name.

When Phoebe came down he was in the middle of shaving. She stood in the bathroom doorway yawning.

'Why didn't you wake me?' he said with a fierce glance in the mirror while he rinsed off his razor. 'Didn't you hear the alarm?'

'But you weren't in bed and I thought you were already up.'

'Do you realize what time it is? I've got fifteen minutes before the nine o'clock service.'

'I'll make you some coffee.'

'No, no coffee! Just bring me a glass of wine.'

She brought him a glass of wine and he drank it straight back like medicine, but his hand was still shaking while he shaved his upper lip.

The early Eucharist service went smoothly, and he returned to his study afterwards and had another glass of wine while he made a few last minute revisions to his sermon, and by the eleven o'clock service he was loose and mellow and sang his heart out during the procession with the choir. During the scripture readings he searched the pews for Julia but it was too difficult to see the faces at the back, and he knew she wouldn't sit near the front. Nor could he find Phoebe and Megan, although Cat had come along with Lola, who had opted out of Sunday School in order to hear her father preach, and the two of them were sitting in the second row just beneath the pulpit. Cat had remembered to bring along coloured pencils and a colouring book for Lola, but the five-year-old sat perched on the edge of the pew swinging her legs while she pretended to read the prayer book, even though she knew most of it by heart.

In the end, Crispin gave one of the best sermons of his career. The congregation sat riveted to the pulpit in a silence so intense it was as if they were all hearing with the same ears and breathing with the same breath. For the longest time there was not a rustle nor the sound of wood creaking nor even a child fussing, and when Crispin sat back down and lowered his head in prayer there was still not a sound but only this full and throbbing silence, and he let out a sigh of thanks and relief.

After the service, as he stood at the door he was pleased and even a little surprised at the enthusiasm with which people greeted him, and the way they pressed their hands warmly into his and recalled parts of the sermon that had impressed them. He would glance over their heads as they passed by and search the crowd for Julia but she was not there, and it was difficult for him to keep smiling.

He mingled only briefly in the parish hall during coffee hour and sent Cat back to the rectory to take Lola home and to see if Julia had arrived, but Cat came back to tell him she was not there.

'I told Mom she missed a really good sermon,' she said, and she pried her way through a blockade of adults standing around the coffee service table to snatch two cookies from the tray.

'You mean your mother wasn't there?'

Caitlin stuffed a cookie into her mouth and shook her head.

'Your mother wasn't there?' he repeated.

Cat covered her mouth with her hand in that fastidious way she had of hiding her braces. Once she had fully swallowed the cookie she answered, 'Nope. She and Megan didn't go.'

'Why not?'

'Mom said she had to cook and Megan stayed home to help.'

'Good grief,' Crispin muttered and thumped down his coffee cup. 'We're having one guest. Not an army.'

Caitlin shrugged again then nudged her way through the crowd for another cookie, and Crispin got caught up in a conversation and tried to keep the hurt out of his eyes, but finally he disengaged himself and slipped through the back hall and up the stairs to his study.

Crispin's study was an enclosed loft built over the Dean's office with just one small lancet window that looked out over the narrow alley and caught the light briefly in the late afternoon. There were quite a few books but nothing like Tom Noonan's extravagant library. What really caught your attention were the photographs of his homeland – images of strange, treeless hills, cast in red by the light of the setting sun, with deep shadows sinking into the valleys, all of it looking like something sensual and flesh-like that gives you odd yearnings you can't quite comprehend. Some of the photographs were aerial and Crispin had taken them himself. There were photographs of an endless sea of tall grasses whipped into waves by the wind. In others there was little more than sky to fill the frame.

There were photographs of his daughters and Phoebe and Crispin on horseback with his father, and his mother before she died. It didn't really look like you would imagine a priest's study to look. There was nothing particularly reverent or scholarly about it, but you knew from the moment you set foot in there that it was a good place to be.

Crispin closed the door, took off his jacket and hung it on the back of the door. Without turning, he began to unbutton his clerical collar. All of a sudden he heard a rustle and before he could turn to face the intruder, he felt her fingers at the back of his neck.

'Here, let me do that for you.'

But his hand caught hers and he turned with a look of astonishment.

'Julia!'

She wore her honey-coloured hair swept into a smooth French twist at the back, and her dramatic eyes were set off by the fur collar framing her face. For a moment Crispin's breath caught in his chest.

'Turn!' she commanded, and he did so, and she said lightly

with a hint of wickedness, 'I've always had this fantasy about defrocking a priest.'

'Shame on you.'

'Oh, I think it's just we all like to think a man would love us enough to give up even his soul. Isn't that it?' She smiled and dangled the collar in front of his nose and he snatched it from her.

'Where were you?'

'I'm so sorry,' she said, and there was honest contrition in her voice. 'I was carrying all these things,' she stepped back and he saw where she gestured to the gift bags clustered on the floor, 'and I was already late so I asked the secretary if I could leave them in your office . . .'

'What's all this?' Crispin said. 'What have you done, girl?'

'Oh, I had to bring gifts. How could I come without gifts?'

'A few posies would have done the trick.'

'And then I was late and missed your sermon.'

'And for once I was darn good.'

'I'm so sorry, really I am. But I came up here and . . .' She walked around behind his desk to where the framed photographs hung and pointed to one of Crispin as a shirtless teenager in jeans and boots and dark glasses sitting on the bumper of an old pick-up. He was a broad-shouldered youth, with muscular arms and chest and the bullish neck of a high school wrestler. In the photo he was suntanned and wore a cocky grin, and you could tell he was proud of his manhood.

'Do you remember who took that photograph?' she asked.

'Of course I do,' he grinned.

'I took it.'

'I know.'

'Did you take these?' she asked, pointing to the aerial shots.

'Yeah, from my plane.'

'Your plane?'

'Yeah. I had my own plane.'

'Oh, Crispin,' she cried. 'That was your dream, wasn't it? To fly.'

'Well, I finished my degree in engineering, but then the air force wouldn't take me. My eyesight wasn't good enough. I'd been selling aviation insurance to pay my way through college and I really enjoyed it – got to meet a lot of other guys like me. Farmers, ranchers, doctors, all with their own planes. It was a good business, and I was making good money. So I stayed with it. Built up a profitable business. Had a good life. Married Phoebe and bought us a big, big house, and filled it up first with furniture, then with kids, and then . . .' He shrugged, suddenly self-conscious, reluctant to continue.

'Go on, tell me the good part.'

'The good part?'

'Yeah. What makes a man give up all that for this?'

He liked the way she was watching him, that teasing smile of hers, and he was thinking how she had grown into her beauty, the square jaw and the long slender neck and the dramatic eyes she had regretted so as a girl.

'You really want to hear that story?'

'More than anything else.'

'I don't tell many people.'

'Would you tell me sometime?'

'If you'd like to hear it.'

The teasing smile had faded, replaced by a softer look.

'I don't have anyone like you in my life, Crispin. I haven't had anyone like you in my life for many, many years.'

'Meaning?'

She quipped, 'Well, Jona has connections, of course, but not like that.'

'I see,' he grinned back.

'Truly. I want to hear what's taken you down this path. You must have given up a lot.'

'And gained a lot.'

Neither of them said anything for a moment, and they held a long look.

Crispin bent to retrieve the gift bags. 'Let's go. The girls are dying to meet you.'

6

Even if you had never seen her act, you knew when she crossed a room that she was someone worth watching. You could try to analyse the parts that made up the whole, but the whole was always the greater. The mouth was too full perhaps and the neck too severe, and the dark eyes nearly eclipsed the face, but when taken together the distortions added up to something undeniably lovely. But most of all you knew when she looked at you and smiled that there was something quite real and good behind the eyes. Quite a few people recognized her on the way through the parish hall and along the cloister. Julia made their heads turn and a ripple of silence passed through the crowd in her wake. Crispin led the way like a bulldozer with a shopping bag clutched in each hand and Julia, close behind, found it touching the way he became all sober and grim like a bodyguard. Once they had entered the cloister garden and closed the gate behind them, he stopped and turned.

'Are you all right?'

She had gone pale, and her eyes had taken on a glassy look.

'Just a little light-headed,' she smiled, dismissing it with a wave of her gloved hand.

'Here, sit down,' he commanded, and he lowered her onto a stone bench in front of the fountain.

'I'm so silly. I should have had some breakfast. Jona's always lecturing me about that. You'd think I'd learn.'

'Just sit for a minute.'

She turned a smile on him. 'Thanks for getting me through that crowd. There are times when I'm just not up for playing the part, if you know what I mean.'

'If I'd stopped to introduce you to anyone, we'd have spent another hour in there.'

He sat down beside her and settled the shopping bags between his feet. 'Still playing the over-protective brother, aren't I?'

'I don't mind.'

She glanced at the old stone rectory on the other side of the courtyard.

'Is that where you live?'

'That's home.'

She cocked her head to one side. 'It reminds me . . . what is it? I know. Sleeping Beauty's castle.'

'That's what Lola said when she first saw it.'

'I can see we have the same references,' grinned Julia. She lifted her chin and sniffed the air. 'This is how London smelled.' She pointed to a shadowy corner of the courtyard where the wall was dark from rain and moss grew over the cobblestones. 'I never get over it, this green smell in the winter.'

'Our winters back home were always so dry,' he said.

'And so cold.'

Crispin's eyes swept up the wall to the spire extending beyond the top of the scaffolding, surrounded by the patch of slate grey sky overhead.

He said, 'What I like about it is the feeling of being enclosed. Enclosure is one of the oldest meaningful forms in the history of architecture. That's one of the reasons why folks find those cluster developments in the suburbs so appealing.' He started to go on, but then he caught a glimpse of Julia's gently mocking eyes.

'There I go again,' he said, reprimanding himself with a slap on the knee. 'Another one of my lectures.'

She studied him quietly and said, 'You haven't changed, Crispin.'

'Is that good?' he grimaced.

'Yes. That's good,' she answered soberly.

Lola had climbed up onto the kitchen worksurface and was on her knees peering through the window.

'Get down,' Megan said sharply and snapped her on the rear with a tea towel. Lola's wail brought Phoebe downstairs and by then Cat and Megan had pushed Lola out of the way and were standing over the kitchen sink peering through the curtains.

'Dad's talking to her about the cathedral,' Megan said over her shoulder.

'That could take a while,' Phoebe quipped.

'Did you see her handbag?' Megan whispered, pulling back a curtain panel. 'That's Dior.'

'I can't believe the things you notice,' Cat answered contemptuously.

'Well, she's a movie star, duh ... It goes with the territory.'

Phoebe interceded and told them they'd all look like fools if Julia saw them peeking at her from behind the curtains. At that moment Crispin bolted noisily through the front door announcing their arrival in his deep baritone voice. The girls at once grew animated and giggled nervously to one another until Phoebe herded them out of the kitchen and into the drawing room.

Much to Crispin's delight, Phoebe and Megan had set the table with their best china and the candy-coloured crystal wine glasses Phoebe had bought at the flea market in Clignancourt. Even the silver was all freshly polished. Megan had cut out star-shaped name cards and labelled them in gold ink, and Julia's was the largest and most elaborate. It was enough to melt Crispin's heart, and he caught Phoebe behind the kitchen door as she was spooning mashed potatoes into a bowl and pulled her into his arms and kissed her. She looked up at him with a pleased smile and told him she knew how important this lunch was to him and that she wanted it to be a special day.

Julia was the kind of person who could make you feel at home with her if she liked you, and if she didn't like you she held herself aloof but still with a kind of discreet charm that fed her mystique. The latter was the persona she presented most often to strangers. But this afternoon, in the company of Crispin and his family, it was as if all those years had never intervened. She was just older, and Crispin was older, and here were his wife and children instead of his parents, and she felt the same contentment she had remembered feeling in his home as a child.

It was clear to all of them that Julia had taken more than a superficial interest in them. She had called Crispin's secretary to find out the girls' ages and tastes and had shopped for the gifts herself rather than send a gofer to do the job. There was a black hip-hugger belt with a rhinestone buckle for Megan, a silver charm bracelet for Caitlin, and a Pooh Bear child's tea set in real china for Lola. For Crispin and Phoebe there was a bottle of champagne and some caviar which Jona acquired in quantity during his frequent trips to Russia. They started with the caviar and finished the champagne with their curried shrimp entrée. For Phoebe's lamb (succulent and pink to perfection) they opened a very nice Margaux for which Crispin had paid dearly, but Julia noticed right away it was vintage and he couldn't help but feel proud of himself.

Although Lola remained withdrawn and ate her meal in shy silence, Megan and Caitlin warmed quickly to Julia and asked her all manner of questions about how films were made — what it was like to kiss men she barely knew, and do it while dozens of strangers looked on, and didn't it make her husband jealous? Julia clearly loved playing up to their youthful curiosity, and she laughed and talked with candid humour, and told countless behind-the-scenes anecdotes that entertained them throughout the meal. She was particularly excited about her next film which she would start shooting in the early spring in Yorkshire; she was to play the lead roll of Charlotte Brontë.

When Cat heard this she hurriedly swallowed her mouthful of green beans and with a hand cupped over her braces sputtered, 'You mean the *Jane Eyre* Charlotte Brontë?'

'Have you read it?' Julia inquired.

She nodded enthusiastically and tucked a strand of dark hair behind her ear. 'Twice.'

'I'm impressed. That's heavy reading.'

Cat beamed and looked down at her plate. Megan threw her a bored look. 'Cat, don't hoard the salt.'

Cat slammed the salt shaker down in front of Megan.

'Girls,' warned Phoebe.

But Julia could not talk about herself without talking about Jona, and it seemed at times as if her pride in Jona surpassed all other things. She wove his life story into her own, and you felt at times she wasn't even aware of the symbiosis. But Phoebe and Crispin noticed it, and it was obvious how much she worshipped him. He had started off as a journalist for the *Wall Street Journal*, she said, and then – seeing he had the instincts for corporate raiding – set himself up as a public relations consultant for hostile takeovers. He was truly brilliant at it, she admitted, was an expert at digging up facts and presenting them to the media in a way calculated to influence the stockholders. But by the time she met him, Jona had already moved into commodities trading, she explained. He specialized in barter arrangements and currency exchange from countries without convertible currency, most specifically the USSR.

Jona's grandmother was Russian, and Jona spoke the language fluently, and back in the days of the Soviet empire he had been one of the few Americans to hold a permanent visa to Russia.

But she didn't dwell long on his business, and Crispin thought perhaps – despite the big words – this was something she understood only dimly. She was most entertaining when she did an imitation of Jona spouting his maxims. She had a prodigious memory and a playfulness that bordered on the comic, and she'd square her shoulders, grip her fork between her fingers the way Jona held his cigars, and mimic in a fault-less Jimmy Cagney Brooklynese, 'You wanna feel the pulse of the world? You watch the little guy. The ones low on the food chain.' Then she'd pause, rock slightly and wave the cigar in your face. 'Your dog knows it's gonna rain before you do. Why? 'Cuz he can feel the drop in pressure. You don't know it's gonna rain until you get wet. So watch the little guy. He's the barometer.' And then she'd talk about his native Brooklyn. 'Underdog capital of the world,' she'd say, sweeping the table with a pugnacious scowl. 'Nothin' in Brighton Beach but hustlers 'n breweries 'n hard-working men bustin' a gut to raise their families.'

Megan was so enraptured that she had hardly touched her lunch, and the slice of lamb Crispin had carved for her lay cold on her plate. 'That must be so cool . . .' she braved, nudging a potato around with a fork, '. . . owning a hotel.'

Caitlin piped up. 'She doesn't *own* the hotel, stupid.'

'That's what Dad said,' Megan shot back.

'Jona's the president,' Crispin corrected gently.

'Oh,' Megan said meekly, and you knew she was burning with embarrassment inside.

'Well, it's almost as good as owning it,' Julia said gently, and you saw she could feel for the girl. 'Actually, Jona really doesn't have to do much of anything. The managing director runs the place. But one of the perks that comes with the title is that we get to live there. And that's pretty cool.'

'Well that's what I meant,' Megan quipped with a cutting glance at her sister.

'Come over and I'll give you a tour sometime.'

'That'd be neat,' Megan smiled, feeling vindicated.

'Or better yet, you girls come for lunch. Or maybe tea would be more fun. They serve formal tea in the gallery and it's a great place to people watch. You'll see all these Italians in their fur coats coming back from shopping carrying their Fendi and Gucci bags. It's fun.'

There was a sudden explosion of enthusiastic chatter while they ran through their schedules and tried to find an afternoon when they were all free, and Crispin finally had to raise his voice to quiet them down. Only Lola remained quiet, although Julia had been careful to include her in the invitation. Throughout the meal Lola had been wary and unwilling to be charmed. She ate only a little of the pasta Phoebe had made for her, and a few moments later while they were clearing the plates she discreetly slipped down from the table and disappeared into her bedroom.

Phoebe followed her roast lamb with a lavish cheese plate and chilled tangerines, and she made coffee while Crispin built a fire, and then they settled into that late Sunday inertia – Julia in the armchair with one of Phoebe's shawls about her shoulders, her hair falling loose around her face and her cheeks flushed from the heat and the wine, and Phoebe nestled up against Crispin on the worn sofa.

'We have more dessert, you know,' Phoebe said, trying to stifle a yawn. 'I made a lemon tart.'

'Oh, Phoebe,' Julia smiled, 'it couldn't get any sweeter than this,' and Phoebe laughed and Crispin's heart swelled, for he could tell when Phoebe truly liked someone, and Julia had won her over like he had hoped she would.

Julia sank back into the armchair with her saucer cupped in her hands and let her eyes drift around the room. Portraits of past rectors and deans hung on sashes against cherrywood panelling alongside sketches of Crispin's father's hunting dogs, and silk-fringed lamps shed their muted light on scarred mahogany tables cluttered with books and magazines and photographs. There were a few mementoes left behind by families who had picked up their lives and moved on, and to this Crispin and his family had added their own furnishings and details, but the clutter seemed to have become a part of the rectory's tradition. With its rumpled sofa and worn armchairs flanking the fireplace, the rectory had the feel of an old country home a little down-at-heel. It was a place that seemed to welcome the effects of the passage of time. It captured the very essence of home: a place that harboured a family in all its intimacy, promising them security, comfort and continuity.

'What a marvellous home,' Julia said. 'How lucky you are.'

'Oh!' Phoebe cried. 'It's a junkyard! Some of the things aren't ours but I'm embarrassed to say most of them are. Or rather they're Crispin's.'

'Some of the things were gifts, too,' Crispin pointed out, too content to rise to an argument. Then, with a lazy grin to Julia, 'Phoebe likes her places to be pretty. I just want it to be liveable.'

'Well, we have a lovely little farmhouse up in Normandy and I'm trying to furnish it bit by bit. I refuse to put any of this junk up there. If it were up to me I'd throw all of this out and start from scratch.'

'You wouldn't!' Julia said.

'Oh yes I would. And another thing, living here is like living in a fishbowl. Everyone notices everything that goes on. You can barely walk out the door without somebody starting a rumour.'

Crispin glanced at his watch and said he had hoped to take Lola to the Champs de Mars to ride her bike, but Phoebe feared it was too late. 'It'll be dark soon.'

'If we hurry we can get in a short walk,' Crispin said.

Phoebe looked across at Julia. 'Julia, go with him if you want.'

'Let me help you with the dishes,' Julia offered, setting her empty cup on the coffee table.

'The girls will do the dishes. You two go. Take Lola. She needs to get out.'

Crispin brought the car around and they loaded Lola's bike into the back and drove across the Seine to the Avenue des Bourdonnais where they parked up a side street. The temperature had dropped and there was a dampness in the air that held a promise of snow; their breath vaporized in the pale light and it felt good to both of them to be walking together like this in the cold at dusk. The lines at the pillars of the Eiffel Tower were short because it was a Sunday in November and bitterly cold. Behind it stretched the wide green lawns of the Champs de Mars, once the parade grounds of the military school, but this too was nearly deserted. They took a gravelled side path that wound through the landscaped gardens where hardy little marigolds and pansies flowered among holly bushes and evergreens. The leaves had fallen all of a sudden, raked from their branches by the sharp wind, and the ground was a heavy blanket of butter-yellow maple, rusty chestnut and bronze elm. In the summer there would be hordes of children crowded noisily around the puppet shows and pony rides, but now there were only darkly-clothed figures hurrying briskly along and a scattering of children bundled up in scarves and gloves. A shivering Yorkshire terrier in a tiny red vest sniffed around the green while his master – muffled up to his eyes – waited impatiently on the path.

Lola walked alongside Crispin holding his hand but she was

quiet. When they reached the wide gravel avenue Crispin set down her bike and she mounted it, then he trotted along behind her to steady the bike as he always did but she pedalled away from him and wove shakily along the path on her own.

'Don't go too far!' Crispin called after her.

Julia had watched this from a distance, and she caught up with Crispin and said, 'Maybe I shouldn't have come along. I'm intruding.'

'No, you're not.'

'I think she wanted you all to herself this evening.'

'Oh, I don't know about that. Lola's not easy to read. You can never be quite sure what she's thinking.'

'I remember how I used to feel when my dad would come to visit me and he'd bring along a friend. I was so angry but I was afraid for him to see I was angry.'

She stopped all of a sudden and dropped her head. 'Listen to me. This is terrible. I haven't even thought about them in so long. It's like I'd almost wiped them off my radar screen.'

'And then I came along.'

'Yeah.' She said it with a smile, but he knew she had not said it lightly.

'I always wondered why you took the name Kramer.'

'It was Jona's idea. He thought Julia Streiker sounded too much like Julius Streicher. He was some big bad Nazi.'

'Yes. I've heard of him. He was the Nazi editor of a German newspaper during the war.'

She gave him a sideways glance of surprise. It was only a piece of trivia (Crispin's brain had soaked up many useless bits of trivia), but however insignificant it was, it meant something to Julia, and Crispin rose even further in her esteem.

'So,' he said, 'Julia Streiker became Julia Kramer.'

'In more ways than just in name.'

She hesitated, but Crispin always had this intense way of

listening to others, listening with his eyes, and you felt encouraged to confide in him even though he said nothing. She continued then. 'I got a contract to model, with this place in Kansas City, but then they sent me to New York. I never even finished high school. I met Jona a couple of years later.' She pulled her collar up around her ears and glanced down the path for Lola. 'He helped me reinvent myself. I couldn't have done it without him. He's my Pygmalion.'

At that moment the lights came on across the city and the tower appeared behind her all of a sudden, its pig-iron girders criss-crossed in perfect symmetry, narrowing to a slender needle at the top. A moment ago it had stood cold and dark and dead, but now it towered lambent gold against the blue-black sky, and despite its monumental size, it awed with a delicate beauty you could never quite grasp.

'Look,' Crispin said, spinning her around to see it.

His touch was brief and he quickly stuffed his hands back in his pockets, but she stood near him and felt his warmth at her back, and she was aware of a sense of well-being in his presence. They were quiet, and they could hear the sound of footsteps in the gravel as people passed by. A gust of wind hit their faces and then swept through the trees behind them, shaking the few leaves still clinging to the branches and sending a handful of them floating to the ground.

In the silence after the wind had passed, Crispin said, 'Julia, we don't have to reminisce about the past.'

She gave a deep sigh as one who has been defeated. Turning back to face him she said, 'You know, there's something . . .' She paused.

'Something what?'

She shook her head. 'I don't know . . . something so *honest* . . .'

'Honest?'

'About seeing you again. Like you're some kind of bedrock.'

He threw back his head and laughed, and his breath roiled in white vaporous clouds.

'That's a good one,' he said. 'I know I'm stubborn, but to that degree . . .'

'Oh, it *is* good to see you again,' she grinned. She linked her arm through his and they turned and continued down the path. Julia felt a lightness she had not felt for a long time.

Suddenly a child's wail cut through the air.

'That's Lola!' he said, quick as a heartbeat. Darkness had fallen sharply and further down the path they could barely make out a huddle of shadowed figures. Crispin broke into a run.

Lola had lost control of her bike and collided with another child. It took Crispin a few minutes to get them untangled and to quieten her, then he picked her up in his arms and they returned to the car.

Even while Crispin loaded the bike into the boot, Lola's little chest was still quaking with sobs, and so Julia asked if she might sit in the rear seat with her on the way home, if Lola would permit it, and Lola nodded that she would. They descended Boulevard des Bourdonnais and followed the flow of cars along the *quai*. Crispin listened as Julia talked to Lola in a clear voice, not that coddled kind of voice adults sometime adopt with children they do not know but want to impress, but one that makes a child feel respected. She told Lola stories about Crispin when they were growing up together. How Julia had once accidentally knocked him out when she was swinging a big aluminium fishnet around her head, and she thought she had killed him, and how Crispin had lain white and still on the old wooden dock and Julia had thought she might die herself from fright.

As they waited in traffic Crispin turned and glanced over his shoulder at them. Lola's sobs had ceased, and her face was transformed: Julia had entranced her.

As they were nearing the hotel, Julia said to Lola, 'Now when you get home, your daddy'll make you some of his magic healing potion, won't he?'

Lola glanced warily at her father. 'Does it taste bad?'

'Bad?' Julia said. 'Hot chocolate? I've never heard of hot chocolate tasting bad. But I do know there's a secret recipe for a very special kind of hot chocolate that has great healing powers. Your Grandma Wakefield used to make it for me whenever I got hurt real bad.'

'You knew Gigi?'

'She was like a mother to me.'

'I don't remember her. She died.'

'Well, I'm sure she taught your daddy her secret recipe.' Julia tapped him lightly on the shoulder. 'She did, didn't she?'

'Sure,' nodded Crispin and he caught her eye in the rear-view mirror and grinned.

'But it only works on big kids,' Julia hastened to add. 'You have to be at least five, I think. Isn't that it, Crispin?'

'That's right.'

Lola jumped in then. 'I'm five,' she said brightly.

'Well then he can make it for you.'

Lola fell into a contented silence, and when they dropped Julia in front of the hotel, Crispin came around to open the car door but the doorman was already there in his black top hat and white trimmed tailcoat. He knew Julia by name, and Crispin felt like she had suddenly separated from him and gone back to her own world.

Lola stared wide-eyed at the doorman and Julia bent down and politely said goodnight to her, the way you would to a real person, and then she turned to Crispin and reached for his hand.

'It was a beautiful day,' she said in a low voice, kissing him lightly on the cheek. 'When Jona gets back, you and Phoebe must come over for dinner. I want you to meet him.'

Crispin watched as she passed through the revolving glass doors into a lobby bursting with light from crystal chandeliers. A dark-suited man hurried to greet her; she said a few brief words to him and he bowed slightly as she passed by. The last image Crispin had of her was of the honey-coloured hair streaked with gold and her coat unfurling in a blur of ambient light.

7

The King George hotel was a grand palace from another era, and like an old crank settled in its ways it had resisted change, so if you wanted to be fashionable and impress people you went to one of the hotels that had been newly renovated in the austere, clinical style favoured by the postmodernist trend-setters. If you came to the George it was because you appreciated the texture of the Savonnerie carpet you noticed even through the soles of your shoes, and the imposing presence of Flemish wall tapestries where medieval princes larger than life hunted stags with hounds. Massive gilt mirrors that dwarfed the human form reflected fine old paintings and wood veneers and crystal drop chandeliers. The George was synonymous with Paris and Paris was in love with its past, and all the city's history of decadence, turbulence and pride was distilled in the aging beauty of these rooms.

As part of the deal he struck when he negotiated the sale of the George to its British buyers, along with the title of President Jona was given a small suite on the top floor which would serve as his primary residence. He had benefited from the same kind of arrangement at the Westchester in London where he and Julia had lived for nearly eleven years. They had never owned a home of their own, and Julia felt the impermanence of their lives very deeply. But there were reasons for this choice of lifestyle, and Julia could not dispute them. Here everything was within her radius of safety, for the entire hotel became her home, and she felt secure within it.

She had learned to feel comfortable in these places, and she had learned how to dress the part, but she had not grown up in this world, and it would never be hers. She felt this even more acutely that night as she left Crispin and walked through the doors of the George, along the hall and past the bar, down the long splendid gallery towards the Prince's Staircase. If Jona had been there she would have taken the elevator, but she would not take it on her own. She could still remember times when even stairs had been impossible for her; once, many years ago in Harrods, she had only been able to get out of the store by inching backwards down three flights of stairs on her hands and knees, oblivious to the stares of passers-by, twenty minutes of sheer terror that had seemed like an eternity to her. She could always feel it coming – like a black cloud – a sentiment of impending doom when fear emerged from its hiding place within her. It oozed out of her very pores and she could taste it in her mouth.

At other times reality seemed to shift to another dimension and she could not function, could not even name the thing she held in her hand, let alone know what to do with it, even if it was only her keys and she was standing in a car park next to her car, and all she had to do was insert the key into the lock. That kind of full-blown panic happened only rarely now. Now she knew what to avoid. But still, there was always the dissembling, the searching for excuses, the pretence of it all.

That very morning she had lied to Crispin. She had arrived only a few minutes late, and she had paused in the vestibule with the gift bags in her hands watching the tail end of the procession through the glass door. A greeter stood on the inside with a handful of Sunday bulletins, and seeing Julia hesitate, she had smiled and reached to open the door, and the stirring echoes of the organ and choir had swept into the cold entrance. That's when the panic seized her. It had hit her so rapidly that she had been totally unprepared. The intensity of it nearly smothered her and she could not breathe, so she spun around and fled down the cloister, taking refuge in the church office where the secretary directed her to Crispin's study. Humiliated, she had waited there, knowing how much she had disappointed him and worried about how to explain her absence.

God knows how she had battled to hide it from all of them. Throughout her career, directors had labelled her capricious and demanding when she had been unable to come out of her dressing room, when she had sent the make-up and hair stylists away and sat paralysed in front of her mirror with a pounding heart, praying for the fear to pass.

There were moments when it had been so overwhelming she felt that if she were to make the slightest movement the world would dissolve beneath her feet. Screams would rise up in her throat and she would try to swallow them down; sometimes she lost consciousness. Once they were shooting a small scene at the top of an escalator; she was to ride it down and then try to race back up. But when they called for action, she had shrunk back and grabbed the arm of the gaffer who had just checked the lighting on her face, then crumbled into a ball on the floor, still gripping his arm so forcefully that he had to drop to his knees beside her. She had covered up, making them think it was violent stomach pains, but she was sweating so badly her make-up was ruined, and a doctor was called in. They had to shoot around her that day, and she didn't make another film for two years after that.

She learned later to accept roles that were far removed from her own personality, self-courageous, strong-willed women or women of another era. She would stay in character even after the cameras stopped rolling, and this enabled her to function without fear, for then she would not be Julia, she would be someone else. She learned to carry with her small objects or scents that triggered her sensory perception, anything that could place her back in her character's world. If she had her own dressing room she asked the set designer to decorate it with props from the set. She read books and listened to music according to her character's tastes. All these things made it easier for her, and no one thought much of it, for all these techniques were part of an actor's craft.

Agents found her difficult; they thought her fickle and too picky, and grumbled that they never had the opportunity to showcase her true talent because they never knew what roles would appeal to her. They were at a loss as to how to market her to audiences who knew her only vaguely. She would pop up in a film here and there, and just when it seemed she was poised for stardom, she would disappear from public view for years, and then the recognition factor was lost and they would have to start all over again.

Julia often joked lightly about her little idiosyncracies, but no one apart from Jona and Susannah Rich, her New York publicist, knew how extreme her distress was and how fear ruled her life. Whenever Julia was tempted to put her trust in a particular director or a producer she admired with hopes they would help her work through the complications, Jona would caution her. He warned that if the truth about her debilitating anxieties became known, she would never make another film.

Papa Jo, she called him in private, the name she had given him seventeen years ago when they first met in New York. She had been modelling for two years but the work was still sporadic, and once, during a long dry spell when she was desperate for cash, she had broken down and gone for an interview with an escort agency. They had sent her out that same evening to the Pierre Hotel for drinks and dinner with an executive who was entertaining overseas clients and needed pretty young women to jazz up the party. The agency made it clear that the escort's obligations did not go beyond dinner.

Nevertheless, Julia knew more would be expected of her; she didn't know how she was going to handle it, and she had been so nervous that she had nearly passed out in the taxi. She had arrived an hour early, hoping to get a little familiar with the place and calm her nerves with a glass of wine at the bar.

It was a little before six in the evening and the lounge was filling up. Julia sidled up to an empty bar stool next to a well-dressed man with a sleek, bald head and Coke-bottle glasses who was hunched over his mobile phone. The television above the bar was tuned to the evening news and he would occasionally glance up and squint at the screen while he scribbled notes on a napkin with a silver pen; it was hard to tell if the notes had anything to do with his conversation, which was in a language Julia had never heard before. He felt Julia's attentiveness, turned a bemused look on her and gave her a wry grin. Then he covered the telephone with his hand and said, 'I've got some Russian friends lost in FAO Schwarz. They're very paranoid, the Russians.' A few seconds later he covered the mouthpiece again and landed a witty little quip that made her smile. He kept up a running commentary, and Julia could picture it all, the Russian and his wife wandering in a daze past Barnies and Barbies looking for Tomb Raider, while this man next to her tried to guide them through the maze over the telephone. The stranger was so hilarious that her nervousness finally broke like a bubble and she was seized with a fit of laughter that she was completely helpless to control. All the stress and tension that had built up in her was released in that one long, glorious seizure of mirth. The stranger cut off his conversation and watched her with growing concern. She kept reassuring him she was just fine, but she went on laughing for a good five minutes. Everyone in the bar turned to stare at her, and the bartender brought her a glass of water, but drinking didn't help, she just kept right on laughing. She fully expected the gentleman to get up and move away; instead he handed her napkins to blot her eyes and urged her to take deep breaths and relax. But Julia had never been so relaxed in her life. It really felt marvellous she said, better than a sneeze and as good as an orgasm.

When it was all over and she had grown calm (with the exception of a few errant snickers) she confessed to him why she was there, and that she had been very nervous having never done this kind of thing before, and now that she had had such a good laugh she would pay for her wine and go home and to hell with the escort agency. And she had him to thank for it.

But she did not go home. Instead she listened in wide-eyed wonder, her face alight, as the man next to her explained complex body chemistry and the changes produced through laughter, and she asked if he was a doctor but no, he scowled, God forbid. Much worse. He was only a humble – albeit erudite – commodities trader who attempted to convert the lessons he had learned from his vast wealth of useless knowledge into useful applications such as making money.

They spent the entire evening at the bar eating oysters and drinking champagne, and Julia thought she had never met a man like Jona Wahlberg and would never meet another like him the rest of her life. He was a ruthless wit and a bewitching storyteller, but what Julia really appreciated was the earthiness hovering just beneath the impeccably groomed exterior, although there was not even a hint of lasciviousness in his conversation and he never once made an unseemly move. All she was wondering was if he was married, and if he would walk away and she would never see him again. Neither proved to be true. The next day he took her to the horse races and spent the afternoon helping her decipher the racing form. When they made love for the first time it was at her place one evening when her roommate was out of town, and afterwards he wrapped his suit jacket around her and held her in his arms and recited a long passage in Russian from *Anna Karenina* about beauty. In the morning he took her out to buy a food processor so she could mix the health food drinks she needed to sustain her (he was concerned that she was already suffering from malnutrition because of constant dieting), and then they went back to his apartment and made love again, and that evening they ordered in Chinese food and – refusing to succumb to her pleas for a fork – he coached her through her first meal with chopsticks. A week later she packed everything she owned into her big blue Samsonite suitcase and three cardboard boxes and moved in with Jona.

In the early days of their relationship they were rarely out of each other's sight. Jona shifted the focus of his prodigious energy to Julia's career, and within a year she was in Hollywood with a contract for a daytime soap. A cynic might have spoken disparagingly of such closeness, but the relationship worked like symbiosis. Rarely did they argue, simply because there never seemed to be anything to argue about. The distribution of power within the couple was straightforward: all the major decisions of their lives were left to Jona. Jona decided where they would live and if they should move, what roles Julia should solicit or turn down and where they should travel on holiday. He read her scripts and reviewed her contracts, and Julia's agent knew that Julia would agree to nothing without Jona's nod. The final decision rested in Jona's hands. Her trust in him was absolute, like that of a child's.

He negotiated her fees, invested her money and paid her bills; he told her what she was making on each film but Julia rarely remembered. Somehow the figures blurred in her mind. Deep down she never thought of herself as an actress, although she worked very hard at it, and even when the studio was promoting her for an Oscar for her role as a mentally challenged young woman who avenges the murder of her beloved teacher, she still didn't feel like she deserved it. She didn't get a nomination, and her response was one of relief.

Despite her insecurities, Julia was a born actress; she was emotional and highly dramatic, and had a great sense of fun. Julia gave Jona all the credit for recognizing her hidden talent, but all he had done was simply follow the natural impulses of a middle-aged man at a crossroads in life who had the blessed fortune to stumble across this sylph-like creature with dreamy dark eyes. He had taken her by the hand, hammered out the rough spots and propelled her into the spotlight.

Julia had not made many films since her debut sixteen years before, and only a few of them had been mainstream successes, but she had eventually earned the respect of critics, producers and directors for her fine portrayals in less than inspiring films. But as far as Julia was concerned, her most challenging role by far was the one she played every day off screen – that of a normal, independent woman.

8

The idea of having tea with Julia at the George delighted Crispin's daughters. Phoebe was hurt that she hadn't been included, and when Julia called to set a date Phoebe weaselled an invitation for herself. When Crispin found this out, he told Phoebe that the occasion was the girls' special treat, and he insisted that they go alone. Phoebe didn't like it but she could always tell when she wouldn't get her way with Crispin, and this was one of those occasions. It never took much to spark a little jealousy in Phoebe, and it struck her straight away that Julia was in a special category by herself, more than friend but not blood family, and this gave Phoebe something to think about.

It was raining heavily that afternoon as the girls walked up the street from the rectory together, the three of them jostling for centre under Crispin's lopsided umbrella and bickering over who was getting wetter. Megan came through the door first, having abandoned Cat to deal with the dripping umbrella, and then Cat followed her in with a disgruntled look on her face and Lola in tow.

They were late because Lola had insisted on wearing the Cinderella costume Crispin had bought her at the Disney store for her birthday that summer, and both sisters had refused to be seen with her dressed like a freak. Their mother was not at home and Crispin was at a meeting with the Dean, and neither sister could dissuade the child, so they dragged her along and arrived at the hotel out of sorts and wet from the knees down. Only Lola seemed unperturbed. She stood in the lobby in her winter coat with her sodden blue tulle skirt drooping down around her ankles, gazing up at the crystal chandelier, believing she was the princess in a fairybook land.

It was not only the King George itself that overwhelmed them, but the reception they were given. Julia had sent the hotel's assistant director to greet them, and he welcomed them graciously before ushering them down the carpeted hall and into the gallery. A receptionist relieved them of their coats and seated them at a round table laid with starched linen and a sprig of lavender orchids in the centre.

Julia appeared just a few minutes later. They watched her descending the grand Prince's Staircase and thought she was the most glamorous thing they had ever seen. She was not dressed in anything remarkable, a polo-neck sweater and fitted black trousers, but she moved with a dancer's grace and never looked down at the steps. She put them at ease immediately, and – seeing that they were wet and bedraggled – she bundled them all off to the powder room where Megan restyled her hair, and Julia dried Lola's skirt with a hair dryer the receptionist brought them. They talked a lot, and giggled when a woman came in and stared at them. It was like a party and they were all having fun.

They ordered a full cream tea, with rich hot chocolate for the girls and delicate tea sandwiches – egg salad, smoked salmon and cream cheese and cucumber – and Lola sat on the edge of her chair with her plate balanced on her knees and her blue tulle skirt spread around her, playing with her charm bracelet and looking very pleased with herself. Julia noticed she would not help herself to a sandwich without being served, but she ate everything that was put on her plate, and when Cat or Megan bit into something they didn't like, they would just slip it onto Lola's plate and she would eat it without a word. There were also bite-sized chocolate tarts, pistachio and chocolate and raspberry macaroons, and pretty petits fours, and Julia could see how Cat was trying to restrain herself, but it was hard for her. She kept eyeing the last remaining chocolate tart, and she bristled when Megan snatched it up and popped it into her mouth.

'You shouldn't take the last one,' Cat scolded.

'Nobody else wanted it,' Megan snapped.

'How do you know?'

'Because it's been sitting there, that's why.'

'Only because everyone else has manners.'

Megan narrowed her eyes and glared at her sister. 'Get off my case,' she said.

Julia quickly intervened. 'We'll ask for more,' she said, looking for the waiter.

'No,' Cat insisted, 'I don't want any.'

'Maybe Lola does,' Julia said.

'Lola doesn't like sweets.'

'*J'aime celui-là,*' Lola said, pointing to an unfinished egg salad sandwich on Megan's plate.

'Here,' said Megan. 'Take it.'

'Speak English, Lola,' whispered Cat.

'Let's order more,' Julia repeated.

'Not for Lola,' Cat said. 'She's a bottomless pit.' She asked her, 'Lola, are you still hungry?' But Lola was watching the piano player who had just sat down at the keyboard. 'Lola, *tu as faim?*' repeated Cat. Lola reflected a moment and then shook her head.

'See, she's not hungry.'

Megan added, 'She was only one when we moved here. She speaks better French than English.'

'I think we'll probably go back next year,' said Cat with a tone of remorse.

Julia looked surprised. 'Really? Your dad didn't tell me that.'

'I don't think he wants to.'

'Then why go?'

'Dad says it costs too much to live here,' shrugged Cat.

Megan jabbed her with her elbow. 'Don't tell people that,' she whispered.

'Why not? It's true.'

''Cause it makes it sound like we're poor.'

'Do you girls like it here?' Julia asked.

'I do,' Cat nodded.

'I can't wait to go back home,' said Megan.

'Only 'cause you won't have to work so hard at school,' Cat said.

'Well only nerds like you like it over here,' Megan replied with that narrow-eyed glare.

'She thinks high schools are like the one in the movie "Clueless",' Cat said to Julia.

'I do not!' Megan denied hotly.

Julia glanced at her watch and reminded them that Megan had to get back for her riding lesson, and she made a call from the hotel phone to arrange for a car to take the girls home.

'At least you'll arrive home dry,' Julia said when she returned, smiling at Lola who was brushing crumbs off her skirt.

'Is it a limo?' Megan said all breathy-voiced.

'Megan!' scolded Cat. 'You are *so* rude.'

'It's Jona's car,' Julia explained. 'A Mercedes.'

'Oh, cool!' Megan exclaimed, and even Cat couldn't suppress her pleasure.

Megan stood up and put on her coat, taking a final glance around. 'I was thinking maybe I'll have my birthday party here instead of at Planet Hollywood. That'd be cool.'

'Who said you could have it at Planet Hollywood?' Cat shot back.

'Mom did.'

'I don't think Dad'll let you have it there.'

'Why not?'

'Because it's expensive, that's why.'

'Since when are you Little Miss Penny-pincher?'

'You're not the only one in the family with a birthday you know.'

'Well I'm the only one who has any friends to invite to their party! That's for sure!'

That's when Cat crumbled, just broke into tears in front of them all. She tugged her coat on quickly and ran off down the hall.

Julia glanced at Megan who was now looking guilty, then she turned and hurried after Cat.

She found her standing outside under the porch, glaring at the dismal rain and crying. She turned wretched eyes to Julia and sobbed, 'She is so mean!'

Julia tried to find something reasonable to say, but in the end she just said, 'That was very cruel of her.' She slipped her arm around Cat and said quietly, 'But you don't know how lucky you are to have your two sisters. Even if you fight and hurt each other.'

Cat's mouth trembled, and she muttered, 'I hate her.'

'Of course you do. But you're still lucky.'

'Sometimes I wish she were dead.'

'No, you don't.'

'Oh, yes I do,' she pronounced bitterly.

Julia stood with her arm around the shivering child. 'I had four brothers,' Julia said in a voice barely louder than a whisper. 'But they all died.'

Cat went very still, and looked up at Julia as she went on.

'They drowned. I would have drowned too if your dad hadn't found me.'

At that moment the car drove up, and Julia went back inside to get Lola and Megan. A doorman held a huge umbrella over their heads while they all bundled into the back seat, and Julia waved them off. She did not see the look in Cat's eyes. It was the kind of look that told you she saw Julia a little differently now.

9

Tom Noonan was behaving a little like a giddy debutante in the spring of her 'coming out'. He had just returned from a round of informal sessions in Washington DC where laymen and clergy were given the opportunity to get acquainted with the three candidates for bishop, of which Tom was one. In his own words the visit had been a 'splendid success', and Crispin had had a hard time keeping a straight face when Tom stood next to him in the men's room zipping up his fly while naming the names of all the Washington power-players he had met, and ruminating gravely about how as bishop he would have far-reaching political influence with national and world leaders.

Much more difficult for Tom was focusing on the day-to-day business of his own cathedral which was now in the untidy throes of renovation. But regardless of his inclination to flee at any given opportunity, he never missed a monthly vestry meeting. The vestry – the cathedral's governing body – was charged with the financial and material responsibility of the cathedral, and the thought of that board of fifteen men and women making decisions without the weight of his influence struck fear into an otherwise iron-clad heart. He also knew it was crucial to his image to arrive at these meetings fully informed in all matters to be discussed. To compensate for his gross neglect and downright ignorance of some issues, he turned to Crispin for regular briefings. This was accomplished under the guise of an invitation for a friendly drink in the

Dean's study, generally a day or two before the vestry was to meet, but these days, because of the intrusive hiss of high-pressure air hoses and the whine of power drills boring through stone, the meetings took place at the Dean's apartment down the street. Like a hard-working chief of staff, Crispin would appear with a heavy briefcase full of memos and notes pertaining to the issues at hand – everything from an upcoming pilgrimage to Syria to the sudden rash of theft of hymnals from the pews. He would sit himself down on the Dean's leather sofa with his back to the view of the Eiffel Tower, and – virtually ignoring the glass of wine Tom always poured for him – he'd get right down to business.

Crispin had long ago learned how to cut through Tom's long-winded banter and bring him back on track if he wandered off into Byzantine history or Tennyson's poetry. The memos were for Tom's benefit, for Crispin, having an intimate working knowledge of the cathedral's operations and an enviable recall of details, had no need of them himself. It had become a tacit understanding between them that it was Crispin's job to make the Dean look good before the vestry, and Crispin did his job well, but it rankled him and he had to sit on his pride at times. There were times when he would shut himself in his office and plot ways to intentionally misinform Tom Noonan before the next vestry meeting so that he would reveal himself to be the ass that he was. But apart from being an ethical man, Crispin was too clear-headed to let his passions rule, and he believed that discrediting the Dean would only discredit the cathedral as well. He also knew that Tom's love affair with his own image had in its own way greatly served the cathedral, had given it enormous visibility and brought in considerable money, and this was something Crispin knew he would never be able to do on the same scale. Whether Crispin liked it or not, they complemented one another. Crispin laboured tirelessly in the Dean's towering shadow, and Tom Noonan reaped the praise in return.

This month the Dean had insisted they meet on a Saturday, and Crispin had felt very imposed upon. He had to leave the girls to walk up the street to their tea with Julia on their own and in the pouring rain while he had dashed down the street to the Dean's building hunched under his trenchcoat, lugging his heavy briefcase and feeling very annoyed. In the elevator he had to work very hard at thinking civil thoughts. The only thing that made him smile was remembering his daughters' excitement as they got themselves ready for tea at the George; hearing them dash around from bathroom to bedroom, squabbling over misplaced make-up or borrowed articles of clothing, lamenting over their hair and generally making all the noises of upheaval girls are known to make when they get ready to go out.

The subject came up while Crispin was providing the background information on the matter of renovating the courtyard garden.

'You are aware of the incident that took place last summer, aren't you?' Crispin asked. He looked across the low coffee table to where Tom sat in his armchair, one long leg crossed over the other, revealing a silky grey monogrammed sock.

'I don't recall . . .'

'The little Romanian boy.'

Tom's eyes widened. 'Romanian boy?'

'The immigrant family we sponsor.'

'Oh, yes,' he nodded, but Crispin knew he didn't have the faintest idea who they were.

'He was playing on one of the old stone planters. The thing toppled over on him and broke the kid's shoulder.'

'We weren't sued . . .'

'Thank goodness no, but we do need to address some safety issues. We need to look at some long-term planning here, maybe bring in a garden designer—'

'Crispin,' Tom broke in, flexing his long, narrow foot with the monogrammed sock, 'tell me, what are *your* long-term plans?'

Crispin seemed not to hear him; he was jotting down a note in the margin of a letter. But Noonan waited, prudently holding his tongue and refraining from revealing what he had already heard from his wife, Gerry, about how difficult the Wakefields' financial situation had become.

Finally, Crispin laid down his pencil and looked up thoughtfully at Tom. 'We haven't made any decisions yet. Though I'll make sure to let you know when we do, of course.'

'Well, in the case of my being called to the bishopry, it would certainly be helpful to have you here while we look for a new dean.'

'I understand.'

'It'd be hard to lose a dean and a canon in the same year.'

'It would.'

'Have you been looking elsewhere?'

'Absolutely not,' Crispin scowled. 'I love this place. I can't imagine being anywhere else.' He removed his glasses and massaged his eyes and it was like he had let down his guard just a little. He put the glasses back on and said matter-of-factly, 'It's a matter of money, Tom. I've got myself a pretty high-maintenance family.'

Tom leaned forward and took a pistachio from the bowl on the table. 'You know Crispin, nobody expects the clergy to keep up with the Joneses.'

The irony of that statement was underscored when the grey clouds outside the window suddenly split apart and a shaft of light streamed into the apartment illuminating Tom's collection of Byzantine icons displayed on the opposite wall. Crispin was an amateur of this particular kind of art and he knew the collection was worth a small fortune.

Tom reached for another pistachio. 'If I can be of any

help . . .' He pried open a nut and popped it into his mouth. 'We're on good terms with the Banque Populaire – if you need to do any refinancing.'

There was nothing to refinance, thought Crispin. They owned nothing except the little farmhouse in Normandy.

'Thanks,' Crispin replied flatly. 'I'll bear that in mind.'

'You know, several years ago we had a fellow here to do a seminar on budgeting. Seemed to have a good turnout. You might want to check into something like that.'

'Yeah, thanks for the tip.' Crispin's smile was stretched thin as he picked through the pistachios, selected one and bit it open.

'Well, not that it's much of a pay raise, but I thought you might like to know you have several members on the vestry who would like to see you elected dean.' He hurried to add, 'Should the position become vacant.'

Crispin dropped the shell into an ashtray and brushed off his hands. 'I wasn't aware my name had come up.'

'It hasn't officially.'

'Official or unofficial, I'm honoured.'

'But there are others who think we need a different kind of personality.'

With a trace of dry humour, Crispin replied, 'Well now, our vestry is never unanimous on anything, is it Tom?'

Tom tilted the glass in his hand and stared soulfully into his wine. 'There are some – quite a few to be honest – who think the cathedral needs someone charismatic. Not just a good pastor. But a truly prophetic speaker. Someone who can inspire with words.'

He rose, went to his desk, snatched a letter from the top of a pile and handed it to Crispin.

'Here. Take a look at that.'

Crispin quickly read it through. It was a letter from a young seminarian who had heard Tom Noonan preach and had consquently been inspired to seek ordination. Crispin had had his own share of that kind of letter back in Chicago, but he had kept them to himself.

'But that's only part of it,' Tom continued, sinking back into his armchair. 'We need someone who can bring in the big bucks we need to keep this place running. And that's where I've been able to put my talents to work.'

Crispin sat still for a moment, riding the silence. He noticed that Tom had started flexing his foot again.

'I'll tell you what,' Crispin began, leaning back into his chair, and fixing Tom with an unflinchingly direct gaze. 'How about a little contest?'

'A contest?'

'If you are called to the bishopry . . . and I'm assuming you'll know within the next few weeks . . .'

'At the most,' answered Tom, reaching for another pistachio.

'Then from that day on I'll match every penny you raise for the ravalement. And I don't mean money that's just been pledged. I mean money that's cleared the bank. If I succeed, you back me for the deanship.'

Tom's jaw stopped working. It also seemed he might have quit breathing for a second.

'Look at it this way,' Crispin continued. 'Whatever the outcome, the cathedral's the winner – right? So, are we on?'

Tom dumped a pistachio shell back in the dish and dusted off his hands. 'Fair enough,' he said, but he wasn't looking Crispin in the eye.

'Good.' Crispin glanced at his watch and began to gather up the files he had brought along. 'I'll leave you that report from the Garden Guild,' he said, rising. 'Vestry meeting's not 'til Thursday. If you have any more questions we can finish up early in the week.'

10

The rain was coming down hard when he stepped out onto the pavement and the sky was a flat grey wash of clouds. Up and down the street a few umbrellas bobbed along, but most of the pedestrians huddled in the doorways of shops and restaurants, and Avenue George V was nearly deserted. With or without an umbrella Crispin was in no mind to wait out the downpour and so he turned up his collar and hunkered down against the pelting rain.

How could he have possibly let his pride get the better of him like that? He would never find time to do any fund raising; it was preposterous to even entertain such thoughts. But the idea of being called to the deanship of St John's sent a thrill of exaltation rushing through his body. He threw back his head and took the full force of the wind and rain in his face, and bounded on up the street swinging his briefcase and muttering under his breath, 'Yes! Yes! Yes!'

Phoebe was home but the girls had not yet returned, and she was in a state because Megan had to get ready for her riding lesson and they were going to be late, so Crispin dropped off his briefcase and hurried up the street in the rain to get them.

A couple of chauffeurs were smoking cigarettes beside a potted fir next to the hotel entrance, and Crispin, now thoroughly soaked, paused beside them to shake the rain from his coat. The twirling glass doors spun him into the lobby and then his glasses fogged over and he had to remove them. When he put them back on he caught sight of Julia in the middle of the foyer wearing a trench coat and fiddling with an umbrella that did not want to open.

'Crispin!' she exclaimed as he approached.

'Hi, Julia. Where are the girls?' he asked, slicking back his wet hair.

'On a joy ride,' she said without looking up. 'I sent them home in Jona's Mercedes.'

'They must have liked that.'

'They're not home yet?'

'Nope.'

'They should be home any minute. Claude just called me from the car. He said the girls had talked him into taking them for another run around the block.'

She was still struggling with the umbrella.

'Here,' he said, taking it from her.

'It's jammed,' she said with an exasperated sigh.

He said, turning it over, 'This looks just like mine.'

'It is. The girls forgot it, and I was sort of in a hurry.'

While Crispin fiddled with the latch, Julia fished a piece of paper out of her pocket and unfolded it.

'Where are you going?' he asked.

'Here,' she said, holding out the list for Crispin, and he noticed that her hand was trembling.

Crispin stopped fiddling with the umbrella and his eyes darted down the list.

'Silicon lubricant? Spark plug gappers?'

'Where can I find that kind of thing?'

'The BHV's probably your best bet.'

'Is it big?'

'A spark plug gapper?'

'No. The BHV.'

'Your usual department store. Big enough. Why?'

'Oh.'

She became silent, folded up the list and slipped it into her bag.

'Something wrong?' He said it softly, and she lifted her eyes to meet his. For a split second he forgot where he was.

'I don't have the faintest idea how to say those things in French,' she said, glancing at two rain-drenched women who had just barrelled through the door.

'What do you need all this for?'

'For them.' He followed her gaze through the lobby to the hall where two men in dark business suits stood in the recess of a bay window.

'That's Jona with the cigar,' she said.

The first thing that struck Crispin was the man's powerful physique, something the photographs had never captured. Then there was the very nice suit, and those Coke-bottle glasses, and the way his baldness gleamed in the light of the chandelier. All together it was a very smooth package. Crispin had an immediate and gutteral dislike for the man.

'I'd introduce you, but I'm afraid it's not a good time.'

'I wouldn't think of it,' Crispin said with a dry smile.

Julia always caught his humour, and she turned her back to them and said, 'That's Boris Tarazov he's talking to. His business partner.'

'That's Boris Tarazov?'

'You've heard of him?'

'Sure I've heard of him. He owns that very controversial independent television station in Moscow.'

'That and heaven-only-knows what else.'

A third man, a dour-looking fellow in a grey bargain-basement suit and a permanent scowl, stood several steps back from them, lighting a cigarette. As he pocketed his lighter, he scanned the room with narrow eyes.

'Who's the thug?' Crispin asked.

'Sergei. He used to be head of the KGB's foreign counter-intelligence. Now he works for Tarazov. Half of Moscow works for Tarazov.'

'What's Jona involved in?'

'Some kind of defence conversion thing. I don't understand it, to tell you the truth. And I don't really want to.'

The dour man was watching them and Julia took Crispin by the arm and turned him away.

'And what do these guys want with spark plug gappers?'

'They're gifts. You know, things that are hard to find over there. Normally his secretary does all the shopping but she's been sick.'

'What? No *foie gras*?'

'A can of Slim Fast is worth more than *foie gras*.'

'Baffling,' muttered Crispin. 'Why can't you send someone from the hotel?'

'Jona doesn't want them doing this.'

'I imagine these hotel employees have been sent after much more titillating things than spark plug gappers.'

'It's not that. He just doesn't want the George business mixed up with his own.' She glanced over Crispin's shoulder. 'I think Claude's back.'

'Here,' Crispin said, slipping the now-functioning umbrella into her hands. 'It's a very devout umbrella. You have to recite a bit of liturgy.'

She gave him a sheepish look. 'I don't remember much.'

'Oh, anything will do. Abracadabra is fine.'

Julia wrinkled her nose in reply, the way she used to do when she was a kid, and it made him smile.

'But now you don't have an umbrella,' she said.

'I'm already soaked.'

'Can we drop you off at the cathedral?'

'You want me to come with you?'

'You mean to the BHV?'

'Yeah.'

Her face lit up. 'Would you?'

'One advantage to having me along is that I know what a spark plug gapper looks like.'

'Don't you have to get back home?'

'Everyone'll be out this evening except for Cat, and she'll be in her room with her headphones on.' He shrugged matter-of-factly. 'I doubt anyone'll miss me.'

Traffic was barely moving because of the rain. The windshield wipers thumped back and forth and Julia stared out the window without seeing anything and kept telling herself all would be fine. They were both quiet and Crispin was enjoying the silence but she was listening and waiting for the signs of the dragon as she called it, waiting to feel the heat of it's breath. That's how it began, a burning like her brain was on fire and then it moved in to devour her. She would try to run to get away, to make it stop, but there was never anywhere to go. It would sit on her and asphyxiate her and she would be wide-eyed and screaming inside but she couldn't let anyone hear. Once she had dug a nail file into the palm of her hand hoping the pain would chase the thing away, but even that did not stop it. It left only when it pleased, just as it came, unpredictably and capriciously, slinking away into darkness and leaving her sweating and shaking and feeling like a limp rag doll, wondering why this was happening and how long it would be until it came again.

They were moving along the *quai* now, heading into a tunnel. Breathe, she said to herself, breathe and become someone else, anyone else.

'You haven't told me about your new film,' said Crispin.

'Fabulous role,' she said. 'I've been waiting all my life to play a character like this.'

'I always thought of Charlotte Brontë as very short and unattractive,' he said, turning to her with a smile.

'Oh, but she had these great big beautiful eyes, and a voracious appetite to see the world. Lord, she wanted so badly to live.' As she spoke she felt the weight on her chest slowly lift.

'Tell me about her,' he said, and he leaned slightly towards her.

'Such a tragic story,' she said. 'She lost all of her family, one after the other, her mother and brother and sisters . . . everyone died except her father . . .' She went on to explain how Charlotte, in her late thirties and well past the marrying age, had received an offer of marriage from a curate who had fallen madly in love with her. 'But her father wouldn't let her go. He was a stubborn old tyrant but Charlotte was devoted to him. Finally, they got it all resolved and Charlotte and her dear Reverend Nichols got married.'

'So it all ended happily ever after,' Crispin said with a glint of humour.

'Nope. Six months later Charlotte got pregnant. She became very ill and died.'

'Seriously?'

'It's a true story, Cris. Nobody had to fiddle with it to make it tragic.'

He didn't say anything in reply, but reached for her hand, and pressed it gently.

A moment passed before Julia said, 'I wanted this part so badly. But nobody thought I could do it. I had to fight tooth and nail for it.'

'When do you start filming?'

'Not until March.'

'Good. Then you'll be around for a while.'

Claude turned around then, pointed out that they were nearing the BHV.

Julia leaned forward and tapped Claude on the shoulder. 'You'll wait here for us, won't you?' she asked anxiously.

Claude rushed to reassure her. '*Oui, ne vous inquietez pas. Je reste là.* I wait here.'

'Are you okay?' asked Crispin. 'You look a little pale around the gills.'

She pasted on a smile and turned to him with the look of a woman revealing her age.

'I have a shameful confession to make,' she said.

'What?'

'I hate to shop. Especially in big department stores. It's just such a . . .' She looked past him towards the entrance where a throng of shoppers moved at crosscurrents.

'We'll be fine. Just hold on to me. We'll make it through.'

He opened the car door. Her ears began buzzing again, and the heat rose to her cheeks.

She managed to get herself through the front door and follow him inside, although she felt her chest constricting. She grabbed Crispin's coat and gripped it tightly as he plowed through the crowd, and kept her eyes on his shoulders as they rode the escalator down to the basement. She didn't hear much of what he said, but he seemed to know how to get what they needed. They bought gaskets and a tune-up kit which was not on the list but Crispin thought it was a nice touch and would be appreciated by the anonymous Russian recipient of Jona Wahlberg's gift. Lipstick was also on the list so they went upstairs to cosmetics, and to her astonishment Crispin set the heavy bag of automotive supplies between his feet and withdrew a tester tube of lipstick from the counter display.

'Rose Nu,' he said, scrutinizing the label. 'Think this would go over big in Moscow?'

He was a man undistinguished by any notable physical traits with the exception of the clerical collar he wore, and yet when he spoke and moved, his eyes and mouth and face were animated by something beautiful. Knowing him and being in his presence, she felt there wasn't a more remarkable man on the face of the earth than Crispin. Through some mysterious charisma he surpassed even Jona.

'Naw,' he frowned without waiting for her reply. 'Too subtle.' He returned the tube to its slot and picked up another. 'Here we go. Red Tango.' He sniffed it. 'Smells nice too.' He held out the tester to Julia. 'What do you think?'

She sniffed it and said, 'I've never known a man to take such an interest in lipsticks.'

'I've got girls, remember? You've got to relate on their level.'

'You're marvellous,' she said. Such blunt admiration took him off guard and for a moment she wished she hadn't said it because he might misunderstand. 'They're lucky to have you,' she added hurriedly, glancing down at the display of lip-glosses. She uncapped a lipwand and dabbed it on her wrist.

'I think I'm the lucky one,' he said.

'That too,' she smiled, but she did not look up.

They bought a dozen each of Fauve Nu and Red Tango and Frivolité. Jona didn't like the Russians to have too much choice, she said; it led to disputes and jealousies and it was better if they all had the same.

While she stood at the counter waiting for her receipt she was aware of how calm she felt; her fears had subsided, and she wondered if it had anything to do with Crispin, if the effect he had on her had somehow reversed all that terror and sent it slinking back to its hole, and although she was tired now and was glad to get away from the press of the hot crowd, she wanted to stay a while longer with him.

From the car Crispin called home and Cat told him that Miia, the cathedral's youth director, had dropped by and that the two of them were heading up the Champs Elysées to McDonald's and maybe to a movie, so when Julia told him that Jona was dining with the Russians he asked if she'd like to have dinner with him.

'I'd like to show you my favourite restaurant,' he said with an inviting smile.

'Oh, Crispin . . .' She stammered to a halt, her eyes averted. 'I'd rather not. Not tonight. Some other time, I'd love to.'

'Is it this?' he asked, laying a hand on his clerical collar. 'You want me to take it off?'

'Oh no,' she cried warmly, and her hand flew out to touch his. 'That's not it at all.'

She was aware of the intense warmth of that touch and she withdrew her hand quickly.

'Are you sure?' he asked.

'I love that you wear it.'

'Not many priests do. Especially here.'

'Why's that?'

'Because at the time of the revolution, the church was as much the oppressor as the King. Churches were ransacked. It's surprising they left what they did.' He was unbuttoning the collar as he spoke. In her eyes it was a transformation; the spiritual man fell away and the carnal man emerged, and she was transfixed. He removed the clerical collar and then unbuttoned the top button on his shirt and loosened the neck; he was muscular and even in the obscurity of the car she could see this.

'But mostly it's my choice,' he continued. 'I realize it's unconventional – wanting people to see you like that.'

'People must respond to you differently.'

'Yes, they do. But it does make them respond, and that's important.'

'What do they do? Do they pour out their hearts?'

'Sometimes. Sometimes I get spat upon.'

'You're kidding!'

'It's happened.'

'Oh, Crispin . . .'

'But I also love the formality of it. We live in such informal times, so I love things that remove us from the street. Sometimes I even wear my cossack around the church. There's meaning behind the tradition of those garments and the altar dressings. Just like all those flying buttresses and pointed arches. They have a structural purpose of course, but there's meaning in the architecture. The place is full of symbols. I love coming in from off the street and going in there. It blows me away. It goes far back and deep in our culture to a time when poverty and asceticism were the economic and spiritual ideals. It's not like that anymore, of course, but I like that it connects me to the past and so I carry it on into the future. Even if you don't understand any of it, if you let it it will wrap you up and hoist you out of despair. Despair is our greatest enemy, Julia. We mustn't ever despair.'

He came around to these last words and then fell abruptly silent; his eyes were fixed on hers with a burning intensity, and his words struck home.

Julia remained silent. What he said had moved her deeply, all the more so because he knew her so well.

All along the Rue de Rivoli the sodium street lamps illuminated the Palais du Louvre with their peculiar apricot light and Crispin turned towards the window, lost in his thoughts.

She thought he was admiring the beauty, and so his next words took her by surprise.

'You have to be wary. It's a godless place.'

The silence hung heavy between them now, as if he had pronounced a death sentence over her imagination, and struck down any naive and romantic image she had of the place.

11

When Julia returned to the hotel, she went up to her room and pulled out a suitcase and neatly packed the things they had bought at the BHV. Jona was leaving in the morning for Moscow. He'd be happy to see she had managed so well. She wanted him to see she could get along here. Pleasing Jona was very important to her and she tried very hard even though it had been terrifying to leave London.

She knew how to handle new places but it was never easy. When they had first arrived, she had established a morning ritual. Still barefoot in her pyjamas, she would kneel on the floor of the suite and unfold maps of Paris and plot her daily walks along the streets outside the George, each day a little longer, a little different. Later a French teacher would come and teach her to pronounce the words. She liked to think that beautiful adventures lay waiting just around the corner if she could only get there safely, and so these maps with their street names held great promise for her. On the maps, the twenty *arrondissements* of Paris were shaded in different colours; the eighth *arrondissement* where she lived was canary yellow, the *métro* lines in ruby red, and seeing it like this made it nicely circumscribed and less terrifying.

On the Avenue George V there were not as many people as there were further up on the Champs Elysées; the George V was a wide avenue with room to breathe, and its orderliness impressed her. The first day she had walked down to the corner and across the street to Claude Maxime where they styled her hair, and she came back and was so pleased with herself that she called Jona and got him out of a meeting to tell him about it. In the days that followed, she learned how to go across the street to the tobacconist to buy Jona's cigars and up the Rue Marbeuf and Rue Pierre Charron. When Jona was away in New York or Moscow, Claude would drive her around the city at night. The beauty was stunning in the winter at night when the chilled damp air shimmered around the street lamps like halos, and bridges and monuments and stone palaces were flooded with light.

Now that Crispin was just down the street it seemed to her that a door had been opened, and Paris was a different world, and it was now accessible.

Julia had the habit of working in bed, and tonight the floor and the bed were strewn with books on Victorian social history, along with biographies of the Brontës and pictorial books on Haworth where they had lived. Anything visual that would bring their world to life. Jona rarely slept beside her. Even when he was not travelling he would be up most of the night. His work schedule was daunting. When he was in the negotiating stage of a deal, he needed only coffee, catnaps and adrenaline to sustain him. Time had no meaning for him. Julia had never known him to rely upon an alarm clock. He wielded his stamina like a tyrant and would wake up anyone, anywhere, at any hour of the night to conduct his business. Sometimes he would call her in the middle of the night just to tell her a good joke.

When he came back from dinner it was late but she was still reading, and they talked while he undressed. Jona was obsessive about his appearance. The cufflinks he wore were solid gold and he had many pairs of them, and all his shirts were custom-made. Even his pyjamas had to be ironed, and he was compulsive about his nails. He went for weekly manicures and owned an assortment of clothes brushes and lint removers and nail-files and clippers. Julia enjoyed watching him dress in the morning. It was a ritual, not unlike a warrior arming himself for battle. Beneath the civilized man in the Italian silk suits and Saville Row shirts was a gorilla at war with other gorillas.

Jona sat down on a chair and loosened the laces on his shoes and told her how Tarazov had lined up some meetings the next day in Moscow which he was happy about. Jona was a maverick and he didn't like doing business in America anymore because there it was the lawyers who played the game; it was dull and not at all like doing business with the Russians. The Russians were in thrall to his American-style efficiency, the way he could get a flight out of New York to Moscow with less than twenty-four-hours' notice, or make a few calls and in no time arrange a private tour of Hewlett Packard headquarters in Stanford for a visiting Russian. The Russians were very attentive to hierarchy and position and they loved Jona's iconoclastic disregard for those very things they held in respect, because he got things done. He liked to brag about how his shortest contract had been handwritten on a KLM notepad and agreed to by a trio of KGB colonels in a St Petersburg hotel room. Russians had little use for lengthy legal documents and Jona liked that about them; trust was built on personal relationships, not legalities.

Julia listened to him, but she wasn't in awe of him anymore. She had reached the age where she wanted an equal but Jona couldn't see her like that, and so she listened. Sometimes she talked a little, but mostly she listened.

Tonight he was not working but got into his pyjamas and she had to clear off his side of the bed. He climbed into bed next to her and she told him about the trip to the BHV and what they had purchased. She told him Crispin's idea about the tune-up kit, and Jona was pleased, like she knew he would be.

'It's too bad you didn't meet Crispin.'

'Was that him I saw you with in the lobby?'

'Yes. We really do need to have them over for dinner.'

'Sure. Fine by me.'

He said he was going to read for a while, but after a few minutes Julia asked him, 'Do we ever give money away to charities?'

'Sure we do. Every year.'

'Which ones?'

'We donate to a couple of foundations.'

'How much?'

'I don't know, sweetheart. The accountant takes care of all that.'

'I want to give some money to St John's.'

'What's St John's?'

'Crispin's cathedral. It's the one just down the street. The one with all the scaffolding out front.'

'Sure. Why not?'

'I was thinking maybe twenty-five thousand.'

He grew suddenly still, closed the magazine and peeled his reading glasses off his nose.

'You want to go into real estate, is that it? You want to buy the church?'

'It's for the ravalement. They have to totally renovate the front facade of the church. All the historical monuments have to do it every twenty years.'

'Give him a grand,' said Jona and he slipped his glasses back on.

'Surely I can afford more than that.'

'Baby, you throw away money like that, you'll be back waiting tables.'

She waited a while before she said anything else. It offended him when she asked him about her money, about how her investments were doing, how much she had. He would say she didn't trust him.

She kept her voice submissive. 'If I can afford it, I'd like to do something really special for him. It's not like it's for him personally. But he cares so much about that cathedral. I think it would make him very happy.'

'You don't need to make him *that* happy,' he replied, and he flung the magazine onto the floor. He removed his glasses and his watch and laid them on the bedside table.

'Can't I do more than a thousand?' she said, still meek.

'You don't owe him anything.' He rubbed his eyes with his knuckle. 'That's in the past.'

She had already thought about that, but she didn't really think it was a gesture premised on the past. If anything it was a renewal. A recognition of something unique between them that had existed then and still existed now. It went beyond friendship. But she decided to say nothing more.

She lay there beside him, listening to the silence and his breathing.

'Did you remember to take your cholesterol pills?' she asked.

He mumbled that he had, and she laid her book on the floor and rolled over, lifted his arm to burrow underneath it and laid her head on his chest.

'Jona,' she whispered, drawing the fingers of his hand around her breast, 'What would you say if I told you I was ready to have a baby?'

'You got your baby already, honey,' he said drowsily, and gave her a gentle hug. 'I'm your baby. And don't you forget it.'

She lifted his hand and kissed it, and his fingers smelled of his cigars.

'But I want more,' she whispered.

'Turn out the light, will you baby?'

She rose on her elbows with her face close to his. 'Talk to me, Jona. Don't dismiss me like you always do.'

His eyes flashed open, and they were as dark as deep cauldrons.

'Don't be angry,' she said quickly.

'What brought all this on? Charity. Babies.'

'Crispin and his family, I guess.'

'Hey, kid, don't go comparing yourself to conventional people. That's a good way to make yourself miserable. And you'll be doing yourself a disservice.'

'But what if I want to be like other people?'

'It's too late for that, baby,' he said. His eyes had fallen shut again. 'Now turn off the light and go to sleep.'

Julia did as he asked. She reached across him and turned out the light.

12

Julia was a little anxious about how Jona and Crispin would react to each other. Crispin with his harmony and aesthetics of enclosure and meaning in architecture, and Jona a shark navigating the treacherous waters of Russian capitalism. Jona met all men on adversarial terms and it was difficult for him to see them otherwise, and here he was meeting a man who had ties to Julia that predated his own and had some kind of unique claim to her heart.

Phoebe was ignorant of all this, although she had her own feminine adversary in Julia. Phoebe was a beautiful woman and came that evening in a short white dress that drew the eyes of every man in the room, so she did not feel defeated by Julia's natural grace. Julia, on the other hand, wanted only to draw them all together as one, to connect them all, and she embraced Phoebe as she had Crispin's daughters and his causes.

Everyone expected Jona to be brilliant at the table and he was, but he was not very flexible and he had to talk on his terms and didn't really have the patience to extend himself beyond that. But Crispin did and he amazed them all. Even Phoebe was impressed because she thought she knew every-thing there was to know about her husband, but she didn't realize he was so knowledgeable about the new Russian economy.

'This business sure as hell isn't for the sissies,' Jona said as soon as the waiter had removed their menus. 'It's for the big risk-takers. But that's what I like about it. The key, of course . . .' He paused then because the wine waiter had arrived. He knew Jona well and knew what Jona liked, and after he had gone they all waited while Jona spread his napkin over his stomach and straightened his jacket. 'The key,' he went on at last, 'is long-term relationships.' He leaned back in his chair and his slick bald head caught the light like varnished wood. 'You get into a partnership because the other guy's there and you're there and you have this sense of opportunity. Sometimes it isn't any more complicated than that. That's how it all starts, but you never know where it's gonna take you. You gotta keep your goals flexible. You can't get stuck in the details. You gotta be flexible.'

Crispin was listening thoughtfully, his hands folded on the table. 'Wasn't Boris Tarazov involved in an embezzlement scheme with some US accountants?'

Jona smiled ever so good-naturedly. 'Boris likes a little danger now and then.'

'I heard the US Justice Department opened up an investigation.'

'Let me tell you something,' Jona said, and even then with Crispin nipping at his heels, he was smooth. He had that air of someone to whom deception came easily. 'Tarazov's one of Russia's unsung heroes. It's men like him who're moving the country into a market economy. Automobile factories, airlines, banking. He's privatized them all. But reform doesn't come without a price.'

'You mean he's looting the economy. Is that it?'

Julia tried to changed the subject then. Several times she made an effort to turn the conversation around to Crispin and his work at the cathedral, hoping Jona might see the value in what he was doing and change his mind about a contribution to the ravalement. But Jona clearly enjoyed sparring with a priest, particularly one as well informed and opinionated as

Crispin, and even Crispin seemed more interested in discussing defence conversion and explosives detection technology than his own work.

Phoebe was thoroughly entertained, as was generally the case when she was given an occasion to look beautiful and mingle with very rich people. She was particularly pleased when Jona gave them a tour of the hotel after dinner, and they were greeted by sycophants every step of the way.

Walking back to the rectory that night, feeling very good in the cold winter air, all warm in her fur coat, she said, 'I do wish you'd learn how to toot your own horn, Cris.' She wound her arm through his and leaned on him. 'Jona's a very interesting man, but he's such a braggart.'

'He's a crook,' Crispin said with sudden contempt.

Phoebe was surprised. 'Goodness, I thought you two were getting along beautifully.'

'You notice how he avoids eye contact?'

'Well it's hard to see his eyes behind those glasses.'

'That's probably why he wears them,' he quipped.

'Crispin!' Phoebe scolded. 'That's mean!' She was mellow from the wine, and she squeezed his arm and giggled, 'That sounds like something I'd say. You're always so generous about people. I'm the catty one.'

'He's mixed up with some foul characters, I know that much.'

'A lot of it's probably exaggerated. You know how men are.'

'He's not exaggerating.'

'Oh, I'm sure he's perfectly respectable.'

'He's not.'

'How can you be so sure?'

'Because anybody who's in business with Boris Tarazov is in business with the Russian *mafiya*.'

'Are they dangerous?'

'If you're in business with them they are.'

'You think Julia knows?'

Crispin shrugged. 'Let's just hope it's a choice she's made.'

'How do you know these things?'

Crispin said, 'The way I know everything. I listen. I watch. I read.'

'Honestly, I'm so impressed. I mean, I think I know everything there is to know about you and then, all of a sudden I find out you know all of these things about the Russian economy.'

'None of it's classified, honey,' he said, but he enjoyed the recognition, and kissed her on the cheek.

She stopped in the middle of the pavement and slipped her gloved hands around his neck. 'I was very proud of you tonight,' she whispered, and then she kissed him. It was the first time they had felt that way in a long time.

At home, when Phoebe came out of the bathroom and got into bed, Crispin looked over at her and said, 'You know what I was thinking? I was thinking I'd like to get Wahlberg and Noonan in the same room together. Two men with an insatiable need to impress.'

Phoebe giggled, 'I'd bet on Tom.'

'I would too,' he grinned back.

She turned away from him and wrestled with her pillow, and then after a minute she rolled back over and said, 'Are you sure you just don't like him because he's Julia's husband?'

'Why do you say that?'

'I don't know. You two have this thing.'

'Julia's like family.'

'I know,' she said.

'He's not a man I'd trust. That's all I'm saying. He's one of those guys who thinks he can operate outside conventional ethics. He's not moral and I don't like that about him. I don't care how smart or well-educated or important you are. If you're a crook you're a crook.'

'Now you're beginning to sound like Tom.'

'Well, square me off against Jona and I suppose I do sound a little like Tom.'

Phoebe gave a big sigh. 'Okay, okay. It was a beautiful evening. Don't ruin it. Go to sleep.'

She gave him a pat and nestled down on her pillow.

He thumped his book shut and turned out the light, then he gently peeled back the covers and slid down on his knees beside the bed. Even in the silence of prayer he was incapable of seeing the truth.

13

Jona travelled frequently that winter, to London and Moscow, but mostly to New York, and Julia turned to Crispin and his family during Jona's absence. Crispin was within the radius of her safe world, and the rectory became a little like her second home. She spent Christmas with them, and you could tell how much it meant to her to be included as one of the family. After that she was frequently invited for dinner, and sometimes she came by with deli food from the Lebanese *traiteur* around the corner, or some gourmet pasta, or sushi, which pleased Phoebe immensely because she wouldn't have to cook. Cat particularly enjoyed Julia's presence. She and Julia would talk about the Brontë sisters, about their novels and poetry which they had both read. Knowing Megan's interest in fashion, she brought over the costume designer sketches of Victorian dresses she was to wear in her film, but Megan kept the actress at a distance. Megan's instincts were firmly on her mother's side, and Julia, for all her innocence, was an intruder, another woman. So Cat became the favoured one, and a real friendship began between the self-conscious girl with braces and the movie star. As preparation for her film, Julia worked every day with a phonetics coach to learn the Yorkshire accent, and when Cat showed an interest, she invited her to the hotel one afternoon to observe a session. Cat came home that evening and entertained them throughout the entire meal with her Yorkshire accent, and for the first time in her life this sensitive and complex child knew what it felt like to shine.

Phoebe latched on to Julia like a trophy, talked about her to her friends, used her in her conversations like a sprinkle of glitter. But Julia defied Phoebe's efforts to parade her around and would not attend any of the guild meetings, nor would she speak at their luncheons. It baffled Phoebe, and she would grumble about it to Crispin.

'She's very snobbish.'

'I don't think that's it at all.'

'Then what is it?'

'She's very focused right now. Preparing for her film.'

'I don't think she likes women very much.'

'She's just reclusive.'

Then Julia stunned them all. She invited Crispin for drinks one afternoon at the bar of the King George hotel and told him she wanted to do something for St John's.

'I've wanted to do something for a long time, but I didn't know what. And then Phoebe told me you have this annual fundraiser coming up . . .'

'Our annual chicken and noodle dinner.'

'I thought maybe, if you wanted to do something a little grander, I could get you a reception room here – at no cost – if we can work out the dates . . .'

Crispin leaned forward and set down his drink. 'If you're going to donate anything I'd like it to be yourself.'

'Myself?'

'Of course. You're an attraction, Julia. People will come to see you.'

She sank back a little in her chair and a dark look fell over her face.

'You don't like the idea?'

She peered at him from beneath lowered eyes. 'I just get a little nervous at those things.'

'You mean fundraisers?'

'Oh, anything where . . .' She sat up straight and crossed her legs and tucked her hands into her lap. She wore a simple cream polo neck over a brown leather skirt and looked like something you might want to frame and hang on the wall of a place like this.

Crispin smiled at this thought, and she caught it and asked, 'What are you smiling at?'

'Nothing, go on. You were telling me why you don't like fundraisers.'

She gave him a probing look. 'You think it would really help?'

'You mean your presence?'

'Would it make that much of a difference to the amount of money you could raise?'

'Yes. I think it would. And if people knew most of their money would be going to the ravalement rather than overheads, then we could justify raising the price of the tickets.'

'And you think, if we did it someplace really sensational like here at the George, and we kept the cost down – I could even try to strike some deal with the caterer – and I . . . I made some kind of an appearance . . .'

'Well, you'd have to do more than that. You'd have to attend the dinner. Maybe announce the winners of a silent auction. Something like that.'

Her hands moved nervously, and it seemed to him she was looking pale.

He reached out to touch her knee. 'Hey, are you okay?'

She smiled at him, 'It's the Scotch,' she said reaching for an olive. 'I didn't have any lunch. I should know better than to drink on an empty stomach.'

'Order yourself something to eat.' He sounded concerned and he looked up to find a waiter.

'No,' she said, 'I'm fine. I'll do it.' He looked back to see her stabbing at an olive with a toothpick. Her hand was shaking.

She gave up chasing the olive and laid down the toothpick, folding her hands back into her lap to keep them from shaking. 'I'll go to the dinner and I'll do whatever I can to make it a huge success.'

Geraldine Noonan, who was chairing the event, loved the idea, but it took more than a little arm-twisting to convince some very tradition-oriented committee members that they should replace their annual chicken and noodle dinner with a sophisticated gala orchestrated around the participation of a film star. For a while the poor chicken and noodle dinner became a kind of cause célèbre, and Crispin and Julia found themselves at the centre of what they dryly called a 'fowl' tasting controversy. But Gerry Noonan prevailed in the end, and the gala was held in February in the ballroom of the King George hotel.

The men grumbled a lot about putting on a tuxedo, but the women loved a formal occasion. Gerry Noonan came dressed in something black, expensive and very unremarkable, but Phoebe shimmered in a strapless lime green satin cocktail dress and pink shoes encrusted with tiny rhinestones. She wore her short hair spiked and gelled and sprinkled with a touch of pink rose petals and looked very young and flirtatious as she bounced energetically around the room giving orders to waiters and overseeing things that had no need to be overseen. When Gerry Noonan saw her she turned to the choir director's wife and said Phoebe's hair looked like it had been styled by the gardener. The choir director's wife laughed but was immediately ashamed of herself, and so she quickly turned away to reach for a caviar-topped nibble and escape Gerry Noonan before she was forced to listen to any more uncharitable remarks.

Rhoderic arrived looking every bit as good in a tux as in a wig and robes.

'You made it,' Crispin said as he thrust a glass of champagne into his hand.

'Of course I did. I'm not totally void of philanthropic impulses.' He glanced around. 'Julia Kramer here?'

'Not yet.'

'You make sure you get me an autograph.'

'Don't worry, buddy. I'll make sure you meet her.'

They were interrupted just then by an old night clerk from reception who approached Crispin and said in a low voice that Mr Wahlberg needed to see him urgently in his office.

The night clerk led Crispin down a flight of carpeted stairs and through a labyrinth of corridors to the lower level administrative offices. They came to an empty reception desk where the clerk stopped and knocked on a door. There was a long pause and then a voice answered, and Crispin was shown into Jona's office.

Jona came around his desk and greeted Crispin with a handshake.

'I wanted to speak to you alone, Cris,' he said. Crispin bristled inwardly; only Julia and his family had ever called him Cris. Nor did he like it when Jona laid an avuncular hand on his back.

'Is everything all right?' Crispin asked.

'It will be. But I needed to clue you in. You see, Julia's got a little problem.'

Crispin felt as if a sledgehammer had caught him in the stomach. There were a hundred and eighty people buzzing around upstairs waiting to meet her. He immediately imagined wardrobe problems, oversleeping, the typical prima dona excuses for holding up the show.

'What kind of problem?' Crispin asked, trying to keep the panic out of his voice.

'Julia's never talked to you about her agoraphobia, has she?'

'What?'

'She has severe panic attacks. You never noticed?'

Crispin was struck dumb; he could only shake his head.

'She hides it pretty darn well. Been hiding it all her adult life. But she's had a full blown panic attack this evening. And now she's exhausted. Once the medication kicks in, she'll mellow out a bit. She doesn't like to take the stuff – has some unpleasant side effects. But she didn't want to let you down.' Jona smiled, all charm and reassurance. He laid a hand on Crispin's shoulder and led him to the door. 'Now,' he said, 'the game plan's this. I'm gonna bring the kid down and mingle a bit with her, but I can't stay. I've got some business to take care of. After I leave, you need to stay as close to her as possible.'

'Of course.'

'She does okay if she's near somebody she trusts.' He flipped off the light and closed the office door. 'And just so you know, Julia doesn't confide in a lot of people.'

'How long has she suffered from this?'

'It started a couple of years after we met. Something triggered her first attack . . . we're not sure what it was. When we were in London she was better. But the move to Paris was tough on her.'

'Where is she now?' Crispin asked as they turned down the dimly-lit corridor.

'Upstairs in the flat.'

'What can I do?'

'Just try to delay dinner for half an hour.'

'I can do that.'

'I'll get her down there as soon as I can.'

Crispin nodded.

'You won't mention this to anyone, will you?'

'Of course I won't.'

'It'd kill her career if it ever got out.'

'I understand.'

'You know, Cris,' he said, and stopped at the foot of the stairs, 'It's been a relief to me, having you around.' He laid his hand on Crispin's shoulder again. 'Julia has special needs. And it's been a pretty big burden for both of us. I'd like to think that . . . well, if ever I'm not around, she could turn to you for help.'

'Of course she can.'

On the way back to the ballroom, Crispin began to put together the pieces of Julia's behaviour, and it all made sense. He remembered the afternoon they met for a drink and talked about this event, and how painful it had been for her to commit to an appearance. He remembered her discomfort shopping in the department store, and her refusal to have dinner with him. And there was the morning he had delivered the sermon and she had not appeared, and he had found her hiding in his study and later she had felt faint when they passed through the crowded parish hall. Phoebe and Gerry Noonan had pestered her to speak at their luncheons, and when Julia had refused, they had accused her of snobbery. How wrong they had been, and it made him wonder how often she had been misjudged.

Crispin delayed the dinner as long as possible, but the crowd was getting restless, and finally, a little past nine thirty, the doors of the mirrored reception hall were swung open by scarlet-coated waiters and the guests caught a glimpse of the candlelit dining room. At that very moment, Julia and Jona entered from the opposite side. They made a striking couple – Jona sleek and preened in his tuxedo that smoothed over the edges of his street-smart toughness, and Julia a head taller than him with her cognac-blonde hair swept into a smooth French twist. Her enigmatic smile was a mask, but such a lovely and deceptive mask it was. Crispin tried to appear casual as he approached, smiling, and kissed her on both cheeks, but he could feel her tremble and she breathed quietly in his ear, 'Thank you.'

Crispin murmured, 'Everything's going to be fine.'

He took her free arm and folded it into his, pressing her hand tightly. With Jona and Crispin on each side they entered the room; heads turned like a ripple through the crowd and the exodus from the halls stopped and chatter died as it does at the sound of glass breaking.

Phoebe broke the ice by rushing to greet Julia with a kiss on the cheek. Crispin gave her a grateful wink and thought again how pretty his wife looked and how proud of her he was. Tom and Gerry Noonan were just a step behind Phoebe, and within minutes the Dean had latched on to Jona. From the beginning it was clear to Crispin what Tom was up to. Crispin tapped Tom on the shoulder and when he turned around, Crispin whispered in his ear, 'Hey, Tom, remember, Wahlberg's my fish.'

Tom appeared startled. 'Of course he is,' he replied, as if snagging a donation from Jona Wahlberg was the last thing on his mind. But Crispin was not fooled. It was just the kind of thing Tom Noonan would do.

14

It didn't take much to fuel rumours at the cathedral, and it never occurred to Crispin that anyone would misread his attentiveness towards Julia the night of the gala, certainly not with Phoebe present and seated on his other side. Phoebe was a knockout that evening, looked more the movie star than did Julia, who had chosen an elegant but conservative cognac lace cocktail dress that picked up the highlights in her hair. No one would have known that he had, several times throughout the dinner, discreetly reached for Phoebe's hand under the table and given it an affectionate squeeze, nor would they have known that, while refilling her wine glass, he had whispered in her ear that she was the most beautiful woman there, which she accepted with a flirtatious toss of the head and a coy smile. People would say he spent most of the evening turned attentively, almost anxiously, towards Julia. Some commented on the obvious intimacy between them, and believed that kind of thing was only possible between lovers. From time to time Julia and Crispin would turn to one another in a quiet and furtive exchange of words. Shrewd observers might even have noticed the moment when Julia replied sharply to something he said, which flustered him, and she must have regretted it because immediately afterward she laid her hand on his arm, a gentle act of contrition, and gave him a warm smile. She would put on an altogether different face when she talked to Tom Noonan who was seated to her right. Of course she was charming enough to Tom throughout the evening and laughed at his witticisms and flattered him, but if you knew Julia well enough you would have detected a flicker of cool scepticism in her eye, and always there was a connection with Crispin.

The rumours most likely originated with the Ribbeys – Tom and Gerry Noonan's closest friends. The Ribbeys were well meaning, but religion had made them self-righteous, parenting left them self-involved, and Synthia's promotion to *Time* magazine's bureau chief and Edward's Pulitzer Prize for journalism had convinced them of their self-importance. Years of writing for the *Washington Post* and *New York Times* had honed their already critical minds to the sharpness of a hypodermic needle; you barely knew they had punctured you until after they had drawn a good deal of blood. Crispin had noticed them at the gala, standing with the others drinking orange juice, her with the pinched unhappy look of a woman who takes herself too seriously, him with a chronic sneer. Neither of them were any fun, and Crispin and Phoebe had always avoided them as much as possible.

After everyone had been seated in the dining hall and the waiters were serving the *Confit de Racan Pigeon*, Crispin caught them observing Julia. It was a hard, blinkless look of one passing judgement, and their expressions were startlingly identical, like something they had perfected through years of marriage and like-mindedness.

It had not worried him at the time, but on Sunday afternoon Cat came home from the cinema in tears after Florence, the Ribbeys' fifteen-year-old daughter, had asked if it was true that her parents were getting a divorce because of Julia. Crispin sat with her for a long time trying to reassure her, and it disturbed him a lot although he tried not to let it show. He explained that she would have to get used to this kind of thing if the vestry voted him dean, because Crispin was convinced the malicious rumour had less to do with Julia than with Tom Noonan's determination to block Crispin's rise to the deanship.

Cat kept the rumour to herself, said nothing to her sister or her mother. She had grown very attached to Julia. Julia championed her, seemed to see something worthwhile in her that the others didn't see, so Cat spread her wing of loyalty over Julia and drew her into the fold. She was very much like Julia in that respect.

If the rumours reached Phoebe's ears, Crispin hoped she would dismiss them. But then on Monday evening, he was in his study when she arrived home in a foul mood. She dumped the groceries on the kitchen worksurface, raced up to their bedroom and slammed the door. Crispin waited a moment, then got up from his desk and ventured into the kitchen. He found Lola sitting on the worksurface with an empty glass in her hand and a milk moustache, while Cat was breaking into a box of chocolate-chip cookies.

'They're for Lola,' Cat said guiltily.

'Your mom still upstairs?'

'Yeah,' answered Cat.

'What happened?'

Cat shrugged.

Placating Phoebe's temper was always difficult to judge. Sometimes, if you waited long enough, she would come out of her room and it would all have blown over. At other times she would smoulder, and waiting was the worst thing to do. It always depended on what or who had set her off, and you couldn't know that unless you braved the flames.

Crispin decided to risk it.

But it was not about the rumour at all.

She was sitting up on the bed with a box of tissues in her lap.

'Do you know what you've just put me through?' she said in a quivering, high-pitched voice.

Crispin took a deep, bracing breath.

'I tried four cards!' The tears broke forth then, and she blubbered, 'Four different credit cards!' She went on to list them for him. 'All of them were turned down! Every one! I was absolutely humiliated! Everyone was staring at me. All these French people lined up to pay for their groceries and I didn't have one single credit card that wasn't refused. I had to put everything back and walk out with what I could pay for in cash!' She yanked a tissue out and blew her nose, and when she looked up at him her eyes were full of contempt. Crispin had never seen her so bitter, and it stunned him.

American Express and Bank of America MasterCard had closed their accounts last summer after Phoebe had continually charged over their limit. Crispin opened his mouth to remind her of this, and then closed it again, because he knew there would be no point. She did not want to hear the hard truth.

'I didn't know we'd maxed out the Barclay's Visa,' he said calmly and sat down on the edge of the bed next to her.

'I give you all my receipts. Every week,' she said with an air of grievance.

'I haven't had time to look at anything. Not for months.'

'Months?' she cried indignantly.

'I've just had so much going on,' he said quietly, and he removed his glasses and rubbed his eyes hard. 'I'll get online this evening to have a look at the accounts.'

It sickened him, all of it, the constant struggles to accommodate them all, and his own weaknesses.

He started to reach for her hand but caught himself. His gesture would only meet with scorn. He stood and settled his glasses on his nose.

'But face it, there are some things we're going to have to do without.'

Her reaction was always the same. She grew closed and

tight and hard. She looked away, at the television.

'Phoebe, be my partner in this,' he urged. 'It'll make it a lot easier on everybody.'

She turned an astonished look on him. 'A partner in poverty? Is that what you mean?'

'You know, I'm proud of the decision I made. You knew we'd have to make a drastic change in our standard of living and you were behind me then.'

'But we didn't!' she cried, sitting forward with a pleading look. 'That's just it! Things went on just like they always had. We had all that money from the sale of your company . . .'

'I know. I'd planned on easing us into a different lifestyle, but we just spent it all. And now nothing's left. We're miserably in debt.'

She turned away again, her jaw set hard.

'Look, I admit, I didn't manage it like I should have. I gave in too often, and now the girls expect things like expensive birthday parties and horseback riding and—'

Her head shot around. 'You're not going to stop Megan's riding lessons!'

'I'm stopping a lot of things, Phoebe,' he said. You could here the genuine regret, but behind it was stone-cold resolve. It chilled Phoebe's blood.

He turned and walked out.

'You can't do that to her!' she cried after him.

He returned to his study and closed the door. It was a cramped little room, with barely enough space for an old leather armchair, a small computer desk and a scratched, ink-stained nineteenth-century escritoire, a worthless antique thing he'd found at a village flea market. But he preferred being here in the evenings, near his family, rather than up in his office. The noises they made never disturbed him; he found them reassuring. It was only silence that disturbed him. He didn't know what he'd do in a silent house, without them. He couldn't bear the thought.

He sank into his armchair, dropped his head into his hands and wondered why he was suddenly so afraid of losing them. As if he might have to make a choice between his calling and his family.

He shook his head to rid his mind of such ugly thoughts, and tried to find that place of peace where he could weather the storm of emotions that threatened to steer him off course. But his mind was far from quiet, and jumbled thoughts clattered through his head, of the girl on the street with HIV; the look on Lola's face the day he came home from the Disney store with her Cinderella dress; Megan on her birthday when she had slipped into his study just before bed, wrapped her arms around his neck and told him how much she loved the horse necklace, even though she had appeared indifferent when she had opened it, but that was because Phoebe was there and Megan was a different child when Phoebe wasn't around. He thought of Phoebe on the night of his ordination as a priest when she had come to him in bed and nestled herself into his arms and told him how proud of him she was; and Julia just several nights ago when she had entered the ballroom on Jona's arm. As Crispin approached her to guide her into the throng, he had sensed her relief and gratitude, and throughout the evening they had shared a silent complicity.

It occurred to him in his turmoil that Julia had brought to him a much needed connection with his past. Because she was here, his life had acquired a sense of wholeness and completion. Where Phoebe constantly left him with doubts, Julia left him reassured. And he believed, regardless of the obstacles, this was where he should be.

15

Crispin was a stubborn man about some things, and he was stubborn about Julia. He wanted people at the cathedral to see her the way he did, not the Julia framed by stardom and sketched by the overheated pens of critics. He had no intention of hiding their friendship; to conceal something implied guilt. But he had been very concerned about the rumours, even though he didn't let on to Cat. It was ironic, those rumours, because he had not been worried about what others would think; his immediate concern had been for Julia. That night, following Jona's revelation, he saw her in a new light, and he had to make an effort not to appear overly protective.

Julia had always brought out that side in him even when they were young, which was strange because as a girl there were so few things that had frightened her. They had waded through murky ponds at night hunting bullfrogs with their torches and dip nets, and huddled together at the bottom of a dry gully as they waited out a summer thunderstorm. And he was always warning her to stay away from the Mackey's prize stud bull, but she loved to taunt the beast and once she had teased him to such fury that the bull nearly overturned their truck as they were trying to escape. That summer day as they barrelled across the field kicking up dust in their wake she had turned to him with eyes shining and cheeks flushed with excitement and announced she'd like to be a bullfighter when she grew up.

But most of the time he recalled other kinds of courage,

like when her father had gone to Alaska to work the offshore oilfields, and Julia had taken over for her mother who cried all the time and never came out of her room. Julia cooked for them all and cleaned up after her four younger brothers, and home-schooled them – taught them to read and write and count – because that's what her father wanted.

The Julia of his childhood had been tough, a scrappy little kid who walked with a swagger and didn't talk much. She never let anyone know how hard things were at home and refused to talk about her mother's depression, although people had their suspicions. Her father only came home for a few days every month, and these visits weighed on Julia; she loved her father and wanted very much to see him, but when he arrived the house had to be immaculate and the five children well behaved with meals ready on time. He did not approve of unhappiness and thought badly of his wife when she cried. He was a proud man of strong convictions and deeply mistrustful of public education, and he would not allow the younger children to attend school in Cottonwood Falls.

Her father was not around to see his wife break down. When Julia was fourteen her mother walked out the door and disappeared for five days. It was Julia who cooked dinner for her brothers, put them to bed at night, and saw they were dressed and did their chores and lessons during the day.

And then the next spring the flood came. It came with the kind of fury that makes you feel very human and small, and at the mercy of the crushing forces of the natural world. Before when the storms came they always blew away quickly; you knew it was only a matter of time before things calmed down and got back to normal. But that spring it seemed like normal was never going to come because it rained for days and nights without stopping. They were holding prayer groups on the top floor of the Presbyterian church. They even gave Redbird Banks permission to hold a native American ceremony in the school gymnasium, and thirty-nine people showed up that night to pray to the gods to dry up the skies. They figured that was a significant turnout seeing as so many roads were washed out.

It was a place where – in times of trouble – everyone depended on their neighbours, but when the river ripped away the trees at its banks and then crept over the fields and advanced on their homes, with the telephones and electricity out, then people had to rely on themselves to manage the best they could. In part that was why things happened the way they did, because nobody was there to know the truth except Julia.

With only the two women and the little boys they hadn't been able to move much out of the way of the water, just the food, toys and books, as well as a silver butter dish and coffee service and the hand-painted porcelain that had belonged to Julia's grandmother. A few neighbours had been over earlier in the week to lay sandbags around the house, but nobody had time to get any appliances or furniture raised up onto concrete blocks, although Julia and her mother did manage to get the television set up the stairs and into the bedroom.

Timothy and Samuel who were seven and eight shared a room, three-year-old Danny slept with Julia, and the baby, Hank, slept with their mother. When the flood came Danny started wetting the bed again, and Julia would wake up in the middle of the night to find the bed drenched in his warm urine. She would have to get up and change his pyjamas as well as her own, and cover the wet place with a towel before trying to get back to sleep. But that night her mother had taken Danny to bed with her so that Julia could get some sleep, but later Julia discovered why she had done it, and that made it worse because she realized how planned it had all been.

Often there were sounds at night; the wind moaned and rattled the shutters and knocked about things that weren't tied down. The wind could sound almost human – very angry, or savage, or mournful, or lustful. They got used to these sounds and even loved them because they were wild and unrestrained, giving rise to myths and tales. But that night there was no wind, and the silence was strange.

Julia had been sleeping deeply, and when she awoke it was to the sound of whimpers and feet in the hall outside her door, but she could not shake off the groggy feeling, and she had fallen back asleep again. She awoke to find her mother looking down at her. Her mother's hair was wet from the rain and it was dripping onto Julia's shoulder and felt cold.

'Mama?' Julia said and she sat up immediately and rubbed her eyes. 'What's wrong?'

Her mother did not answer but stood gazing down at her daughter with a ghostly solemnness.

'Mama, what's wrong?'

'Can you see me, Julia?'

'Yes . . .'

'I'm not invisible?'

'Mama, what have you been doing? You're all wet.'

'I'm hollow,' her mother whispered. 'There's nothing in me. I'm empty.' She turned shivering towards the mirror over Julia's dresser and gazed at her own reflection. Julia noticed her nightdress was muddy at the hem and the damp nylon clung to her hips and legs. Even like this she was beautiful. She made Julia think of floating Ophelia and her whispery soul.

'I can see myself,' her mother said with a hand on her pale throat, 'but I'm not there.' Then she gave a violent shudder.

Julia was on the edge of her bed feeling for her slippers with her feet.

'Mama, let's get you a dry nightgown,' she said soothingly. 'Then you go back to bed.'

Julia pulled her dressing gown from the back of her

wardrobe door and tied it around her as she swept into the hallway. The door to the boys' room was open, and as she peered in to check on them she saw that the bed was empty.

Julia knew then something terrible had happened. She raced into her mother's room and flung back the sheets on the bed but she knew before doing it that her brothers were not there.

Julia spun around to find her mother in the doorway watching her.

'You mustn't ever tell your father,' she said in a frightened whisper.

Julia's mouth suddenly felt very dry, and the words she spoke seemed to stick in her throat. She cried, 'Where are they? Oh, Mama! What have you done?'

When her mother did not answer, Julia pushed past her, raced down the stairs and threw open the front door. She ran out onto the front lawn and stood in the rain shouting their names until she was hoarse. Then her mother opened up the screen door and came out, and Julia followed her around the side of the house to the cellar entrance. The old wooden cellar door had been swung back, and Julia watched in horror as her mother pointed down into the dark pit. Julia stood in the cold drizzle with her bare feet sunk in the mud, feeling as though her knees had turned to jelly. The cellar was flooded up to the top step, and as she peered over the edge she saw a tiny white hand floating in the murky water below. She began to scream and her mother grabbed her and shook her, told her to be quiet, but Julia shoved her away and dropped onto her knees. She reached down into the hole for the hand but it was too far down, so she swung her legs around, scrambled down the first few steps and waded into the water. Her heart was racing with terror and the icy-cold water knocked the breath out of her; for the longest time she felt like she couldn't breathe and that her head was exploding. She grabbed the pale hand – by the size she knew that it was the baby – and she pulled him up into her arms and crawled out of the cellar. She sat rocking on her knees with Hank in her arms, and then raised her eyes to her mother.

'Where are the others?' Julia cried.

'Put him back,' her mother said with a trembling voice.

'Where's Danny? And Timmy and Samuel? Oh God, what have you done?'

'They weren't good enough for your father. None of them were good enough.'

'Are they all down there?' Julia nearly gagged on the words.

'Put him back, Julia. Your father likes things tidy. Put him back where he belongs.'

She flew at Julia and tried to wrestle the limp body from her grasp but Julia clutched Hank tightly, rolled on her side and kicked at her mother, while her mother screamed at her to put the baby back where he belonged. Julia fought hard but the ground was slippery and her dressing gown was wet and covered with mud and it dragged her down. She was screaming for help but there was no one to hear. Suddenly her mother backed away, and as Julia raised herself on her knees and struggled to stand she felt herself shoved from behind. She fell head first through the cellar opening, down the narrow concrete steps and into the dark water with Hank in her arms. While she floundered, trying to find her footing and to get her head above water, she heard the cellar door squeaking on its hinges and then a thundering crash as it fell shut, and she was immersed in total darkness.

The water rose that night, and all the next day. Light seeped through the cracks in the rotted planks of the cellar door, and Julia tried not to look at what was in the water around her. Things were floating there, things they had not bothered to salvage when the cellar began to flood, and somewhere in the vast pit of the house's foundations floated her three brothers. She cradled Hank in her lap while she crouched on the top step, immersed in water up to her waist. From time to time she would shout, hoping someone would pass by and hear, and she wondered if her mother were still outside. She pleaded with her to let her out; she made promises and begged forgiveness for all the bad things she had done, for her laziness and her selfishness and her disobedience. But no answer came. There was only the sound of the rain outside and the wind that had turned blustery, and the water around her, lapping at her waist. After a while hypothermia set in and she stopped shivering and grew sleepy. She was afraid she would fall asleep in the water and drown, and she tried to think of things to do that would keep her awake. She sang all the church hymns she could recall, and Christmas carols, and she recited bible verses she had memorized, and the pledge of allegiance and all the nursery rhymes she had sung to the boys, but these made her cry. Later it seemed the water had risen a few inches and she began to panic but then the panic passed and she was very sleepy again. Hank had long ago drifted away from her. She could not feel her body anymore; her head was heavy and her neck very tired, and she grew weary of trying to save herself.

That was the spring Crispin turned seventeen, and he had grown to be good-looking and muscular like his father. He played football and wrestled for his school, taking home awards and trophies, and girls liked him a lot. Things had begun to change for him that year, and he had not seen as much of Julia.

Crispin's father was a veterinarian and when the flood came and the river made its advance on their homes, Crispin would be up before dawn with his father helping neighbours move their livestock to high pasture, or helping him on his rounds. Twice they were called out in the middle of the night for horses with colic, and both horses had died before they had a chance to operate. The nights had been long and he and his dad were weary and sad. They were worried about the flood and they had a lot to keep them busy, and Crispin felt bad that he had not taken the time to drop by Julia's and give them a hand.

Crispin came home late and went straight to bed, too exhausted to eat his dinner or take off his clothes. But tired as he was, he kept thinking about Julia and her family. It nagged him, that he hadn't even called, and he hadn't heard from her. He tried to turn his thoughts away from her and not feel the guilt, and go back to sleep. Finally, he dragged himself out of bed and stumbled downstairs to the phone and called. It was after midnight but Julia was always up late, and besides he didn't give a damn. He just wanted to ask if they were all right and get it off his chest so he could go to sleep. But there was no answer. He called again and again. It worried him because it was late and there was always somebody to answer. If they had abandoned the house and moved in with another family, Julia would have let him know.

He returned to bed, but worry got the better of him, and finally he got up, took the keys to the truck and slipped out of the house. He didn't tell his parents where he was going. He knew they'd tell him to go back to bed and get some sleep, that they'd check things out in the morning. But Crispin didn't want to wait.

The temperature had dropped that night but the rain had cleared and he went through patches of mist, but when he turned down the road towards the Streikers' place the moon appeared through breaks in the clouds. From a distance the Streiker house looked dark; he could see no lights, and he began to think they had simply gone away and left the place to the rising water, that all his worry had been for nothing.

Nonetheless, he knew he'd feel better if he could see for himself. The driveway was flooded, so he parked on the road, got out of the truck and slogged through the shin-deep water towards the house. Straight away he noticed the family's truck was still parked near the shed, but their Toyota was not in sight. And then he noticed the front door was wide open.

Inside, the house was quiet; he tried the light switch in the hall but it wasn't working and he thought their electricity must have gone out. He could see they had done their best to save some of the furniture and he felt bad that he had not been there to help them. He called Julia's name and then her mother's name, and when there was no answer he climbed the stairs. Stacked along the hallway upstairs were boxes and paper bags filled with things they had emptied out of the kitchen cabinets – tins of pineapple and green beans and brownie mixes and plastic bottles of Coke – and it seemed odd to him that they had gone away and left everything like this when the water had not yet flooded the house. Julia's bedroom was the first on the left: something about it struck him as strange, but he wasn't sure what – something about the way the room had been left, with the bed unmade, her tennis shoes on the floor in the middle of the room, and her jeans hanging over the footboard of her bed. The boys' room and her mother's room were the same. The beds were unmade and clothing had been left as though they had simply vanished in the middle of the night.

Crispin knew the family well. He knew how their mother fretted about keeping the house tidy, even when the father wasn't home, and he knew they would never leave the house like this when there was no imminent danger.

He walked back downstairs and out onto the front porch. The wind had come up and was chasing the clouds across the sky, and the moon lit the hills with a dappled light. The river had flooded the fields behind the house and it lay upon the earth like liquid silver. It was beautiful but Crispin did not notice it. There was a tightness in his throat from fear. He thought he might check the stables but he didn't know what he was looking for. When Julia's father had gone to Alaska, they had sold their two horses and the few cattle they owned, and leased their land, so now there was no livestock to tend. There was no reason for anyone to be out there, and certainly not at that time of night.

This is silly, he thought. *You're being paranoid. They've gone, that's all. They would have called if they needed help.* He was cold now, and he tugged the collar of his jacket up around his neck and trudged down the front steps through the flooded front lawn towards his truck. But then he hesitated and looked back. *Come on*, he thought, coaxing himself into action. *Just take a walk around the house outside. Make absolutely sure no one's around. Then you can go back home and rest easy.*

He remembered how slight and insignificant his decision had seemed at the time. He had acted more in response to his own feelings of guilt than any cosmic sense of fate. But his hesitation had saved Julia's life.

And then, had there been no moonlight he might never have noticed the curious object protruding from the cellar door. It appeared as if someone had wound some sort of cloth around a stick and then wedged it between the boards. As he drew near and bent down to look he heard a faint whimper from below, and then he realized with a start what he was examining: a flat stick used to stir paint had been tightly wound with the fabric belt of a dress and rammed between the slats from below.

'*Julia!* ' he cried as he crouched and struggled to raise the cellar door, but it would not open and he realized with horror that the latch had been secured with a padlock. With trembling fingers he fumbled with the lock but it would not release, and all the time he was imagining the chilling stories of families dragged from their beds and murdered in the middle of the night. He called out Mrs Streiker's name, then Julia's, and the whimpering grew a little louder and he knew they were down there. He found a pair of hedging shears in the shed and then splashed back to the cellar and used the long metal blades to pry the latch loose from the wood. The wood splintered easily, and it didn't take him long. The cellar door was unusually heavy, as if something was weighing it down, and he could only lift it a foot or two. It was dark below but as he peered into the pit he realized something was attached to the door. Suddenly the stick pulled loose and there was the muffled splash of a body falling into the water. He was able to lift the cellar door then, and he looked down to see Julia's white face sinking below the water.

As he lowered himself through the opening and grabbed for her, he saw what she had done: she had tied the belt from her dressing gown around her chest, securing it underneath her armpits. She'd then wound the other end around the stick and jammed the stick between the wood slats, thus fashioning a kind of harness to keep her head out of the water. She had hung there until she had finally fallen into a state of semi-consciousness.

She was like ice when he dragged her out and laid her on the ground. She groaned and her eyes fluttered. 'What happened?' he cried. 'Where's your mom? Where're your brothers?'

Finally, convinced there was no one else in the cellar, he lifted her into his arms, carried her up the front steps and into the house and lowered her onto the sofa. He called his father from his mobile phone and told him what he'd found, and his father said he'd call an ambulance and then he'd be right over.

As the son of a veterinarian, there were things Crispin had learned from his father. He knew Julia couldn't survive the loss of any more body heat, so he ran upstairs to her room, tore the blankets from her bed and dragged them back to the sofa. He hesitated only momentarily, then he slipped the wet nightdress over her head. As she lay there naked and pale and cold, it was not a sexual longing he felt, although she was beautiful and no longer a child; it was a kind of deep anguish and rage that anyone could do this to her. He was relieved to see there were no marks on her body . . . only a redness over the top of her breasts where the belt had been tied. He wrapped her in the blankets but he knew that was not enough, so he went into the kitchen and tried to light the gas stove to heat up a kettle of water, but the burner wouldn't ignite and he assumed the gas had been cut. Finally, he stripped off his shirt and lay down beside her on the sofa. He began to rub her bare arms and her face and hands, even her feet, working with frenzied motions, trying to bring back the heat that had been lost. He kept it up until he heard his father's truck pull up outside.

Julia could not face what her mother had done. She retreated into an autistic silence and would not speak to anyone, not the doctors nor the psychiatrists, nor the detectives investigating the case. Crispin was the only visitor allowed in her hospital room, and he would sit in the corner doing his homework after school while Julia slept. Her father flew back from Alaska and went to visit her at the hospital, but when he walked into her room she became hysterical and they had to make him leave. That evening they found her on the floor in the corner, curled into a ball and hugging her baby brother's teddy bear that Crispin had retrieved from the house for her.

Eventually she talked to Crispin, and through him revealed what had happened that night. But there was never any need for a trial. Her mother's mutilated body was discovered five days later in a tunnel in a Colorado mountain pass where she had thrown herself down on the railroad tracks.

16

Trying to change his family's spending habits was by far the greatest challenge of Crispin's adult life. For two weeks after Phoebe's outburst over the rejected credit cards, Crispin was barraged with a heavy, sullen silence. But he held out against the assault. He treated Phoebe with pleasant, even cheerful civility, and nothing she did could break his resolve. And the more determined he became, the easier it was for him.

Finally, one evening he took Megan into his study and told her that he would not be able to pay for her to ride on the competition team the following year. Maybe, if they found a less expensive club, she might be able to continue with just one lesson a week. But there would be no more purchases of expensive tack, of bridles and special bits and monogrammed saddle cloths.

He did not even attempt to soften it by telling her how deeply he regretted this, that he knew how much she loved the sport and how good at it she was. There was no way of making it easy on her, and so he told her the way it would have to be from now on, and that was it. He waited for the blast of temper but it didn't come, and he figured her mother had already warned her, perhaps even coached her on a response. Megan sat quietly, staring at him with vengeful eyes, and then rose and started out the door. But she stopped, and you could tell she was fighting with herself, and finally she gave in to the impulse.

'You know what?' she said, her eyes dry and full of rage, 'As a dad, you really suck.'

Then she left the room. She didn't bother to close the door.

Next he called Cat into his study. Cat would adapt – if for no other reason than to spite her older sister. What hurt Cat the most was that they wouldn't be able to return to Santa Barbara for their summer holiday. Ever since they were born, Phoebe had taken the girls to her parents' place for the holidays. Cat had made close friends there, and the friendships were renewed each summer. Santa Barbara was home.

'I'm so sorry Cat, but three round-trip tickets to Los Angeles . . . Honey, we just don't have the money.'

'Mom said maybe Grandma and Grandpa would pay.'

Crispin reminded her that they had a great country house in Normandy, and suggested she invite her friends to fly over for a long visit in the summer.

'They're old enough to travel on their own now, Cat. They'd love it,' he urged, but Cat didn't see it like that, and she left his study in tears.

Later, when he was trying to focus on his work, Lola came in, barefoot in her dressing gown with peanut butter on her cheek, and she stood and quietly stared at him until he looked up. He asked her what was wrong, and she said it was her turn, that she didn't want to be left out.

Only one thing boosted his morale these days, and that was his documentary about the cathedral. It had been Julia's idea; she came up with the plan after Crispin told her about his wager with Tom Noonan. She jumped at the opportunity to champion Crispin in his fight for the deanship, and threw herself into it heart and soul. They collaborated on the text, which Julia would narrate, and together they combed the cathedral for the best interior shots; Julia even consented to put on a hard hat and take the elevator up to the scaffolding to get some footage of the restoration in process. She brought in a director who offered to donate his time to the project – at least that's what she told Crispin – in reality, she was paying the director's fees out of her own pocket.

The morning before the shoot Crispin arrived at his office to find Julia waiting for him. She was standing by the stained-glass lancet window with the light filtering through onto her face, and when she turned to smile at him it struck him how much she resembled Mary Magdalene in the painting behind the altar.

'There you are,' she said.

'This does not bode well,' he said as he dropped a handful of message slips onto his desk.

'What makes you say that?'

'Just my antennae talking. What's up?'

'Oh, Crispin . . .' she said.

'Oh, Julia . . .' he mocked, giving her a peck on the cheek.

'You're going to kill me for this.'

He stopped cold then, and the amused gleam in his eyes faded to a worried look.

'What's wrong?'

'It's my schedule. They moved up the shoot by two weeks.' She gave him a pained look. 'I'm sorry. I don't have any say about it. I have to leave for London tomorrow. I have a week of make-up and costume tests and then I have to go directly on to Haworth. I'm so sorry.'

Crispin sank into the chair behind his desk and his eyes fell on the script they had written together. He was feeling a little stunned.

'Oh Crispin,' Julia said again, and she was standing there with her eyes squeezed shut and her brow tightly furrowed, and when he looked up and saw this he couldn't suppress a grin.

'Does it hurt?' he asked.

'Yes,' she whined.

'Good. This is a huge disappointment.'

'I know, but listen.' She pulled up a chair and leaned across the desk towards him, all earnestness. 'I've got it all figured out. I'll find someone else to fill in for me. I've already got somebody in mind. And I talked to the director and he's still available next week.'

'Hey, Jules, whoa. You don't have to do all this. You've already given so much. You struggled through our fundraising dinner and I know how difficult that was.'

She unsnapped her handbag, pulled out an envelope and laid it on his desk.

'Here. This is for you.' She sat before him, smiling and clutching her bag, wearing the glow of a child at Christmas.

He picked up the envelope and turned it over.

'What's this?'

'Open it.'

He tore it open and took out a cheque, and his mouth dropped open.

'What's this for?'

'For the ravalement.'

'Twenty-five thousand dollars?' he breathed, his mouth still hanging slack.

She leaned forward, laid her hand on his arm and looked at him with pleading eyes.

'You won't refuse it, will you?'

'Of course I won't.'

'I didn't know for sure who to make it out to, so I made it out to you directly . . .' She jabbed a finger in the direction of Tom's office below. 'That's so it's perfectly clear as to who's bringing in this money.' Then she pointed to the cheque. 'But there's a note at the bottom indicating it's for the cathedral renovation.'

He looked up from the cheque and saw the delight on her face.

'Julia,' he murmured. 'You never cease to amaze me.' His eyes kept returning to the cheque, and then up to her radiant face. He stood up, walked around the desk and pulled her to her feet. He took her in his arms and held her.

'Don't,' she said gruffly, pushing him away. 'I'll start crying.' She dabbed at her eyes with the back of her hand.

'Is this your money?' he asked, still a little stunned.

'Yes.'

'My goodness . . .'

'It's okay. Jona takes care of me. I don't need it.'

'I'm just . . .'

'I know how much it means to you. And since I can't do the video, it's the least I can do.'

'Do you have time to go and get a coffee?' he asked. 'I could use a bit of caffeine.'

'I'll make time.'

They found a booth at the rear of a scruffy little workers' *café tabac* squeezed between a gaudy Cantonese restaurant and a stationer's on the Rue Marbeuf. The café was narrow and deep and there was little room to navigate between the tables and the counter, but Crispin liked the place because the young *patronne* smiled easily and made an effort to talk to you even if you didn't speak French very well. It was easy to grow accustomed to places in Paris because it was all about establishing relationships, not about making money. Crispin came in a couple of times a week and had a coffee at the counter, and from time to time he came by at lunch and had the daily special. It felt familiar and he liked to come here even though the furnishings were cheap and the bathroom lock was tricky, so there was always someone banging to get out because they thought they were locked inside.

Crispin had never brought anyone to his café. Not Phoebe or Tom Noonan or any of the good people he worked with all day long. He had never given much thought as to why this was so. And he didn't give much thought to it that morning when he opened the door for Julia and the *patronne* looked up from behind the counter where she was towel-drying glasses and greeted him.

'This okay with you?' asked Crispin as they seated themselves and Julia unbuttoned her coat. 'Would you rather be nearer the front?'

'This is fine,' she answered, glancing around with a smile. Ever since the fundraiser, Crispin had been solicitous of her comfort. But he was always discreet about it.

'It's a bit different from the George, isn't it?'

'A welcome change.'

Crispin ordered coffee for both of them and a croissant for himself and when the waiter had gone he said, 'So, you're off to England.'

'I'm off to England.'

'Jona going with you?'

She shook her head. 'He's not even in town. He's in New York. He goes to New York an awful lot these days.'

'Are you flying?'

She nodded.

'You okay with that?'

'No,' she said bluntly, and then laughed.

'How do you handle it? The flight I mean?' he asked, and there was a matter-of-factness in his voice that she liked. They had never really talked about her anxieties since that night of the fundraiser, but Julia wasn't in the habit of talking about it. She was always trying to cover it up, pretend it didn't exist.

The waiter brought their coffee then, and there was a moment of silence before she said, 'I have to work at it. I have methods – techniques I've learned.' She dropped a lump of sugar into her coffee and looked up at him with a broad smile. 'But once I get to England I'll be Charlotte Brontë and then I'll be this terribly complex little woman with a gargantuan appetite for life, and I won't be myself at all.'

She stirred her coffee quietly while Crispin waited for her to continue.

She said, 'I'll transform myself into someone else. That's the way I do it. The clothes always help. I'll be wearing Victorian silk dresses with petticoats and bonnets and tiny pointed shoes.' She dropped her eyes long enough to raise her coffee to her lips. 'Have you ever been to Yorkshire?'

'Nope.'

'Neither have I. But the photographs I've seen remind me a little of home. It's not so vast, but you get this sense of isolation. It really comes through in Emily's poetry.'

She set down her cup and grew very quiet, and in a rough Yorkshire accent she began to recite:

In all the lonely landscape round
I see no sight and hear no sound,
Except the wind that far away
Comes sighing o'er the heathy sea.

She looked up at Crispin with glowing eyes. 'Doesn't that remind you of the Hills?'

He had never seen her quite like this. She was often animated and expressive, but something in her mannerisms when she spoke of her work hinted of a passion he had never witnessed.

'So you memorized her poetry?'

'Emily's. Charlotte's poetry wasn't nearly as good.' She smiled broadly at him. 'I remember how I felt when I got the script. It was like a physical reaction. I knew there was something in that story that spoke to me at some profound level. These passionate, obstinate children isolated on harsh moorland and cut off from normal social interaction. They were so intellectually refined, so different from the rest of the villagers. Charlotte was always dreadfully nervous and shy with strangers, to the point of offending people sometimes. I imagine there were times when she was downright odious. But she had such a passion for life and adventure.'

'Reminds me a little of someone I know,' he grinned.

'It's sort of the same soup, isn't it?'

'Yep.'

She sighed, greatly relieved, and she seemed to unwind a little. 'I knew you'd get it. Jona doesn't, though. He didn't want me to take the role.'

'Why?'

'He says audiences like films with cute, wacky heroines or sexy, power-house kind of women, and the last thing they're going to flock to see is a film about two English clergymen fighting over a middle-aged Victorian spinster. And he's right. It's not likely to be a blockbuster.'

'Do you care?'

'I do. I want it to be seen. But that's not a reason to turn it down.'

He was watching her intently and with such earnest compassion that it made her smile.

'I bet you do a lot of this, don't you?' she said.

'What's that?'

'Don't you Anglicans have confession?'

'This isn't confession.'

'No, but you're such a good listener.'

'I do listen a lot. People tell me things.'

'I remember that about you from when we were kids. When everybody else was being a jerk, you had the ability to empathize. That's a real virtue.'

Crispin shrugged in that self-conscious way he had when listening to good things said about himself.

'I always thought it was a bit of a curse,' he replied. 'When you see things from somebody else's point of view, it can weaken your own perspective. Sometimes I envy people with really rigid mindsets. I envy that arrogance.'

'Jona's like that. He never seems to doubt who he is. Even when you prove him wrong. He just doesn't hear it. Like he's tone deaf to anything that challenges his authority.'

Crispin raised a dubious brow. 'And you married this man?'

'Actually, we never married.' She studied him to see his reaction. He only dipped the last of his croissant in his coffee and cocked his head and replied, 'Could've fooled me.'

'We almost did. Years ago. Jona wanted to get married. Do the family thing. I couldn't. I was so afraid I'd end up just like my mother.'

'You'll never be like her.'

'But she still pretty much rules my life. She's always there. Jona made me go through therapy. I guess it helped a little.'

She shrugged with a smile of resignation. 'Meanwhile, as far as I'm concerned, what Jona and I have is as sound and committed as anything on paper. Or consecrated before God, if you want to see it in those terms.' She reached out and laid her hand on his arm. 'Oh, Crispin,' she whispered, 'you are *so* where you're supposed to be.'

He stared at her a little stunned. 'I'm glad you think so. It does me good to hear it.'

'Why? You mean others don't agree.'

He was a long time replying, and she withdrew her hand and gently asked, 'Is it Phoebe?'

'It's difficult sometimes,' he replied. 'It's been a radical change in lifestyle from what we used to have.' He drank down the last of his *café crème*. 'I spoiled them rotten, when I had the money to do it. I loved to see them happy. I was never very good at that tough love stuff.'

'Crispin, don't ever doubt what you're doing with your life. You have a gift for it.'

He was a little taken aback. 'What makes you say that?'

'I don't know. Something about the way you respond to

people. Like you're able to cut through the crap that always stops us from loving. It's like you just knock your ego out of the way and love them.'

There was a long and solemn pause. At the next booth, the waiter was setting the table for lunch.

Crispin replied, 'Thanks, Julia. I needed to hear that.'

The first thing Julia did when she got back home was call their accountant. She told him she had just written a cheque on her New York bank account for twenty-five thousand dollars and he'd have to cover it. She told him to sell whatever he needed to in the way of stocks or bonds to make the cheque good.

When she had finished speaking, there was a long silence on the other end of the line. Julia waited anxiously, knowing she was defying Jona, and that Jona would know about it before the end of the day. When Phil finally replied he asked if Jona had authorised this.

'It's my account, Phil. It's my money. I'll do what I please with it. Just cover the cheque.'

She hung up then, and she was glad she was already sitting down because she felt light-headed. She took a few deep breaths to calm her nerves and then she got up and turned on the radio. She found a station with some good rock and turned it up loud and then went into the kitchen to make herself a tuna sandwich. She was smiling to herself, and was feeling light and giddy, and free.

17

Julia fell in love with the moors at first sight. The landscape was that of her abandoned homeland distorted through the prism of myth and her own fertile imagination. Set within this new landscape, the painful memories surrounding her past were tinted by a sentiment of nostalgia, and she found in the bleak little village of Haworth, with its dramatic sweep of rugged moorland, a wrenching beauty that tugged at her heart in much the same way the Kansas grasslands had once done. It was a landscape of shifting moods, one moment luminous and drenched in colour, the next thunderous and grey, and always with clouds wrestling overhead. And there was always the wind, a wind so ever-prevailing that the lack of it was cause for comment, and the few isolated trees on the tops that survived the elements grew gnarled and stunted and lonely. Everything man-made seemed to crouch low and solid and unobtrusive as though hoping to retreat into the natural landscape. The wind had its poetry too; it knew how to dance with the clouds, sending cloud-shadows flying over hills that seemed to stretch to the end of the world. But in the end, it was the sky that held your rapt gaze; all the land was in thrall to the sky.

The landscape moved Julia deeply, and she had been in Haworth less than a week when she wrote the first of a series of letters to Crispin in which she expressed these sentiments. She wrote nothing of this nature to Jona; the idea of writing all this to Jona never even crossed her mind.

March 12th

My dearest Crispin,

How I wish you could see Haworth Moor. It would not appeal in the slightest to the sophisticate but rather to the mystic, and although we have never spoken of those things I assume a priest must have some kind of inclination in that respect, and therefore I conclude this is a place for you. You have the sense of being drawn into the place, it stirs something strange in your heart, a kind of desire for oblivion, a deeply romantic longing for something unreal and unattainable. Only now, being here, do I fully grasp Emily's poetry. The place had a hold on Charlotte as well, but how difficult it must have been for her to reconcile herself to a life so lacking in refinement. It strikes me as both prison and oasis – confining and liberating.

I'm staying in a cottage in Haworth just down the street from the parsonage where the Brontës lived. My assistant finds it depressing and wishes I'd move into the hotel in Bradford with the rest of the cast. It's true the cottage is cramped, the ceiling low, and the windows narrow. The staircase is treacherous – narrow with shallow wooden stairs, and Fiona, my assistant, has already fallen once. Every sound can be heard, the floor creaking above (Fiona's room), or the housekeeper setting the table for dinner downstairs. But I love the confined feeling, as if the house is just a second skin that protects me from the harsh elements outdoors. I feel so much better here than in big places where I rattle around in empty, meaningless space.

I am sitting here in a very Victorian nightdress, similar to something I imagine Charlotte might have worn, with a shawl over my shoulders and a coal fire burning in the grate, writing to you in period fashion – by hand (although I'm not about to mess with an inkpot.)

I will email Megan and Caitlin as I promised, with news from the set. There's not much happening yet, but I have a very gossipy make-up artist who just finished a film with Ryan Phillipe and he has some juicy stories Megan would love to hear. Also when I was in London for costume fittings I found a beautiful little Victorian child's dress that the costume department is willing to sell me for next to nothing, and I thought I might get it for Lola . . . unless you think it's excessive. As for Caitlin, there's so much Brontë memorabilia flapping on stands in the streets, as well as books and photographs . . . I don't want to come off as a doting non-aunt, but I sort of like to think of myself as almost family. When spring break comes around, would Phoebe like to bring the girls over to visit the set? I am in so many scenes that I can't promise I'll have much time to spend with them, but they might still enjoy all the hoopla.

Much love,
Julia

March 18th

Dear Crispin,

Your letter warmed me so. Jona has not been able to visit; he has spent a lot of time in Moscow recently trying to salvage some deals, and although he tells me very little, I sense he is worried. His silence means all is not well. I am so thankful for my work just now. I would be terribly anxious if I were back at the George in Paris waiting to hear from him.

I'm getting along fabulously. I knew once I threw myself into the character I would shed my anxieties, and so far so good. Have not had even a tremor of panic in weeks. I do so love exploring Charlotte's mind. She was such a romantic, and so vulnerable to tyrannical men of genius. And Mr Nichols – the clergyman she finally married – I've concluded he was really a remarkable man beneath all his conventionality. He must have had the tenacity of a pit bull to pry her away from that infuriatingly selfish father of hers.

I am disappointed with the actor playing Arthur Nichols, however. Heath McEwan is a fine British stage actor, but so lacking in subtlety (he has done very little film). He plays Nichols as a bit of an arrogant twerp which is so wrong. Actually I envisioned Arthur as more like you in nature. Michael (the director) keeps having to tone down Heath's performance. He strides around the set like Goliath when just a cocked eyebrow would do the trick. And he has an ego to match, which also disappoints me as it can be so fantastic when everybody just loses themselves in the story, and then we're all working towards the same goal.

I get my email every day, although I don't get online myself – it takes me too far out of character. My assistant prints out my email and I read hard copies, and I always look forward to receiving something from you.

Must get to bed and get some sleep. I'm up at five for make-up.

Love to the girls and Phoebe,
Julia

April 8th

Dearest C,

Got your email. (Yours are the only ones I have time to read and answer.) Tried to call you half a dozen times to get the details but you were out. Your secretary was getting annoyed so I thought I'd best write.

So, Tom Noonan will soon be bishop. Washington DC, right? This means the way is clear for you, and I do hope you will charge ahead. Please don't underestimate yourself, my dear Crispin. Different priests have different gifts. Personally, I think Noonan is full of crap – I don't care how charismatic he seems to be. I felt I learned a lot about him just from the little interaction with him and his wife when we organized the gala. But my perception is undoubtedly clouded by my loyalty to you. You never say an unkind thing about him, but I sense this is only because of your generosity of spirit. I'm sure he is plotting behind your back to keep you out of the Dean's chair, even in his own absence. What does Phoebe think of all this?

Going out to dinner this evening. Pub up the road. Yorkshire pudding and roast beef. Very English. I have fun speaking to the locals in my Yorkshire accent. Have fooled a few of them.

Must go,
Love
J

April 12th

Dearest C,

Got the girls' thank you notes. That was so thoughtful. You've really brought them up well.

I do love your emails. I love hearing what's going on around the cathedral and what's happening with Phoebe and the girls.

We are well into the shoot. One major problem I'm having is that I don't trust my own judgement when

Michael sees it differently. He makes me doubt my instincts, and then I give in, but later I go back to the cottage and storm around and get all worked up because I didn't trust myself. Sometimes I think he's testing me, seeing if I have the confidence to stand up for myself. Sometimes I think he respects me more than I respect myself.

But the more we get into the shoot, the less this is a problem, because there is less and less of me the actor. With every scene I grow with the character. Charlotte was rather unattractive, you know. A tiny thing. So short as to seem stunted. Bad teeth and poor vision but beautiful eyes. The men she adored found her appealing only on an intellectual level. What heartache that must have been for her. And despite what you may think, I can identify. I think most girls can. We always see ourselves the way we were at thirteen, and I found myself so ugly. That image never seems to die.

More and more I think of my own family and what might have been had we all survived. Like Charlotte's family, we were a close-knit group, even though my brothers were all considerably younger than me. I always felt it was this extraordinary closeness that gave us a sense of privilege even though we were outcasts in that rural society. Father had us reading the *New York Times* even before we understood what we were reading, and at dinner he drilled us on the capitals of countries we would never see and could barely pronounce, and he would pass a globe around the table and play games with it. Somehow he made it such good fun. Even though we were all terrified of him, oh how we loved him. But then you remember all this, don't you? You were the only kid we dared invite over because we knew all the other kids found us so weird.

Everyday I become more of Charlotte and less of

myself, and there are no more shackles. I'm free to fly off to where Charlotte lives and leave myself behind, and those are the most beautiful, the headiest of moments. Her life was so scorchingly painful and yet she had an inner life that was so rich and rewarding. At times I am drunk with her. I feel I'm doing my best work ever.

Love,
Julia

PS I can't tell you how much your encouragement means to me. You are a great support. I just hope I'm not burdening your life too much these days. You already give so much of yourself to so many people.

18

It was a long, lonely month for Crispin because he was trying to right past wrongs. He was trying to love his children and his wife without indulging them the whims they deemed their due, but they did not understand what he was trying to do and they were bitter. For the first time in his life he felt prepared to do whatever it took, and the battle was as much with himself as with his family. He traded their new SAAB with its cream leather seats for a Renault with 70,000 kilometres and a fabric interior. Phoebe was appalled and Megan said she wouldn't ride in it, that she'd rather take the bus or walk all the way to the Bois de Boulogne for her riding lessons than embarrass herself in that car. Crispin pointed out that the difference in car payments and insurance might permit him to continue paying for her riding lessons, but adolescence is blind to reason, and this fact did nothing to mitigate her indignation.

Cat countered her sister's petulance with an Herculean effort at cheerfulness, which was not at all in her nature, and it hurt Crispin to see her act like the little mother at dinner, attempting to hold up the conversation with tales of her school day. You could see Megan itching with impatience to start a row with her, but it seemed part of her mother's strategy to withdraw into silence, to freeze Crispin into compliance, and with just a look or a pat on the knee, Phoebe brought her eldest daughter under control.

Lola could not be reached for comment. She ate her meals in silence, obediently, without prodding, although at times

Crispin thought he saw tears in her eyes. Then he would tell her she didn't have to finish, that she could leave the table if she wished, and she would immediately put down her fork, slide down from her chair, carry her plate to the kitchen, then scamper off to her room. She got into the habit of changing into one of her play dresses as soon as she came home from school. She would become Cinderella or Ariel, or Sleeping Beauty, wearing the dress through dinner, until it was time to change for bed. Crispin knew it meant something, that she must feel the tension in the family. One day after a staff meeting he left the cathedral and marched up to the Disney Store on the Champs-Elysées where he rummaged through the racks to see what they had in the way of new costumes, but he forced himself to leave without buying anything. He hated how he felt on the way home.

As his domestic life slid into decline, his esteem among his parishioners rose. The news of Julia's generous donation on top of the success of the fundraiser had given Crispin the cachet he needed, establishing him as a viable successor to Tom Noonan. You could feel the difference in the way people around the cathedral addressed him, and they seemed a little more apologetic about taking up his time. Crispin had always commanded respect, but now the respect was just a shade more deferential. Tom Noonan was too consumed by his status as Bishop-elect to bother challenging Crispin's candidacy for the deanship, and although the vestry would interview other candidates out of necessity, it was common knowledge that Crispin was already assured the majority of their votes.

During this time, news from Julia came as an enormous relief from the frenzied intrigue surrounding his bid for the deanship. He took mental refuge in his ongoing exchange with her and would try to find time several evenings each week to whip off replies to her letters.

He never saw any danger in his attachment to Julia. When

he first met Phoebe, she had immediately dazzled him with her physical charms, and this was the experience of love to which he compared all others. But a love affair of the mind and spirit is another thing altogether; it creeps up on you in small increments, in minor epiphanies of shared insights and intimacies. Crispin's loyalty to his wife and his firm belief in the sanctity of marriage had always acted like a firewall to physical temptation. But he was a man open to intimacies of the heart, open to beauty of the soul, and this was how Julia came to him, penetrating him and filling him even when he did not know he was empty.

Both of them were vulnerable to certain weaknesses and at the same time on the threshold of realizing deeply revered dreams. They relied heavily on one another for support and encouragement. Jona was not there for Julia, and Phoebe had long ago failed Crispin. She had proven herself incapable of withstanding the only real crisis in their marriage. It was not in her nature to weather difficult seasons – hers was not an heroic nature, nor a sacrificial one – and her sense of survival was as much a factor in the destruction of her marriage as any person or event. As time went on, and the breach between Phoebe's illusions and their humble reality began to widen, Crispin's resentment grew. To renounce his calling altogether and return to a lucrative business of some sort in order to make peace with a family who revered status, would make him a man he did not wish to be.

No one in their narrowly proscribed world could have foreseen the events that followed, and yet they were all connected, linked through people and time to a place where other dramas were unfolding, centred around people they never knew and would never meet. The time was early that spring, and the place was a noisy street in central Moscow, an office in a concrete monolith of a building hidden in a

yellow haze of smog and dust. There were only two men –
a General Streletsky who had consented to meet with an
Oleg Yavlinsky, a man the General neither liked nor
respected, and who he greeted with barely concealed contempt. Oleg Yavlinsky was a man who invited mockery; he
always entered a room with the same hunted look on his
face, and sidled up and quickly slipped into a chair. He
always carried the same thick briefcase even if he had nothing
to deliver. This had become a running joke among the
General and his friends, and they would mimic Yavlinsky's
mannerisms, how he would sit opposite, staring at them over
his briefcase, fidgeting with his glasses throughout the
meeting, taking them off, putting them back on, cleaning
them. There was something weak about Oleg Yavlinsky, an
unsavoury hint of perversion. His mannerisms were unsuited
to men in power, men like the General who played rough
sports and served in the army.

The General knew why he was here. For over a year
Yavlinsky had been discomforted by the rising success of his
competitors Boris Tarazov and Tarazov's American partner,
Jona Wahlberg.

'Tarazov is scum,' Yavlinsky said, his hands tightening
around the briefcase balanced on his knees. 'We can't let men
like him rule Moscow. We have to eliminate him.'

'Oleg Alexandravich, my good friend, our security forces
were not created just to eliminate your competition.'

'Tarazov's no threat to me!' Yavlinsky cried, as if he had
been personally insulted. 'His television station is no competition for mine! But the man's dangerous. He's out of control.'

Yavlinksy's tiny gimlet eyes bore down on the General over
the top of his briefcase. 'Everyone's complaining about him,
even the President's family. Poor Tanya can't even drive into
town without having to pull over and stop while his cars go
by.'

That much the General knew to be true. Every day Tarazov's convoy of armoured Mercedes and Jeeps and armed bodyguards could be seen speeding through Moscow, streaking through red lights and stop signs.

The General reflected for a moment, and then said, 'If this poses a security threat to the President or his family, of course we can put him under observation.'

'That's not enough. Tarazov must be eliminated. And I'll show you why.' Yavlinsky opened the briefcase and with fumbling fingers withdrew a slim document and laid it carefully under the General's eyes.

'Here,' he said. 'I told you he was a dangerous man. Now you'll see what I mean.' He jabbed a finger at the document. 'That's what the Americans call a position paper. That's what Jona Wahlberg drew up and presented to the American Federal Aviation Authority. He's been Tarazov's partner for a long time. They've done a lot of business together.'

General Streletsky was skimming through the paper. His brow knotted and his face went pale. He read on, his habitual composure shattered.

Yavlinsky nodded eagerly. 'Yes, it's worrisome, isn't it? They're talking with your deputy defence minister about converting our Typhoon nuclear subs into oil drill subs.'

'We have other plans for those subs,' Streletsky said in a steely voice.

'Of course you do. But wherever you go, Tarazov and Wahlberg will follow. When I formed my joint venture with the Americans, Tarazov did the same. Then when I established my bank, Tarazov opened his and stole our most lucrative accounts. Then it was the television network. And now this. Tarazov and Wahlberg undermine everything we do. As long as they're around, all our efforts are useless.'

Again the General glanced through the proposal Yavlinsky had set before him, and his face hardened into a deep scowl.

Yavlinsky knew he was getting close to the mark.

'We're losing time,' Yavlinsky pressed on and his voice modulated into a whine. 'If Tarazov and Wahlberg go ahead with this, do you realize the opportunity we'll have lost? And not just this one. Tarazov starts with this, and soon he'll be doing all the defence conversion. He'll be walking away with the contracts for all our technology. And all the money will go into his pockets, not ours.' Yavlinsky leaned back and slapped his briefcase. 'Time doesn't stand still. For things to move ahead we need certain decisions to be made on your part, decisions which I've been trying to get for almost a year now.'

'You'll have them,' the General replied, and he closed the proposal with a determined and final gesture.

Several weeks later, Boris Tarazov was leaving his office at his bank's headquarters. He always travelled heavily guarded by a personal security team of one-time professional boxers or hockey players, or ex-KGB or special forces from the swollen ranks of the army's pensionless and unemployed, men with scarred faces and broken futures. They armed themselves with handguns or Kalashnikovs, and moved by caravan, with Tarazov in a black armoured Mercedes and a Jeep Grand Cherokee doing the bodyguard drive. They drove fast and hard and it was not unusual to see them pass by on the wrong side of the road, at times even on the pavements. They ignored traffic lights and policemen. None of the vehicles displayed number plates and they were never stopped.

Tarazov knew it was coming. Streletsky had given him ample notice. First there were attempts on his life by snipers or drive-by assassins, but Tarazov always escaped. Finally, Tarazov's enemies grew tired of being subtle; they crammed explosives under the seats and in the trunk of a Volvo sedan, parked it near Tarazov's television station and then detonated the bomb by remote control when his car passed by. The explosion was massive; it rocked the entire neighbourhood and tore the facade off a nearby office building, killing two shoppers and a garbage collector. They found pieces of Tarazov's body clinging to the top of a telephone pole.

The news was brought to Jona that night as he dined with two American venture capitalists in the Marriott Grand Hotel. He quietly laid down his napkin beside his plate and excused himself, then he went up to his room and made a call on his mobile phone. When his secretary called back half an hour later to confirm he was booked on a morning flight back to New York, Jona's suitcase was already packed.

He left before dawn for Sheremetevo International Airport and passed unnoticed through the security and passport control. As he sat in the airport lounge waiting for his flight to be announced, he was approached by two men in uniform. A French banker waiting for the same flight who witnessed the encounter told the embassy officials that the American seemed perfectly calm and the uniformed men treated him quite respectfully. The American even looked a little relieved when they introduced themselves. He left willingly with them; in no way did it appear to be an arrest. The Frenchman could not say for sure which branch of the police it had been, although he was sure it was not the *militsiya*, the regular Russian police. They may have been military security, he said, but again he couldn't be sure.

Two days later a taxi driver feeling an urgent need to relieve himself pulled over to the side of the motorway a few kilometres south of the airport. He crept a little ways into the woods, and as he unzipped his fly and casually glanced around, his gaze settled on a muddy heap sprawled at the foot of a tree, partially concealed by a clump of bushes. The body was identified as Jona's. He had been stabbed numerous times, and then eviscerated.

*   *   *

It was mid-afternoon the following day when Susannah Rich, Julia's New York publicist, arrived in the village of Haworth in northern England to break the news to Julia. She sent word to the director that she would wait for him in the Black Bull Inn, and then holed up in a back room making calls and taking care of business until he could get away to meet with her. To her dismay the producer was also visiting the set, and although her plan had been to consult Michael Langham, the film's director, before she took any action, Larry Turman's presence on the set meant she would have to bring him into the picture. Susannah dreaded the idea of confiding in Turman. A crass and notoriously underhand man, with an unctuous, affected manner, Turman's name was synonymous with sleaze. Susannah knew the only reason he had bought the Brontë script was to lure an A-list director like Michael Langham into working with him in the hope of transforming his image into something with a little more class.

They arrived together a little after six in the evening. Langham walked in looking like a man who'd spent a hard day at work; he was a bit on the heavy side, a little bald, slightly rumpled, with an Englishman's ruddy complexion. Turman had the suntan, and didn't look at all sixty, which he was. He wore a smart sports jacket and black polo neck sweater and sunglasses although the sky was a mist-filled grey.

Susannah closed her Filofax and stood up. She had the well-groomed appearance and perfectly scripted responses of a television broadcaster, which she had once been, and she commanded considerable respect in the business. Both men greeted her with a kiss on each cheek.

Langham sat down with a heavy sigh and searched his pockets for his cigarettes. 'This can't be good news if you've flown all the way across the Atlantic to deliver it,' he said as he tapped a Marlboro out of the pack.

Susannah told him about Jona's assassination, about finding his eviscerated body, and Tarazov's car bombing.

'Geez,' whistled Turman.

Langham listened, absolutely motionless, the lighter halfway to the cigarette between his lips. 'Oh God,' he said, shaking his head. 'What a bloody awful thing.' Finally he lit up his cigarette. 'Bloody awful timing too,' he groaned.

Turman asked, 'Who is this guy of hers? Some Russian *mafiya*?'

'That's an inaccurate description,' Susannah answered, feeling suddenly defensive of Jona, a man she had never much liked. 'Jona Wahlberg's been doing business with the Russians for decades.'

'So, do we have an image problem here? Is our star a mob moll?' Turman said, smiling at his own twist of humour.

Susannah levelled a look at him. She dealt with despicable men daily and she was adept at dissembling.

'Image isn't really what I'm worried about just now,' she answered with composure. 'When the press makes the connection between Jona and Julia, then we'll do what we need to.'

Turman sat up in his seat a little. 'Oh, I think we might get some good mileage out of this. I don't see this necessarily as a negative image thing. Do you?' He turned to Michael for a response.

Michael took a long drag on his cigarette and played the silence deftly. He knew Susannah hadn't come all this way just to discuss image.

Susannah leaned towards him, ignoring Turman. 'I'm very concerned about what will happen to Julia when she hears the news.'

'So, she takes a few days off for the funeral, you shoot around her,' Turman said callously. 'These things happen.'

He leaned back in his chair to flag down a waitress and

Susannah took advantage of the moment to throw a meaningful glance at Michael. 'I doubt if it'll be as easy as that.'

'She's got a contract. She's a professional, isn't she?' Turman answered.

'She was very dependent on Jona. It'll be tough for her.'

Turman was craning backwards in his chair to see the bar in the adjoining room. 'What does it take to get service here?'

'This is a pub,' Langham told him. 'You've got to go up to the bar to order.'

'Christ,' he groaned, sounding miffed. 'Well, I'm gonna go get a beer. You two want something to drink?'

Susannah shook her head.

'Sure, I'll have a pint,' answered Langham. 'Thanks.'

As soon as he was out of earshot, Susannah turned to the director and whispered furtively, 'There's something you need to know. I'm really risking it by taking you into my confidence, and if I do you have to swear you'll keep this strictly between us. And above all, don't tell Turman. I could lose Julia as a client if this gets out.'

'Is this something other people will have to know?'

'Absolutely not. You can work around it. Trust me.'

'All right. Go ahead.'

'Julia's got a severe anxiety problem. She's agoraphobic. She has absolutely crippling panic attacks.'

Langham screwed up his brow in disbelief. 'But she's been fine. Shows up on time for make-up and costume. Always prepared. Absolutely professional.'

'She does a remarkable job of hiding it. Believe me. I know. But I also know she's been feeling very good about this film. She's called me a few times since you started shooting to tell me how well she's been getting along. You can take a lot of the credit for that. She knows you respect her . . .'

'Let me tell you something,' he interrupted, pausing to reach for a metal ashtray on the next table. 'Julia wasn't my first choice for this role. Nor the second. But every night I go back to my room and thank God my first two choices turned it down. That first week I could see her shifting around a little, testing herself and testing me, but then one day she walked on the set and there was Charlotte Brontë. I swear to God. Sometimes when I watch her I forget who she is . . . I forget she's my actress. Hell, I even forget I'm directing. She's totally relaxed. And I'm relaxed. Everybody's relaxed. It's like she isn't even working at it anymore. She *is* Charlotte Brontë. It's spooky. God knows, if she doesn't get an Oscar nomination for this . . .'

'Of course she'll get a nomination.' It was Turman, back with their beers and a bowl of peanuts. 'We'll all get Oscars for this baby. Peanuts anyone?'

Susannah shook her head.

'No. Thanks,' Michael answered, taking a long drink of the beer Turman had set down in front of him. He turned back to Susannah. 'So, you think Jona's death might . . .' he prodded, without finishing the sentence.

'Yes, I do,' she replied cryptically. 'It could be very disrupting.'

Turman spoke with a mouthful of peanuts. 'Don't you worry. We'll handle her.'

Langham asked gently, 'What's the best way to break this to her?'

'She'll need support. Someone she's close to.'

Turman butted in. 'Get her a therapist. They've got people specialized in dealing with these things.'

'Has she developed a close relationship with anyone on the set?' Susannah put the question discreetly, hoping for a discreet reply.

'Yeah,' grinned Turman. 'She fucking anybody?'

Langham pretended he hadn't heard, and Susannah was grateful. 'She's strictly professional,' Langham answered.

'Doesn't go out much. Pretty reclusive, really.'

'How about her assistant?'

'Fiona gets along with her well enough. But I don't think they're particularly close.'

'Does she ever talk about Jona?'

'All the time. Like he's her North Pole.'

Susannah nodded knowingly.

Turman was finally beginning to get a little nervous. He said, 'Hey, look, if you think this guy getting himself murdered is gonna jeopardize the production, then just don't tell her. Simple as that.'

'We can't do that,' Susannah said.

'Why not?'

Susannah looked at him with unconcealed contempt. After a cool pause, she said, 'Because we don't operate by the same rules.'

'What rules?' Turman replied indignantly. 'I'm a producer. That means my goal is a marketable product. Not a bunch of celluloid in the rubbish bin.'

You're a shit, thought Susannah, but she only stared at him impassively.

'Look,' Turman said, 'how many more weeks of shooting do we have left? Two? Three?'

'For Julia, about that,' Langham answered.

'What are you suggesting, Larry?' Susannah probed, sensing where he was going with this.

'Michael just said she doesn't go out much. Hell, let's just hide it from her. Screen her calls. Limit her contacts.'

'You can't hide that kind of news from someone,' she answered, seriously alarmed. 'This is her husband we're talking about.'

'I didn't think they were married,' Turman replied.

Susannah spoke quietly, struggling to remain composed. 'They've been together for seventeen years. That's longer than all your little bimbos put together.' She punctuated it with a smile.

Turman's tanned face lost it's colour, and his jaw hardened. He quietly edged his chair back from the table and rose stiffly, pausing only to give Langham a fraternal pat on the shoulder. 'Call me tonight, Mike,' he said, and strode out.

Susannah's fair cheeks were burning. 'Forgive me,' she apologized quietly. 'I'm short on sleep.'

'Don't worry about it. He'll get over it.'

She brushed a dark curl back behind her ear and said, 'Look, Michael, I want Julia to finish this film as badly as you do, but I don't know what will happen when she finds out about Jona's death. All I'm saying is you'd better be prepared.'

'I'll look over the production schedule this evening. See how we can work around her for a few days.' He ground out his cigarette and looked up at her hopefully. 'Are you going to stay on?'

'I can't,' she answered firmly. 'I'm supposed to be in LA right now. I'm flying out tomorrow. I can break the news to her, but you'll need some kind of support after I leave.'

'So you'll tell her?'

'That's why I flew over here.'

'I appreciate that.'

'I'm just terrified she'll find out from somebody else before I get to her.' Susannah unzipped her bag and dropped her agenda inside. Then she headed for the door with her face set in a look of grim resolve.

19

On each side of the village's steep, cobbled main street rose soot-blackened stone cottages that had once housed combers and weavers of the wool trade, where Victorian women once sat dawn to dusk over their hand looms, their livelihood dependent upon the meagre light cast by a grizzled sky through rows of narrow stone-mullioned windows. Most of the cottages had long ago been converted to tourist shops or inns; the Heather Cottage was one of these. There were fresh lace curtains at the lower windows and pansies in brightly painted window boxes, and this relieved the bleakness of the town. Susannah rapped upon the door, and after a moment there was the sound of hurried footsteps and the door was opened by Julia's assistant, Fiona, who announced in an exaggerated hush that Julia was napping, and she was not to be disturbed. Susannah dropped her bag onto the stone floor and, unknotting the belt of her trench coat, summarily informed the young woman that she had flown all the way from New York with a message that could not wait, and would she please show her to Julia's room and then bring up some tea for both of them. Fiona led the way up the narrow wooden stairs, tiptoeing in a ridiculously dramatic fashion that Susannah would have found amusing under other circumstances, but at the moment it only irritated her.

The floral curtains had been drawn and the room was nearly dark. Julia was sleeping. She looked very childlike, sprawled on her back with one arm hanging over the edge of the bed, a bare foot sticking out from beneath the quilt. She stirred as the door opened, and her fingers twitched.

'Fiona?' she said groggily, rising on her elbows and squinting at the light from the doorway. 'Is it time to get up?'

'Julia, it's me,' Susannah replied, drawing back the curtains. The fading light of day flooded through the windows and Julia sat up and blinked. Her hair was brown now, and it made her seem unfamiliar.

'Susannah?'

'None other.' Susannah leaned down and hugged her. Julia could tell then, by the way that she clung to her, that something was wrong.

'What is it?' Julia said anxiously. 'Is something wrong?'

Susannah reached for her hand. 'I have some very sad news for you . . .'

Julia did not expect it to be Jona. She thought it had something to do with the film, and she had that terrible anguish in her stomach at the anticipation of some great disappointment.

'What's happened?'

Susannah sat down on the edge of the bed. 'I don't know how to tell you this.'

'Tell me what?'

'Jona's been killed,' she said softly.

Julia's first reaction was a nervous laugh. 'You're kidding,' she said, stupefied.

'No, honey, I'm not.'

'Jona? Papa Jo?'

In the hovering twilight Susannah could see the confusion on her face, the sudden mental leap as her mind fumbled to orient itself within new and terrifying surroundings.

Susannah told her everything she knew, about Tarazov's murder and about how Jona had tried to escape the country, how he had safely made it to the airport, then been lured away and killed.

Julia listened but there was disbelief in her eyes and she responded with soft utterances of denial. It was pathetic to see her grapple with something for which she had no defences.

'They killed him?' she muttered. 'I don't believe it! No. They wouldn't have done that. Not Jona. They all knew him. He helped them. He did so much for them.' She rambled on like this for a while, but then came the moment when realization hit her; stripping the disbelief from her face and leaving her features softened, as though sculpted by a sickening agony, and she became unrecognizable. Susannah touched her but she recoiled. The pain was too private and powerful. She turned her head away and withdrew behind a dazed wall. Curled in a ball, she wept quietly.

The silence in the room was heavy. Outside a dull, muffled rain had begun to fall.

After a while she wiped her face with the sleeve of her dressing gown. 'Where is he? Where's my Jona? What'd they do with him?'

'The embassy's returning his body to Paris. You don't have to worry about any of that. Do you know where he wanted to be buried?'

Julia shook her head.

'That's okay. Don't worry about it, I'm sure he had a will. His lawyer will sort it all out.'

Julia began to cry again; the muscles in her face drew up in terrible spasms of pain, and Susannah had to avert her eyes. Fiona returned with the tea, but she only set it on a table next to the window and left quietly.

After a while Julia composed herself; she wiped the tears from her cheeks and with a kind of blank helplessness asked, 'What am I supposed to do now?'

'We'll have to get you back to Paris.'

'Oh, no. Not again.' She took another deep, shuddering breath.

'I'll send someone with you.'

'You can't come?'

'I'm sorry, sweetie. I have to be in LA tomorrow.'

'Oh my God, the film . . .' Julia rushed to say, anxiety creeping into her voice. 'I can't leave it . . .'

'They'll shoot around you. I've already spoken to Turman and Langham.'

It came sweeping back over her again. She could be distracted for only a few seconds, and then it returned like a keen blast of cold wind.

'Oh, God,' she muttered, struggling to halt a new flood of tears.

'Do you want me to call a doctor? You want something to help you sleep?'

'Maybe I should. For the flight.'

'I'll get someone over here right away. Don't worry. We'll get you through this.'

'Just stay with me,' she begged softly as she pressed Susannah's hand.

'Of course I will. I'm not going to leave your side until we put you on that plane tomorrow. Are you taking any medication? For your anxiety?'

Julia shook her head. 'I haven't needed any. I've been doing so well. I had a short relapse in Paris. But since then . . .'

'If you need to start again, let me know. I can get it in New York and send it overnight express.'

Julia gave her a grateful smile. Susannah knew exactly where to situate herself in the chaos of crisis; it made her friendship priceless. A bit of light broke into Julia's eyes and she said. 'I'm so glad you're here.'

'You'll pull through this.'

'I have to finish this film.'

'You should have heard Langham gush about you this evening.'

'He did?'

'I wish I'd recorded it.'

'I haven't seen the dailies, but he's sounded really enthusiastic.'

'He loves it.'

'I have to come back. I have to finish.'

'That's what Jona would have wanted.'

Julia nodded, but she knew better. Jona had never encouraged her to take this role.

But Crispin had; he had understood its significance, how it resonated with her past. Crispin had always understood her. This realization cleared her head and brought a brief moment of serenity. *Dear Crispin*, she thought. She held Susannah's hand and in her mind she held onto the thought of him; if she kept Crispin in her thoughts, she could get through it all.

The return trip to Paris exhausted Julia, and she was relieved to be back at the George where she was received with kindness. At the George they would take care of her. And Crispin was nearby.

She wasn't quite sure of the order of things, how to handle death and burying the dead. She spent the morning with the concierge of the George and a rabbi, going over the funeral arrangements. Fiona, the assistant who had accompanied her from England, was kept busy answering the door and the telephone, and keeping track of the extravagant arrangements of flowers that poured in. There were calls from Julia's friends, from directors and actors in London and New York who had been informed of Jona's death by Susannah, but the people who passed through the King George Hotel to offer their condolences that morning were basically men from Jona's world. He had chosen their friends just like he had chosen their wine and physicians and brokers. He had taken care of her and relieved her of the dolorous burden of making decisions. Julia didn't trust her own judgement, but she had trusted Jona's. She had believed him to be a superior judge of character and motive. But now, without Jona, these men and women seemed like total strangers, and their gestures of sympathy struck her as meaningless and hollow. She felt adrift in her own world, and she longed for something or someone to anchor her. Most of all, she longed for a quiet moment to call Crispin.

Then in the afternoon Maître Albert arrived, and the others left. Maître Albert had come to read the will. He was nervous, but Julia didn't notice this.

Julia had never liked Maître Albert though she wasn't sure why. He had always been perfectly discreet and utterly self-effacing. He was a small man with a moustache that covered his upper lip and he had a tic that reminded her of the twitching of a rodent. Now, dressed in a sober black dress, her legs tightly crossed and her hands curled into a ball on her lap, she sat stiffly in the corner of the leather sofa while he rifled through a batch of files in his briefcase. He withdrew a large, sealed manila envelope and ripped it open. Then he searched his inside pocket for his glasses, settled them on his nose and began to read.

At first she tried to follow, but the legal language bored her, and Maître Albert spoke English with a marked accent that made him extremely difficult to understand. First there was the will, but the will bequeathed his entire estate to his trust. Maître Albert finished the will, and then he asked if he could have something to drink. He downed the water that Fiona brought him, and put the glass down gently, delicately, on the glass table. Then he picked up a copy of the trust. He took off his glasses and rubbed his eyes, and when he began to read again, his hands were shaking. Julia noticed this and she became instantly alarmed; in that brief second she knew something terrible was about to happen.

In the time it took to read the trust agreement whereby the

majority of Jona's assets would be distributed to his legal wife, one Raza Lichovich, and his son by said wife, Alexander, the world Julia had created for herself was utterly and completely eradicated. The pallid little man read through to the end of the lengthy trust, and then Julia excused herself and went to the bathroom and vomited. She had eaten nothing over the past twenty-four hours, and her sickness was only dry heaves. Fiona tapped meekly on the door, asking if she was all right, and Julia replied that Maître Albert mustn't leave, that she would be out in a minute. She splashed her face with cool water, rinsed her mouth and brushed her teeth, and then she went back into the living room.

Maître Albert stood near the door ready to leave, his coat slung over his arm and the briefcase weighing him down, looking very formal and awkward. When he saw her, he adopted a deep air of chagrin but there was a noticeable trace of relief in his voice.

'Call me if you need me, Madame. I am at your service.'

He bowed slightly.

'Who is this woman?' Julia asked with an unsteady voice.

'I did only as I was instructed.'

'You can't walk out of this room until you tell me who she is. You must know. You're the executor of his estate. You must know who she is.'

He had misinterpreted the hesitation in her voice; it was not grief but rage. He set down his briefcase.

'She is a Russian lady. She lives in New York.'

'How long have they known each other?'

'I only know that they were married last summer, just before the birth of the child. I believe he felt it was his obligation.'

'I don't believe this! Not for one minute do I believe this. Jona wouldn't do this to me. He didn't want children. She must have tricked him into it.'

He hesitated, then replied with a slight air of apology.

'Monsieur Wahlberg was a Jew. The mother is Jewish. He gave me the impression that he was very proud of being a father.'

'*How can you say that?*' Julia screeched, and the sound of her voice startled both of them and brought Fiona out of the kitchen where she had been nibbling from a plateau of canapés brought up earlier by room service. 'Jona always tried to hide his Jewishness! He even changed his name! He ignored all the holidays! All the years we were together he never once set foot in a synagogue!'

The little man was clearly embarrassed by Julia's outburst. 'The child is not inheriting very much,' he added with a twitch of his moustache, as if this resolved the matter.

'He left him his entire estate!'

'There will not be much left, Madame, once all is settled.'

To Julia's stunned silence he replied with a shrug of the shoulders, and leaned down for his briefcase. 'After the funeral you must call his financial manager and discuss it with him. There may be certain limits imposed on your expenditures until after the estate issues are settled. He will explain all of this to you.'

'Are you telling me I don't have any money?'

His hand was on the doorknob. 'I cannot answer that, Madame.'

He opened the door and fled.

Julia picked up the telephone and called the front desk. She asked them to hold all her calls and to make no more deliveries to her suite, and then she sent Fiona away. She needed to be alone now, she explained. When Fiona had gone she disconnected the telephone and hung a DO NOT DISTURB sign on her door.

When she was alone she opened the door and stepped out onto the balcony. Earlier in the morning, the sky had held the promise of a blue day, but now clouds had turned the day grey and dim and there was a chill of rain in the air.

Piano music drifted up from the lounge below. Across the courtyard were other suites, as opulent and privileged as her own. This was Jona's world. She kept seeing him before her eyes, strutting into a room wearing an iron-clad arrogance that suited him so well, a barrel of a man with a heart-bending smile and infectious laugh that swept you up and never let you go. Everyone wanted to be a part of Jona's world. No one could ever resist him.

A light rain began to fall but she did not go back inside. For a long time she stood there, feeling the rain penetrate her hair and trickle onto her scalp, down her neck and into her eyes. She focused on the edge of the balcony, willing herself to approach it. The spire of Crispin's cathedral rising above the skyline caught her attention. Suddenly she heard his voice, as clearly as though he were standing beside her.

Don't ever despair, Julia, he said. *Don't ever despair.*

Suddenly panic seized her. Her heart pounded mercilessly in her chest, and the marble floor beneath her feet seemed to give way. The thought of taking a step in any direction terrified her. Unable to move, she sank to her knees. If she stayed close to the ground, she would not fall. Cautiously, her heart still racing, she crawled back inside on her hands and knees. She was able to close the door and then, still on hands and knees, she inched her way to her bedroom.

She was cold, and she sat on the bathroom floor while she stripped off her dress and her underwear, then she crawled back to her bed, clutching a phial of sleeping tablets in her hand. But she could not sleep in the bed. Jona was still there. He was everywhere. She pulled a blanket and a pillow from the bed, crawled into her dressing room and closed the door.

With a trembling hand, Julia counted out just enough capsules to make her sleep. And until she slept she fought away the despair by imagining herself in the sanctuary of the cathedral. How beautiful it must be, she thought, to live up there, high above the crowds, close to the heavens. Crispin had told her there were rooms up there, and she imagined them inhabited by hermits and saints who painted their walls with visions of God. She thought of her impulsive and extravagant donation to the cathedral restoration; at the time she had been racked by guilt and even a little fear, and Jona had been furious with her later. But now it stood out against the backdrop of her life as a single significant act of great import. Not only for its altruism, but because it was strictly her own decision. It was the only time in her life she had openly and unequivocally dared to defy Jona.

20

During the hours that passed, Julia's grief turned to rage, and her rage was titanic. The cocoon of the dark dressing room and the mental image of the cathedral spire had soothed a little of her pain, and the suicidal impulse had passed. But she did not know how to hate Jona without hating herself, and when she awoke late that night, she sat naked on the floor of her dressing room with scissors in hand and meticulously set about shredding each and every strip of clothing. She cried while she ripped the beautiful dresses from their hangers and hacked away at them. Jona had been with her when she bought these things; his taste had moulded hers, and his taste had been superlative. Twice she had been featured in best-dressed lists, and Jona had been proud of her. Both times he had thrown a lavish dinner party at their suite in London although it was his own ego he was celebrating. With time she had grown into the clothes and the image, learned how to walk with attitude, her head high and her eyes skimming over the tops of the looks that followed her down the street. She never saw others stare at her but Jona did and it gave him enormous pleasure. He liked her to wear soft colours to blend with her hair, and cashmeres lasciviously moulded to her breasts with light English wools that fitted snugly around her hips so that when they walked side by side he could discreetly slide his hand down her rump and feel the thrust of her hip. He abhorred things that were ostentatious and vulgar and she was only permitted simple albeit expensive accessories – her Cartier watch and a strand of Christian Bernard pearls or simple gold jewellery. Her clothes were an erotic pleasure for him as well as a totem of status; in Julia he could emulate that unabashedly snobbish aesthetic of upper class Britain that he so envied but personally, as a foreigner and a Jew, could never achieve.

And so that night she whittled away at herself. When she had purged some of her anger, she pulled on a sweater and went into the kitchen and ate the rest of the caviar canapés that Fiona had put away in the refrigerator. It had taken years of coaching from Jona before Julia had learned to disregard the cost of things; but he was dead and his death was both terrifying and liberating for her. As she ate the caviar and *foie gras* and drank a little of his wine she began to feel bad about her rampage because it occurred to her she could have given the clothes away to one of Crispin's charities. She felt guilty that she had not thought of this earlier. Jona had always criticized her impulsive generosity to strangers; he said it was a character flaw, a sign of weak sentimentality. In their early days in New York, she would dig into her handbag for coins to give to beggars on the street, but Jona would give her his trademark scowl of disapproval, and eventually she learned to pass on by.

She still saw that scowl that night as she wrestled trunks out of wardrobes and suitcases down from the top shelves and packed up all the remaining clothing, along with her alligator shoes and Prada and Dior handbags. Even when she could not see his face she felt his disapproval weighing down on her, but she battled with it, and tried to see Crispin's face instead and Crispin's joy. Crispin would not dismiss such an act as transient madness. Or perhaps he would, but he would call it divine madness.

She knew now what had to be done. She would go back to Haworth and finish the film. The greatest struggle would be to get out of town. Shedding Jona's image of her was not the same as shedding her fears, and she knew she would have to summon every skill she had learned in order to make her way, alone, back to England. She wanted desperately to do it on her own, without Fiona, without anyone.

Once she had emptied her wardrobe, saving only a few pairs of shoes and some sweaters and jeans, she sat down at her desk and made a list of what needed to be done and how she would do it. She called Air France and made a reservation for the next morning, billing the ticket to her account at the George. She rarely did these things for herself, and she was nervous over the phone; she felt that she was doing something wrong, and that someone would catch her up and she would not be able to get away. But when it was done she put down the telephone and felt an immediate rush of elation. It was such a tiny thing and yet she was so proud of herself.

She bathed and dressed, and brushed her dark hair back into a simple ponytail, then she sat down and wrote a note to Crispin and told him what had happened and what she was doing. She would send the letter over to the cathedral in the morning along with the suitcases of clothing. By then she would be gone.

It was much easier to leave at night. She instructed the porter to take her holdall and call her when he had loaded it into a taxi. When she went downstairs, there was no one in reception and she attracted no attention. The desk clerk nodded respectfully and then went back to reading his newspaper.

As the taxi left the hotel, she sat in the rear gripping her bag as if it were an anchor. She was afraid to take one last glance at the hotel for fear it might trigger some emotion she couldn't handle. However, she instructed the driver to cruise slowly past the cathedral, and she rolled down her window and looked up at the now dark spire and thought with sudden lucidity how this place had entered into the small but complex pattern of her life. How Crispin was at the centre of it.

She rolled up the window, then pulled her bag closer, hugging it to her breast. It seemed as though her world were now reduced to only this.

'Oh my goodness,' Phoebe cried as she read Julia's letter over her husband's shoulder. The letter had been addressed to both of them, and had been delivered to the rectory in the afternoon along with the trunks of clothing. Phoebe had not dared open the letter without Crispin, and she had called him out of his study to see what it was all about.

The letter briefly told of Jona's betrayal, and Julia's need to cleanse herself of him and his influence. Crispin was baffled that she had not called, but he knew she must have been reeling from shock and humiliation. In her innocence she had chosen to include Phoebe in her confidence. Phoebe, as Crispin's wife, was an extension of him. Julia wanted to believe in Phoebe's goodness too. But now Crispin took one look at his wife's face and immediately recognized his mistake. He should have opened the letter in private.

'Don't you breathe a word of this, Phoebe,' Crispin warned. 'Not to anyone.'

'Of course I won't.'

'Can I trust you?'

'Of course you can!'

Crispin wasn't so sure. During the early years of his ministry in Kansas City and Chicago, she had been a true helpmate, and she had handled the joys and tragedies of their parishioners like an earnest acolyte, a little naively perhaps, but with genuine concern. But that had changed. There were many extraordinary women at the cathedral, but Phoebe had chosen to make friends with women much like herself, women capable of neither great sin nor great saintliness, women whose only interests were the petty struggles of power within an insular world.

'Can I open them?'

Phoebe was referring to the luggage the porter from the George had deposited in their living room. There were two trunks and four suitcases, all of them full of Julia's discarded clothing.

'No,' he replied curtly, stuffing the letter back into its envelope.

'They're not Jona's clothes,' she begged. 'They're Julia's. She's not dead.'

'I think we should just leave them alone until she gets back. She's overreacted. I'm sure she'll change her mind.'

'There are mountains of clothes here.' Phoebe was visibly swooning at the treasures buried behind lock and key. '*I* sure wouldn't do anything that stupid.'

'I'm sure she'll want them back.'

'Well, if she doesn't, don't you dare give anything away until I've had a chance to look at it.'

'If she doesn't want it, then it'll be considered a donation to the church.'

'Oh, come on Crispin. Don't be so stubborn.'

'*Don't you have enough clothes as it is?*' he shouted.

Crispin never raised his voice, and Phoebe was stunned. She spun around and marched out.

He stuffed Julia's letter into his jacket pocket. It was raining as he dashed across the courtyard and out the front door. He needed to be alone, away from eyes and ears. He was hating Jona Wahlberg just then. It was such a violent, disturbing sensation, and he didn't like having it inside him. He could only imagine what Julia must have gone through when she had learned of his betrayal. Lord, he thought, the bastard was married with a kid. And all of it had been done behind her back. She hadn't deserved this.

He stormed down the street, rain pouring down his neck, stomping through puddles like they were Wahlberg's face.

He would never admit to the jealousy that had clouded his judgement of Jona Wahlberg, and now he could boast that he had been right all along. He dashed across the avenue, cutting between the cars. He needed to find the words to describe such despicable behaviour. Julia's life had been a constant struggle to overcome a fragile sense of self-worth, and Jona had built her up and then shattered her. What names do you call a man like that? Sure, she had chosen to delude herself. She had even admitted as much. She had made him into God-the-Father. But if he *was* God-the-Father, then that girl-child had just been cast into utter darkness and abandoned.

It was no different from what her mother had done to her.

Rarely had Crispin been angered to the point of physical violence, but he was now. He wanted to slam his fist into something, or kick something, or knock someone down. Finally, he stopped halfway up the Rue Marbeuf and turned to stare at a window display. People were bustling down the street with their heads down because of the rain, so no one could see he was fighting back tears.

That evening after the rest of his family had gone to bed and he could be alone, he sat up late in his study and sent Julia a long email. He was just closing down his computer when he heard Phoebe coming down from their bedroom. She opened the door and gave him a sweet smile.

'You're working late,' she said, and crossed to him and laid her hands on his shoulders as if she cared, but he knew she was just reading the screen over his shoulder.

'I was just sending an email to Julia.'

'That's all so sad,' Phoebe said, and Crispin could almost believe she meant it. And then she ruined it all by adding, 'We should have taken her up on her offer to visit the set. Now it's too late. I don't imagine she'll want us up there now.'

Crispin hid his dismay and gave a tempered reply. 'I agree with you there.'

'I know she's a glamorous film actress and all that, but frankly, I always felt a little sorry for her. She just sort of latched on to our family, and I found that sort of sad. I think she wanted what we have.' She gave Crispin's shoulders an affectionate squeeze.

There was a frozen silence, and Crispin was tempted to say, 'Just what do we have, Phoebe?'

Then she said, 'Why didn't she have any children?'

'I suppose that was their decision. I don't know.'

'She's such a needy person, isn't she?'

'Did you want me for something?' he asked a little sharply.

'I was thinking about the girls' Easter holidays. I thought I'd take them back to Santa Barbara to visit my parents . . .'

'That's out of the question.'

'Let me finish,' she said with strained patience. 'I already talked to Daddy. He'll pay for our tickets.'

The news hit hard, and it hurt. He turned around in his chair and looked at her. 'But you'll miss Easter service at the cathedral,' he said, unable to keep the surprise from his voice.

'The cathedral isn't the only place they celebrate Easter, you know.' She said it flippantly but avoided his eyes.

'I thought we were going to our house in Normandy,' he said. 'That's what we do every year after Easter.'

'That place depresses me.'

'Depresses you?'

She shrugged. 'Yeah, it depresses me.' Her voice lacked conviction. 'I guess if I'd had a chance to redecorate it . . .'

'You liked it when we bought it.'

'I saw its potential. But you've never let me do a darn thing with it.'

'It's simple. And cozy.'

'Oh for goodness' sake!' she cried in exasperation. 'Spare me, will you?' She marched out and caught the sleeve of her dressing gown on the doorknob and was jerked back. It was the kind of thing they would both have laughed at before, and the row would have been over, but now she whipped her wrist loose and stormed off with her white silk dressing gown billowing behind her.

Days passed and Crispin received no answer to his email. It had wounded him that Julia had returned to England without calling or trying to see him. Perhaps he had assumed too much, imagined himself to be more important to her than he really was. He wanted very much to hear her voice, to know she was all right. He missed her.

The girls' Easter holidays were upon them and Phoebe found a mountain of things to do before they left for Santa Barbara, most of which necessitated money – visits to the hairdresser for herself and the girls, new clothes and shoes, gifts for her parents and friends. But Crispin was resolved that they should sink no deeper into debt, and there was little money for these things. Phoebe seemed determined to inflict her anger and disappointment upon him, which in turn only heightened his sense of failure as a husband and father.

It seemed to Crispin that things were unnaturally complicated right now. Before, he had always been able to establish his priorities and stick by them, and things had always worked out. He was a happy sort of guy. That was his nature. He'd been able to adapt, even when the choices were tough. But he wasn't happy anymore. He had the feeling something was being asked of him, and the fear that hovered deep down in the darkness of his thoughts told him the sacrifice might be more than he was willing to pay.

21

With Tom Noonan soon to decamp for Washington DC, the vestry was now actively interviewing candidates for the deanship. Three of them, two from the US and one from Malaysia, were flying in for interviews, and Tom had repeatedly commented to Crispin on their résumés, saying they all seemed to be exceptional. It needled Crispin, and Maddy Cartwright, the senior warden, picked up on this and invited Crispin out to lunch the day after the first candidate had come and gone, with the intention of reassuring him. She asked Crispin where he'd like to go, and Crispin took her to his café beneath the Chinese dragon where he had taken Julia.

Maddy was a woman in love with the things Crispin loved, with the ritual and the beauty of the cathedral, but she also loved the people, and when her husband died she had turned her benevolent spirit towards the good of others. Every Friday she was up before dawn doing the shopping and supervising the cooking for the Friday lunch for the homeless. She did anything anyone needed of her, and she did it humbly and in the spirit of sacrifice, and on occasions she went with Crispin on his Tuesday rounds when he ventured out into the city, ministering to the sick and the destitute. She always brought along Piaf, her tiny Yorkshire terrier, and it was the sweetest Yorkshire terrier you'd ever meet. She'd hug the dog under her arm while they talked to people on the street, and Piaf looked like she could understand everything. She had big soulful eyes and ears that listened and she never yapped like

Yorkshires do, but she'd whine a little now and then. Sometimes people on the street would want to hold her and she'd go to them and sit in their arms and she sort of loosened their tongues. They'd stroke her and suddenly it'd become easy to talk about their troubles, and there would be this priest and this bosomy old lady with angel-white hair and this Yorkshire terrier all willing to listen. Once somebody called the three of them the Holy Trinity.

Piaf had that effect on Crispin that day as he sat opposite Maddy in a booth at the rear of the café, lunching on Madame Meriot's home-made *hachis parmentier*. The waiter had given them a saucer and Maddy had scooped a little of the ground beef onto it and set it on the floor for Piaf.

'I appreciate this gesture, Maddy. It means a lot to me.'

'What? Feeding Piaf?'

'No. Feeding me. Not that I'm not well fed at home. It's the meaning behind your gesture. Your support.'

'Tom hasn't given up the battle yet, you know.'

Crispin raised his eyes from his plate. He was chewing slowly, reflecting on this.

'You think not?' he said at last, and took a swig of his beer.

'I know not. He's got his bloodhound going through the restoration expenses as we speak, seeing if he can find the slightest trace of an irregularity.' The 'bloodhound' was Maddy's nickname for Edward Ribbey.

'You must be joking,' Crispin said as he offered the bread basket to Maddy and then took a slice for himself.

'I'm afraid I'm not.'

'Waste of his time.'

'Oh, we all know that. He knows he's not going to find anything. It's all show. Tom probably thinks if word gets around they're scrutinizing your expenses it'll give a subtle impression that you may have perpetrated some wrongdoing.

But everybody knows it doesn't have a darn thing to do with anything, except that Tom'd rather see the devil himself up there on his little throne than cede the deanship to you. He's desperate. He knows you've got it in the bag now, and there's not much he can do. You're his Achilles heel, you know. You succeed where he fails.'

'I always thought it was the other way around.'

'That's what he wants you to think. But you're what we need. You're exemplary, Crispin. Really you are.'

'Thank you.'

'But there is something you'll have to be on the watch for.'

'What's that?'

'We have a lot of unhappy women among our parishioners. A man with your qualities could easily find himself the subject of controversy.'

The way she said it put Crispin on the alert. He laid down his knife and fork and leaned back with his arm rested on the top of the seat and gave her a long querying look before he spoke.

'Maddy, I target people's hearts and souls, not their bodies. I thought people knew that about me.'

'Of course they do.' She leaned towards him, her ample bosom nearly dipping into her plate. 'But that's what makes you so appealing. Sweetie, you're a lot cuter than you like to think you are.'

'Well,' he was sounding uncomfortable again, 'that's nice of you to say, but I certainly hope I've never abused whatever physical charms I may possess.'

'Of course you don't. You hide 'em under a barrel. Like all good priests. Pity, though.' She looked sincerely chagrined.

Piaf was whining softly at her feet. Maddy reached under the table, fished the saucer up from the floor and scraped the last of her *hachis parmentier* onto it.

'Are you hearing rumours?' Crispin asked.

'You don't know who I'm talking about?' she said as she replaced the dish on the floor.

'I assume it's Julia.'

'It's just jealousy,' she said.

'Damn them,' mumbled Crispin. He picked up his fork and poked at a sprig of parsley. 'They better leave her alone.'

'You two go way back, don't you?'

'I didn't have any brothers or sisters, you know. Julia was like a sister to me. We had this thing. We always seemed to find each other. Like needles in a haystack.' A look of reminiscence passed over his face and he gave a light laugh, but then the smile faded. He picked up the parsley and twirled it between his fingers. 'Julia had four brothers.' There was a long pause, and then he said quietly, 'Her mother drowned them all. Julia was the only one who survived.' Crispin dropped the parsley and wiped his hands on the napkin.

Maddy let out a soft gasp and her hand flew to her heart. 'Oh my goodness,' she whispered.

'Yeah,' said Crispin. 'I was the one who found Julia. She still thinks she owes me her life. I don't feel it that way. Sometimes I think I owe her mine. Don't ask why. I can't explain.'

Maddy had become perfectly still. After a while Crispin threw off the heavy silence and looked up at her with that beguiling grin of his.

'You should get to know her, Maddy. You'd like her a lot.'

'I'm sure I would.'

'And besides, if I left my wife for anyone – which I won't – it'd be for you, Maddy.'

For some unknown reason, Piaf squirmed at their feet and emitted a slow and unexpectedly deep growl.

Crispin drove Phoebe and the girls to the airport, and stayed to see them and their excess baggage off to California, and he came back a little lighter in spirit, feeling like he could get a lot of work done. He worked late at night after everyone had left, and then he went into the cathedral and kneeled at the altar of St Paul the Traveller for a good half-hour. Afterwards he returned to the rectory, and he was nosing around in the refrigerator for something to eat when the telephone rang. He couldn't understand the woman at first, because he had the television on in the living room, and he had to locate the remote control and lower the volume, then he heard her introduce herself as Susannah Rich. She said she was Julia's publicist, calling from New York.

'I understand you're a close friend of Julia's,' she said. The line was crystal clear, and it sounded like she was in the same room.

'Is something wrong?'

'I sure hope not. You're a priest, right?'

'Yes. I am.'

'You know about Jona's death?'

'Yes. I got a letter from Julia about five days ago. But I haven't spoken to her.'

'Could you make a trip up to northern England to visit her?'

'When?'

'As soon as possible.'

'What's happened?'

'I don't know. She won't let anyone near her. She's locked herself in her room and hasn't come out for four days.'

'Did she ask for me?'

'She won't talk to anyone. But her assistant remembered you'd been corresponding during the shoot – before Jona's death.'

'Yes. That's right.'

'Well, we took the liberty of pulling up your emails, and we thought, given the nature of your friendship, she might open up to you.' Susannah's voice became much more anxious and less controlled. 'I'm really worried about her. Everybody is. But the last thing we want is to send her off to a mental ward, and I'm afraid that's where they're heading.'

Crispin slammed the refrigerator door shut and said, 'Look, I'll get the first train up there in the morning. Tell her I'm on my way. Tell her I'm coming.'

While he was rushing around trying to think what he should pack, he kept seeing images of Julia hanging in the dark water in the cellar, and Julia at fifteen, naked and stretched out on the sofa, her skin cold like snow.

When he called Eurostar and found there was a train that night at 21.13, he booked a seat even though it meant he'd have to spend the night in a hotel somewhere in London. The train was nearly empty, and he tried to read a little but he couldn't concentrate, so he spent most of the journey drinking coffee in the lounge car, watching his reflection in the darkened glass window and feeling anxious about Julia. In London he had to pay an exorbitant rate for a hotel where he got only four hours sleep, and he was back at the station at six the next morning buying his ticket for Leeds.

He changed at Leeds for Keighley and from there took a private steam train on to Haworth, arriving in the village centre well before noon. From the train he caught only a glimpse of the moors which Julia had described for him, but he was disenchanted by the grim blocks of houses and flats that obscured the land. The horizon was interrupted by tall smoke stacks from the regions' many mills and factories. Smoke drifted over the towns, blown by a high, steady wind, and the beauty of the morning was lost in a dull industrial haze.

In the village the narrow cobblestone street was swarming with tourists. There were Japanese out in packs, and Germans, and lone Americans in Birkenstocks. Everywhere you looked there was a tourist shop selling all kinds of useless things.

Crispin found Heather Cottage and knocked on the door. He glanced up at the window above and thought for a moment he had seen a movement, but it was only a plump cat sitting on a window ledge, blinking down at him and twitching his bottle-brush tail.

It was not Fiona who answered, but Mrs Ingilby, the proprietor. She was expecting him, and she graciously took his jacket and hung it on a rack behind the door and told him to have a seat at a small round table already set for tea.

'You can go up in a moment, Father,' she said, 'after you've had a cup of tea,' and it was the quiet kind of voice that you listened to and heeded. Her voice didn't go at all with her appearance, which was a little brassy. She was one of those ladies who wore her lipstick bright and thick and drawn beyond the outline of her mouth.

When she came back from the kitchen with a pot of hot tea, Crispin asked, 'Is she all right?'

'You can hear her moving around.' She poured his tea artfully, like someone who enjoyed serving. 'She's been crying a lot.' She set the teapot down and stood facing Crispin with her hands folded across her apron. 'I went up last night and talked to her through the door. I told her you were coming. I think it upset her. She said we shouldn't have bothered you.'

'No. It was the right thing to do.'

'I thought so too.'

'Where can I stay? I'd like to freshen up.'

'The room at the top is yours. No one else is here except me. They sent that young woman who was her assistant back to London. Poor dear.'

She left it at that. Crispin finished his tea and carted his bag up the squeaking steps to his room where he had a quick shave and changed his shirt, then went down to Julia's room.

'It's me, Julia,' he said. 'Can I come in?'

There was a long silence, and then he heard a quiet tread

and the door opened slightly. The room was dark; the heavy curtains were drawn, blocking out the light.

'I can't believe they called you,' she whispered from behind the door. She sounded very tired.

'I'd cross mountains for you,' he said. He reached through the opening in the doorway. 'Give me your hand,' he said. She took his hand, and hers was warm and damp. 'What's wrong? Why don't you want to let me in?'

'I don't want anybody to see me,' she said. She lifted his hand, and he could feel tendrils of wet hair, and then she ran his fingers over her cheek, and whispered, 'See what I did?'

Gently, he pushed open the door. She had recently taken a shower and the room was humid and smelled faintly of perfume.

'Let me see,' he said. He drew her towards a small bronze lamp on a dresser and turned on the light.

'Here,' he said, lifting her face. There were long inflamed gashes down each cheek. 'Did you do this to yourself?'

She nodded, unable to look him in the eyes.

He reached for her, and she buried her face in his chest, clinging tightly to him.

'You take it all out on yourself, don't you?' he whispered, and she nodded, her face buried in his shoulder, and he could smell the shampoo in her hair.

'Oh God,' she muttered. 'I'm such a mess.' She tried to laugh, but the sound came out raw and cracked.

'What? You're not telling me this is your fault?' he asked, stroking her hair.

'I never saw it, though everybody around me must have. I'm so humiliated,' she muttered. 'That's why I never called.' It was so much easier talking about it like this, with Crispin's arms around her. 'But I still can't believe it. It's just not like Jona to do something like this. But he did. So I'm a fool. And I guess, in a way, he was protecting me, because he knew what would happen if he left me. He knew I'd fall apart.'

'No. You would've grown up. And that's what's going to happen now. It just would have happened sooner. And I promise you, you won't fall apart. The Julia I know has courage like no one else I've ever met. She just parked her common sense in the deep freeze for a while. That's all.'

She shook her head, a vague, helpless gesture.

'And don't ever despair,' he pressed. 'Ever.'

She grew very still, and lifted her eyes to his.

It takes a strong soul to bear the weaknesses of others without despising them. Man can be so despicable, to himself as well as others, and not many people had that gift of seeing with love, but Crispin did. Julia knew this; she had known it since they were young, although it had not yet been formulated in her mind then, as it was now.

'Oh, bless you,' she said, her red, swollen eyes glistening in the lamplight.

'My gosh,' he teased lightly, touching a lock of her wet hair, 'they've turned you into a brunette.'

She tried to smile but couldn't. He folded her back into his arms and held her while she cried. He had cradled many people in his arms, women who had lost children, husbands who had lost wives, but he had never felt his heart so full of sorrow as he did when he listened to Julia cry.

After a while he helped her back into bed. She confessed that she had been up most of the night, and she was worn out and needed a nap. He covered her with a blanket and then pulled a chair up beside the bed. She rolled over to face him.

'Don't leave me yet,' she whispered.

'I won't leave you at all.'

He stroked her hair, and gradually she relaxed, and soon she was asleep. Crispin thought about going up to his room. He needed sleep badly, but he didn't want to leave her. Quietly, so as not to awaken her, he stretched out on the bed beside her. He was careful not to even touch her, but he could not sleep. He lay there listening to her breathe, praying that the proximity would not arouse passion, because he knew he could feel that for her, and he didn't want to feel it. Not now, not in her condition. Not ever. He could hear Mrs Ingilby moving about downstairs, opening and shutting cupboards, running the water, preparing dinner for them. They would have dinner tonight, Julia and him, just the two of them. It would be nice. Mrs Ingilby would shield them. She would keep the world in abeyance for another night. He fell asleep.

22

Mrs Ingilby knew things would be all right. She had faith in Father Wakefield from the first moment she laid eyes on him, and she went to a good deal of trouble to prepare a special dinner, hoping he would coax Julia into eating. So when Crispin appeared in the kitchen and asked if they could have dinner upstairs that evening, Mrs Ingilby felt greatly relieved, and she bustled happily about the small kitchen as though she'd been asked to serve the Queen herself.

Mrs Ingilby's rabbit stew came nowhere near Madame Meriot's *lapin chasseur* but it was good nonetheless. Crispin did not press Julia to talk, and there were long silences between them, but they were not awkward silences. His arrival had revived Julia's appetite, and she ate a small portion of the stew and drank her wine. He could tell when she was thinking about Jona because there would be a moment when she seemed to detach, but after a while she would come around again. After clearing their dinner plates, Mrs Ingilby lit a fire for them, and Crispin sat in an armchair and read the London *Times* while Julia sat on the bed and dried her hair, watching him. His silent presence, his undemanding acceptance of her, the way he just came in and shared her life without judgement, without hurrying her along to some cure or another, brought her reassurance in a way no one else could have done. She marvelled at the way he fitted into her life, effortlessly, and at his patience.

Crispin caught her gaze and he lowered the paper and said

something to make her laugh, and then she began to talk. At first she didn't speak about Jona but about her fears, because it somehow seemed to her that they were at the root of her failure.

She told him how everything beyond the walls of Heather Cottage terrified her, but her greatest fear of all was that she wouldn't be able to finish the film, that she would never make another film again. All the techniques that had worked for her before, everything she had learned to do to reduce her anxiety had all failed her once she had arrived back here in Haworth. It was as if she had used up every last ounce of courage, and she was doomed to be a prisoner within these walls for ever. She knew of extreme cases of agoraphobics who never left their homes again, and she could not bear to think of her life like that. Daily, even hourly, she fought against despair, against the urge to take her own life. At times her despair turned to rage, and she imagined herself confronting Jona with his lies; she'd scream at him and dream up ways to hurt him, but then the grief would return and she'd succumb to tears. There were moments when she could almost believe he was still alive out there, that he'd walk through the door and explain it all to her. There would have been some terrible misunderstanding, and none of this would be happening. She heaped all the blame on to herself, reproaching herself for withdrawing into a make-believe world and turning her back on her intuition. Because there had been times when she had suspected Jona was something other than she believed him to be, but to doubt her image of him would have destroyed her world. And she had sought, at all risk, to keep that world intact.

Since his death, she had begun to re-examine her relationship with Jona, and was slowly coming to grips with the disastrous consequences of relying so completely upon his guidance, of believing in his infallibility. She confided in

186

Crispin how, when she was younger, Jona had attempted to educate her and fashion her interests to suit his own tastes. She had been like a sponge, soaking up Jona and his world. He chose books for her to read, books to sharpen her mind and form her opinions, just as another man might have chosen stylish clothes for his mistress. Julia didn't care much for the things he made her read, but it was a way of becoming a part of him.

But as the years passed and her docility gave way to maturity, she began to desire an equal rather than a master. Jona couldn't see this. To challenge his supremacy was an act of treason; questioning his judgement implied she didn't trust him. If she tried to raise herself to his stature, it was interpreted as an act of rebellion. When she was younger and yearned for an adult to care for her, she willingly gave him control over her finances. He had her sign entire chequebooks, and Julia never questioned how the money was being spent. But years later, when she asked him to explain how their investments worked, he made a ruthless game out of it, purposely confounding her with rhetoric far beyond her grasp. He gave her investment periodicals to read, set them down in front of her like bait, knowing she had neither the inclination nor the time to study them. Eventually she quit asking him to explain anything, and relinquished her hopes of self-reliance. Nevertheless, if she was still under his influence after all these years, it was because she thought he was the best man in the world – the best lover, the best friend, the best father. She was still in thrall to his sharp mind, his complexity, his ego, his sheer energy. He had been everything to her.

But Jona's betrayal had sparked a homicidal anger of which she had never believed herself capable. It was fortunate they had taken his body away, because her anger could have raised the dead; at times she believed he was not dead but hiding somewhere, perhaps from his assassins, perhaps from her. Perhaps he had made it all up to be rid of her, to be able to live his life with the other woman. But then she would remember the way they had been, and she knew this wasn't true, and that he was dead and she would never see him again. Then her rage felt hollow and impotent, and grief rose inside her like an insurmountable wall.

The hours swept by without notice, until finally, around eleven, Crispin began showing signs of drowsiness and Julia urged him off to his room.

'How long are you staying?' she asked.

'As long as you need me. Phoebe's back in California with the girls, visiting her folks. It's the Easter holidays.'

'What about the cathedral? All those people who rely on you?'

'Why are you worrying about others? You think you're not important?'

'You came all this distance. I never would have asked you, you know that.'

'I want you to be safe. I don't want anything to happen to you. I don't want anyone to hurt you, not ever again.' He touched her swollen cheek gently with the back of his hand, and he felt himself suddenly aroused. He tore his hand away. 'Don't hurt yourself again, Julia. You must be good to yourself.'

'I know,' she said, her hand rising to her cheek where he had touched her. 'What I did was terrible.'

'But I understand.'

'You do?'

'Of course I do. But what's more important is to know how much you are loved.'

He leaned forward and kissed her on the forehead. 'Try to sleep.'

'I will.'

He headed across the sitting room towards the stairs. Then, before she had closed the door, he turned and said, 'I was thinking maybe I'd get up early and go for a walk before all the tourists descend upon the town.'

'Oh, you should. It's so beautiful. Even if it rains, you should go. Mrs Ingilby has a lot of old hiking boots lying around. She'll have your size, I'm sure. And anything else you'll need.'

'Good. I'll see you when I get back.'

But in the morning, when he opened his bedroom door, he found an envelope on the hardwood floor. Inside was a poem, copied in pen and ink. He recognized the poem, one of Emily Brontë's, perhaps her most oft-quoted.

No coward soul is mine,
No trembler in the world's storm-troubled sphere:
I see Heaven's glories shine
And Faith shines equal arming me from Fear.

He found her waiting in the parlour. She was dressed in a period costume she had worn during the first week of shooting, a grey muslin dress with wide sleeves and white lace collar, and her hair was pinned back in a tight bun. She had taken pains to cover the scratches on her face with foundation, but apart from that she wore no make-up. She smiled at Crispin's surprise.

'I'm coming with you,' she announced. She pointed to some boots and a hunter's all-weather coat on a bench. 'Those are for you. Mrs Ingilby's still asleep, so I pulled out some things we're using for the film.'

'Good,' he said with a restrained smile, trying to conceal the immense joy he felt.

'I suppose you think I'm being very dramatic, going out

like this. But . . .' She faltered, and looked down at her hands.

'Don't explain. I understand. You told me. Back in Paris.'

'It's the only way I can handle it.' While she spoke, she dusted at her long muslin skirt. 'It's really hard, getting to that place in my head where I'm free. But when I'm there . . .' she heaved an enormous sigh '. . . when I'm there, everything becomes possible.'

As he was lacing up his boots he said, 'It's odd, how you seem to change, just watching you, I can see what you mean. You're not Julia anymore.'

'You look very Victorian in Reverend Nichols' coat.'

'Do I?' he grinned, glancing at her dress. 'You're sure you'll be warm enough?'

'I have a cloak. And I packed us breakfast. Some cheese and bread. And some beer.'

He straightened, picked up his hat, and solemnly offered his hand.

They set out under the pale mist of dawn, with the cottages huddled in shadow, the streets quiet and the windows dark. The hill was steep and the wet cobblestones slippery, and Julia clung to Crispin's arm, gripping her skirts with her free hand while they climbed. At the head of the village the street levelled out, and they followed it past the Black Bull Inn and around the church, turning into a lane flanked by the sexton's house on one side, the graveyard and parsonage on the other. Here Julia picked up her pace, her skirts raised above her ankles, as though eager to be away from the depressing little village. Once she stumbled, and Crispin caught her and looked down into her face. He could see the anxiety building in her eyes.

'Are you okay? Do you want to go back?'

She shook off his hand. 'I'll be okay once we're out of the village,' she replied, hurrying past him.

They turned off the lane onto a footpath beside an avenue of trees, and finally, at the crest of the hill, with the morning light filtering through grey-cast sky onto the moors, Crispin caught his first glimpse of the distant hills. They rose in great rolling sweeps, one horizon beyond another, receding into paler, mistier shades of blue. The air that hung between the place where he stood and the farthest, faintest hill seemed almost liquid.

He looked around for Julia, and she too had stopped, a little further down the path. She looked up at him and smiled and waved, then she turned and hurried on.

Crispin and Julia had been raised in a place not unlike this, a land with a grand beyond, a place in thrall to the sky. But this was not a hostile land; here there were no extremes, no floods or droughts or plagues. The hills were steep and the moorland wild and uncultivated, but there was in this bleak and dramatic landscape a heart-wrenching beauty that gripped their souls. For both of them, land offered a profound connection to life, and here was a land of expectancy and change where nature was at its most unpredictable. It was a land of ever-prevailing winds, of sudden, violent rains, of winter snow and starry nights. They had never outgrown their love for these things, and they became like children again, delighting in every aspect of nature around them, the spring-green dells carved up by low stone walls, a stream coursing down a cragged slope, knee-deep heather, a lane bordered by foxgloves, a field dotted with buttercups. Every turn or rise opened up a new vista, and when at last they reached Top Withens, Julia led him to a high slope behind the ruined farmhouse and its lone, gnarled tree, and they stood side by side and gazed out at the dim blue chain of mountains surrounding them.

They spread Julia's cloak on a grassy knoll and ate the picnic breakfast she had brought along. It was late morning by then, and the sun was warm, and after they had eaten they stretched out beside one another, Julia with her head resting on Crispin's arm. The beer and the meal had made them drowsy, and they both fell asleep and slept until the sun disappeared behind dark clouds, and they were awakened by the wind rising from the north and drops of cold rain. They gathered up their belongings and hurried down the slope to the farmhouse ruins. The roof and the upper storey had collapsed long ago, and they took shelter in a corner and watched the dark sky and the wind-driven rain.

Crispin said, 'Maybe it wasn't too wise. Coming this far.'

'It'll pass. It won't stay like this for long.'

'You're cold,' he said. He threw her cloak over her shoulders. 'Put this back on.'

'This doesn't frighten me, you know,' she said earnestly, her eyes on the roiling clouds above.

'I know. You were never afraid of the truly dangerous things,' he laughed.

'I'll never really be cured, you know.'

'But you'll learn how to cope again.'

'I hope so.'

'You will.'

'It feels good, not being afraid.'

'You can finish the film now.'

'Not until my face heals up.'

'Let your make-up people handle that.'

'I don't want them to know.'

He took her chin between his fingers, and turned her face towards him and studied it. 'They'll heal quickly.'

Her eyes were wide like liquid moons, and tendrils of her hair had come loose and hung around her face. She had unbuttoned the collar of her dress, revealing the hollow at the base of her throat, and he had a sudden desire to kiss her there. He looked away quickly, and withdrew his hand.

Julia stared quietly at him. Thunder rolled in the distance. The storm was passing. Suddenly the clouds separated and a shaft of sunlight fell upon the moorland.

'See,' she said. 'I told you it wouldn't last.'

They were both still for a moment, and then she whispered, 'You should go back home tomorrow, Crispin.'

He knew she was right, but he was sad, and for the rest of the day he carried that sadness around like a stone on his chest.

They returned to the village mid-afternoon, and the tourists on Main Street gawked at them. Julia hid her face with the hood of her cloak and kept her head down. Someone stopped Crispin and asked if they were making a film, but he only hurried past, trying to shield Julia from their curious stares. A tourist snapped photographs of them as they entered Heather Cottage.

They had dinner downstairs that night, in the dining room, and you could tell subtle things had changed between them. Finally, halfway through dinner, Julia laid down her knife and fork and buried her face in her hands and cried out softly, 'Oh Crispin, let's not ruin this, please. Let's not let anything come between us. I couldn't bear to lose you too.'

He knew what she meant and that was the first time he knew that she felt it too.

'It won't,' he said confidently. 'I love you too much.'

'Don't let it turn on us.'

'I won't.'

'Promise me.'

'I promise.'

'We're strong like this. Just like this.'

'Yes. We are.'

'When you're beside me, I feel like I can take on the world.'

He felt the same way, although he couldn't say it, because it sounded too much like a betrayal, but it was true all the same.

'Where will you go when you finish the film?'

'I don't know.'

'You won't go back to the King George?'

She shook her head emphatically. 'No way. I couldn't go back there. Besides, now that Jona's gone they wouldn't let me stay.'

'You can have our farmhouse. The place up in Normandy. It's not very glamorous . . . and it's not Paris, of course . . .'

Her eyes lit up. 'Phoebe wouldn't mind?'

'Hardly. She doesn't like the place.'

Julia reflected on the idea in silence while she toyed with the creamed peas on her plate, herding them into a little mound on the side. 'Gosh, I sure miss French food.'

'What about all your things at the hotel?'

'I don't want anything.'

'You'll regret it later.'

'I'll only go crazy again and do something stupid.'

'There must be things you want to keep. Photographs, letters.'

'Right. Like I want to see his face right now.' She laid down her fork and gave him a heartbroken look. 'I don't even know who she is,' she said. 'Who is she? How on earth did she get him to marry her? And have a baby . . .' Her voice rose and then trailed off. Then, bitterly, she added, 'She's Russian. He was always so damn dewey-eyed about those Russians.'

'Wasn't his family Russian?'

'His parents emigrated and his grandmother died in St Petersburg. But Jona was a pure New Yorker.'

'Sometimes those things become important when you get older.'

'And she was Jewish. I never thought it mattered to him. I guess I was wrong.' Her voice had hardened, and she sat back with tears glistening in her eyes. 'Wow, was I ever wrong.'

'You can fight this legally you know.'

'There's no money, Crispin.'

'What?'

194

'That's what he meant.'

'Who?'

'That little geek of a lawyer. He said the estate didn't amount to much. I don't know. I'm supposed to be meeting with some bloody financial advisor.'

'Would you like me to handle it?'

'Oh Crispin . . .'

'I have a buddy who's a lawyer. He can take care of it. He'll do it as a favour.' He was thinking of Rhoderic. Rhoderic would never bill a friend. It would have been ungentlemanly. 'Let him meet with the guy.'

She nodded, relieved. 'I'd like that, if you could arrange it. I can't trust any of them now. They were all Jona's advisors. They must have known about this all along.'

'You have to build your own world now. It'll take time. But you'll do it.'

His encouragement put a glimmer of a smile on her face.

'And I never thanked you,' he said.

Startled, she replied, 'What on earth for?'

'For your donation. All your clothes.'

She laughed lightly. 'Oh, that.'

'You've got a heart, girl.'

She reflected for a moment, and then said quietly, 'That's funny. Nobody's ever said that about me. They tell me how great I look, or how much they like some film I've done . . .'

'That's because they don't know you.'

'Or maybe I changed. Maybe my heart got buried under all this . . .' She struggled to find a word, something to express the anger and bitterness and confusion, but finally she gave up and only shook her head, perplexed.

'You were just trying to protect yourself. So you built walls. Walls aren't always a bad thing. They're necessary to survive. And you're a survivor.'

'Not without you,' she said, unabashed, and her eyes locked

on his and they felt it again. Crispin couldn't look away but Julia did, and it made her want to cry because she recognized in that brief instant all the beauty life could hold with a man like him, and she knew it would never happen.

'Do you want me to go back for you?' he said quickly, to cover the awkwardness.

'Go back?'

'To the George. Pick up the things you left behind. Anything personal you might want later.'

'You don't have time to do that.'

'I do now. With the girls gone. I could box up your things. You could keep them at the place in Normandy. We've got a big empty attic. You don't want to just abandon everything.'

'You're the voice of reason speaking.'

'Then call the concierge. Tell him to let me in.'

'If it'll make you feel better,' she mocked with a grin.

He left early the next morning, took the train back to Leeds, then on to London. He caught the Eurostar to Paris and was back in his office just after five in the afternoon. He had been gone a little over forty-eight hours but it felt like he had been gone for weeks. The next day, people teased him about disappearing as soon as Phoebe had left town. He didn't take it seriously. And then word got around that he had gone to England to see Julia, and the rumours spread like wildfire, growing in intensity and consuming and destroying, so that when the flames were finally extinguished, it was too late, and the landscape of his life had been disfigured beyond recognition.

23

After Crispin's visit to England, he and Julia frequently exchanged calls. He always spoke to her in private, behind closed doors, and sometimes the conversations were long. He took calls from lawyers and financial advisors 'with regards to the estate of Ms Kramer'. Unmarked cardboard boxes appeared in his office, stacked behind his desk, and when asked what they were, he replied evasively. One afternoon Edward Ribbey got the choir director to call Crispin out of his office and distract him while Edward snooped around in the boxes. All he found were photographs and scrapbooks full of newspaper clippings and publicity material about Julia's films, as well as some old address books and fan mail. There was nothing at all to indicate an intimate liaison, but to Tom Noonan and his supporters it all added up like a simple mathematical operation with only one possible solution.

If Maddy Cartwright had been around she could have controlled the damage; she would have alerted Crispin and he could have addressed the rumours. But Maddy was in Atlanta attending her granddaughter's wedding, and his other supporters, of which there were many, were too embarrassed to approach him on the subject. To confront Crispin with suspicions of something as serious as adultery was a mission none of them wanted to undertake.

By then everyone knew about Jona's death, and later Maddy Cartwright said it was all so absurd. Anyone with anything to hide would never be so obvious, and if Crispin was silent about what it all meant, it was only out of discretion, and respect for Julia. Julia was like family, Maddy said, and he was only trying to protect her the way one protects family, and to keep her business out of the reach of busybodies. Maddy stopped short of actually naming names.

She didn't need to. You didn't need to do much sleuthing to deduce who was spreading the slander. Gerry Noonan and Synthia Ribbey led the campaign, although everyone knew that Tom Noonan was behind it all.

Gerry was truly fond of Phoebe, and she meant her no harm, but she was fonder still of her husband. She never saw it as slander or gossip-mongering, but as upholding her husband's ideals.

Tom had put it to her quite clearly one night after dinner when they were discussing Crispin's hasty flight to England.

'It just reeks of deceit,' Tom had said sourly. He was knotting a big plastic bag full of kitchen rubbish while Gerry scoured out the sink.

'But he didn't really try to cover it up, Tom,' she reasoned. 'He didn't lie about where he was going.'

'All the same, the whole thing's just gotten out of control. I've heard too much from too many parishioners to ignore it. It's been very damaging for the cathedral. All these salacious innuendos whenever his name comes up. It's all anyone wants to talk about.' He was getting all worked up now and Gerry turned off the water and swung around to look at him. 'After all, I'm the Dean. I shouldn't have to run around after my canon as if he were some incontinent child, cleaning up after him every time he soils himself. I find it all very, very distressing.' Distressing. That was the key word, and it landed in the air like a hammer blow. When Tom found something distressing, it meant he was not in full control of a situation, and he would take any action necessary to regain control.

'Do you think it's true?' Gerry asked. 'You think they're having an affair?'

'The fact that he's given so many people reason to suspect an affair is what matters.' He straightened and stood there tall and righteous with a bag of rubbish in each hand as though he were weighing up the truth. 'I'm just afraid he's going to slide into the deanship on his personal popularity, dragging all this baggage with him, and that would be a downright calamity.'

'You really think the vestry will vote him in?'

'I do. Unless something catastrophic happens.'

'Like what?'

'Like Phoebe leaving him.' The idea had just occurred to him, and it brought a brightness to his face as though he had just found the solution to a particularly knotty problem.

'I doubt if Phoebe knows a thing,' Gerry said. 'She's still in California. They won't be back for another week yet.'

'Maybe she should,' he said with a smile of satisfaction. 'Yes. Maybe she *should* know.' Then he went to take the rubbish out, leaving Gerry with those words and that look, like a mandate.

After that it all became political.

Normally the girls would have been on the beach, but California was unseasonably cool and rainy that spring. Their friends, whose holidays did not coincide with their own, were in school, and so they spent their days moping around their grandparents' house, watching videos and eating too much. If the weather had been better, they could have taken advantage of the beauty of the place. The Darr's home was a splendid Palladian villa, set deep in the interior of a vast maze of separate gardens; there were vine-covered pergolas and terraces, fountains and creeks, and even a Tuscan-style grotto. There was a turquoise pool for swimming and a reflection pool for reflecting and palm trees for the sound they made. There was a gardener and a housekeeper, and a mechanic on retainer for their four cars.

Phoebe loved her visits to Santa Barbara, even more so after they left Chicago and moved to the cramped rectory in Paris. So when the girls grumbled about the weather and moaned that this was no different from the Easter holidays they spent at their cottage in Normandy, Phoebe was quick to point out that their property in Normandy was an old farmhouse with rotting wood beams, slanted floors and creaking steps, and that when there was no sun in Normandy they always ended up spending their days working on the house. Phoebe also made a point of reminding them that their activities were being limited because of budget restraints imposed by their father.

Phoebe had never tried to hide Crispin's financial difficulties from her parents, but on this visit she began to voice her complaints openly, and she gave the story a new spin. Phoebe had a gift for manipulating perceptions, and the husband she portrayed to her parents was an infuriatingly unreasonable man who was taking self-denial to the extreme and forcing them to live a life not of their own choosing.

It was painful for Hilary and Richard to see their daughter struggling with something as humiliating as loss of status. In the past, when they had offered financial assistance, Crispin had adamantly refused. Now, all they could offer was temporary relief. They all drove into Los Angeles to have lunch at the Polo Lounge at the Beverly Hills Hotel, and then Phoebe's mother took Phoebe and Cat and Megan shopping at the Beverly Centre while her father took Lola to see the latest Disney film. Next, Hilary and Richard drove their three granddaughters down to Anaheim to Disneyland, including an overnight stay at the Disneyland Hotel. Lola returned in a state of exhaustion and bliss, wearing a new costume and clutching a stuffed Tigger, and she wanted to call Crispin in Paris to tell him about it, but Phoebe wouldn't allow it. It was still the middle of the night in Paris, she explained, but the real reason was that she didn't want to talk to Crispin.

Phoebe took to spending her mornings at a local health club where she ran into Cecilia Glass, one of her old sorority sisters from UCLA who was now living in Santa Barbara. Their morning workouts were generally followed by fruit drinks and long chats at the bar. Cecilia had been through three divorces and each husband had been wealthier than the last, so she had all sorts of sound advice for Phoebe, all of which was predicated on greed. Phoebe listened with interest. She did not really want to divorce her husband, but she was very discontent. Being back in Santa Barbara, surrounded by a level of comfort and luxury of which she had been long deprived, only heightened her discontent. By the time Gerry Noonan called from Paris, Phoebe was already primed for action.

Phoebe was sunbathing by the pool that morning. She sat up to take a drink of iced water, and squinted into the sun. The weather had turned again, and it was a fine, warm morning with only a thin haze in a brilliant blue sky. Then the housekeeper came out and handed her the telephone; it was Gerry Noonan.

Gerry approached the subject obliquely. She inquired about the children and Phoebe's parents and declared how much they were missed. Then she talked about Crispin, emphasising how busy he was and how little they were seeing of him around the cathedral. Only towards the end of the conversation did she mention Julia.

'Isn't it awful about Julia Kramer? That man of hers dying?' Gerry said.

'I know!' Phoebe exclaimed, lowering her voice; all of a sudden the conversation took on real interest. She reached for a cigarette. 'Isn't it dreadful? He was murdered!'

'Is that true?'

'Absolutely!'

That's terrible!'

'Did you hear about the clothes she left?'

'No . . .'

'She sent over these trunks full of her clothes and asked Crispin to donate them to the cathedral.'

'Why on earth would she do that?'

'I can't tell you, and you wouldn't believe it anyway.'

'Why not?'

'Crispin doesn't want any of it to get out.'

'You mean about his murder?'

'Oh, Gerry, there's a lot more to it than that,' Phoebe said with tantalizing secrecy. 'It was absolutely mind-boggling what Jona pulled on her.'

Gerry lowered her voice. 'Oh Phoebe, I won't tell a soul. You know I can keep a secret.'

So Phoebe told all. She explained how Jona had led a double life, marrying another woman and having a child, all while living with Julia. And that he had left his entire estate to the child.

'So I suppose all those clothes were things he'd bought her,' Gerry surmised.

'I'm sure of it.'

'I think I'd torch a few things myself.'

'I don't know for sure, but from the letter she wrote us, I got the impression she may have tried to kill herself.'

'Oh my goodness!' Gerry exclaimed. 'So that's what all the urgency was about. Crispin didn't say anything when he got back from England.'

'England?'

'Yes, when he went to visit her.'

Gerry paused, and you could hear Phoebe's stunned silence on the other end of the line. Gerry went on. 'Of course, no one had any idea she was threatening suicide. But it makes sense now. The way he just raced up there overnight. Right after you left.'

'Well, I know Crispin's been counselling her,' Phoebe replied, believing she had concealed her surprise. 'You know how he is. He gets so wrapped up in other people's tragedies.'

There was another pause, and then Gerry said, in a low, confidential tone, 'You didn't know, did you, Phoebe?'

'Didn't know what?'

'That he went up to see her.'

A long tentative silence hung in the air. Finally she replied, 'We haven't talked in a while. We've been missing each other. He's called but we've been out. It's difficult, with nine hours time difference.'

'Well, of course,' Gerry said.

There was another awkward silence, and then Gerry said, 'Look, I'm sure he would have told you. It's just, well, you need to be prepared for all the rumours. They're flying all over the place. I didn't want you to come back with all this going on behind your back, and not know what everyone's been saying. There's nothing worse than being the last to know.'

There was a long silence on the telephone, and then Phoebe started to speak, but her voice broke.

Gerry said then, 'Oh Phoebe, I'm so sorry. But don't "shoot the messenger". Please. I'm your friend. Somebody had to tell you.'

Phoebe was crying now. 'Oh, Gerry, I'm so glad you did. If I came back, and didn't know all this was happening . . .'

'Particularly if you run into her. Those situations are just so odious.'

'She won't ever set foot in my home again, I promise you that much.'

'But I heard she's moving into your house up in Normandy, after the film's finished.'

'What?' Phoebe cried.

After she hung up, Phoebe lit up another cigarette and sat at the edge of the pool with her pretty brown feet dangling in the water, watching a waterbug skitter over the surface and hating her husband for something she wasn't even sure he had done. It didn't matter that she herself was most clearly guilty of infidelity, that she had once, years ago, indulged in that very same behaviour herself. The affair had lasted five months. It had been an immediate and intense attraction, something wild and inexplicable. Day after day she had drowned in illicit pleasure, aroused to extremes she had never imagined possible; she had allowed him to videotape them together, doing things to one another on beds they never slept in. It was not Phoebe but another woman who slunk in and out of those hotel rooms, leaving each time with his smell on her, naively believing she had concealed the affair with a lie or two and a little perfume, until she found out she was pregnant with Lola. She had never loved the man, she had not even liked him, although he was in love with her. At the end he disgusted her, even though she was convinced Lola was his child. But she never really felt ashamed of what she had done. Her betrayal sat in a tightly sealed little cubicle at the back of her mind, far removed from the rest of her life.

She met Cecilia for lunch that day in a nice little courtyard restaurant across from the beach, and she swizzled her mango punch and cried while she told Cecilia her husband the priest was having an affair with the actress Julia Kramer. (The fact that he was doing it with someone with a certain amount of celebrity soothed a little of her injured pride.) Cecilia reacted by ordering Phoebe a double margarita, then she reached for her mobile phone and called her lawyer and made an appointment for Phoebe the very next day.

'But I don't know if I want a divorce,' Phoebe sniffed. 'I need to find out the truth first.'

'You think you'll ever know the truth?'

'Crispin wouldn't lie to me. He's not like that.'

'Where their dick's concerned, they're like that, honey. Believe me. They'll lie all the way to the grave.'

When Phoebe told her mother, Hilary's dear maternal heart sank in her chest. She had always been fond of Crispin and found his decision to enter the priesthood an admirable one, but now Hilary felt betrayed.

'Oh Lord,' she said, 'I think I'm going to be sick.' Her hand flew to her mouth. 'What are you going to do?'

'I don't know, Mama.'

'Oh, honey. How awful. And living in a fishbowl like you do . . .'

'I know. Having to face all those people.'

'Will you run into her?'

'Crispin told her she could move into our house in Normandy,' Phoebe sobbed.

'What?'

'He didn't even ask me,' she said, tugging a tissue from the box beside her bed. 'Can you believe it? He's putting his mistress up in our country house! That's *our* home!'

'I'm sure this isn't the first time he's rushed off to console some poor unfortunate woman. And I can see how they might fall for him. He has such a good heart, and he is such a good-looking man. But I can't imagine him doing this.'

Phoebe buried her face in her mother's breast, and broke into tears again.

'You just need to go back and get this all sorted out with him,' Hilary soothed, stroking her daughter's hair.

Phoebe shot up. 'I can't stand the thought of going back there.' She unwadded the tissue and blew her nose. 'It's all too awful. I hate that place!'

'I thought you loved Paris.'

Phoebe heaved a long sigh. 'I do. But I'd love it a lot more if it we weren't always fighting over money. It's such a struggle, Mama. Being married to a priest. It was so different when he had his business and we had the money to do whatever we wanted.'

'But you know, I seem to remember, even when he was making a lot of money, he wasn't really attached to it. He just wanted to see all of you girls happy.'

'He doesn't seem to give a damn now. He seems to think there's some kind of virtue in being poor. I didn't want to raise my children like that. I wasn't made for that kind of life.'

'What are you saying, sweetie?'

'I don't want to go back there, that's what I'm saying.'

'Honey, the girls have to go back to school.'

'There are schools here, you know, Mama.'

'How would the girls feel about that?'

'They'd love it.' At least Megan would. And Megan was the only one she'd really have to deal with.

'Are you sure about this?'

'Mama, if he wants to sort this out, he can come here. After all the misery he's brought down on me, he can damn well come here and explain himself.'

'Well, I do see your point, honey. Rather than all four of you flying back there and having the girls exposed to such a nasty situation, and you too. If these rumours are true, you couldn't possibly continue, now could you? I mean, in a way, it's really too bad for you that it all got out. If he'd been more discreet in handling the situation, it would have saved you so much embarrassment.'

Phoebe had a prickle of conscience then, remembering her own liaison, but it quickly faded. After all, Crispin had never known. She had never let it hurt him. She had been discreet.

'You're so very right, Mama,' she said.

'I have a little experience in these things, sweetie,' Hilary said sadly, and she squeezed her daughter's hand.

'And if none of it's true, then I'll just go back.' Phoebe said it with such sad regret that it prompted Hilary to take her daughter into her arms and wish, as mothers do, that she could make the pain go away.

24

There were some at the cathedral who were close observers and reasonable people, and all of them noted later that Crispin did not act like a guilty man, but rather like a man burdened with responsibilities. There was the ravalement and critical decisions to be made with the chief architect and engineers, and his ongoing efforts at fundraising (during the week since his return from England he had written two requests for grants from private charitable trusts – paperwork which took him two all-nighters to complete). He performed weddings and visited the sick and the dying, and lent his comforting ways to the families of the bereaved, as well as meeting with those who just came looking for someone to listen to them. And when Miia, the youth director, came to him in tears because she was carrying the entire burden of planning for confir-mation classes – a duty the Dean was mandated to share with her – Crispin jumped in and shouldered Tom's share of the load. He did all of these things because he loved the people, and he thought that if he did his job well, he might briefly uncover the face of God so they could get a glimpse of a world he had once seen himself. Then they would know what he knew, and it might get them through life with the courage they would need, and with a little more kindness for their fellow man. Yet he never felt exhausted, never resented the demands made upon him. He was a little like the miracle of the loaves; the more he gave of himself, the more there was to go around.

Amidst all of these things he still found time for Julia. As promised, he met with Jona's lawyer and brought in Rhoderic to represent Julia's interests and find out all he could about Raza Lichovich and her son, Alexander. He looked over financial statements and spoke with bank trustees to try to unravel the whole mess, but he could see right away that no one person knew all there was to know about Jona Wahlberg's business matters. Crispin was convinced there were illegal activities buried deep within the web of Jona's affairs, and that the only men who knew anything about this were either dead or sitting in a fortified office in Moscow with armed guards stationed at the door.

He was also hoping to get up to the house in Normandy to do a little painting and some repairs before Julia moved in, so this too was weighing on his mind. Bringing her to Normandy was a way of making Julia a part of his family. He wanted everyone to see that there was nothing clandestine about their affection for one another.

Phoebe and the girls were to return on Saturday morning, on a direct flight from Los Angeles, and Crispin was at the airport early, but the flight was late and he sat in the café at the *Point de Rencontre* plowing through *Le Figaro*. He was a little nervous about seeing Phoebe again, because she always came back from the States with a freshly critical eye for all that was French, and the girls would pick up on it. They'd complain about the taste of the milk and the awful beef, and how small the rectory was compared to their grandparents' home in Santa Barbara. He had not spoken directly to Phoebe since the very beginning of their holiday, but he had spoken to the girls several times and to Phoebe's father once, and everything was fine. Nevertheless, he had been feeling a little guilty about the tight budget he had imposed upon them. He had sent Phoebe off to California with a modest amount of cash and no credit cards, and she had been furious. They had fought about it the morning she left, and now he was thinking perhaps he had overdone it a little. At the same time he knew that without draconian measures, he would never be able to pull them out of the mess they were in. At times, when it got too much for him, he'd think about quitting the priesthood and going back into business for himself. But the very idea of abandoning the cathedral and its community left him feeling like he'd been catapulted into utter darkness, a place without hope and joy, a place he never wished to be.

He dwelled on these thoughts while he waited in the airport café, staring at the crowded hall where family and friends waited for arriving passengers, when he heard his name paged over the loudspeaker. It made his heart bash into his chest because he instantly assumed there had been an accident of some sort. He sprang out of his chair and rushed from the café, tripped over a dog and forgot the shopping bag under his table with the 'welcome home' gifts he had bought for them. At the airport information counter there was a young man dressed in motorcycle leathers waiting for him. The young man opened a courier pouch, handed Crispin an envelope, and waited while he signed for it.

Crispin's hands were shaking when he opened the envelope and read the letter. Suddenly he felt dizzy, and the young woman behind the counter asked if he was all right because he went very pale. He knew he was going to have to sit down because his legs felt like they wouldn't hold him up. He found another café and he went to a table at the back and sat down and read the letter again, and then he felt it, the whole crushing weight of what was happening. It was like an explosion of bright light in your mind when everything momentarily becomes clear, and you see into all the corners and you see things that had always been there but before had been concealed by shadow.

He waited until their flight arrived. They never came

through the door, but still he waited, hoping they had been delayed, when all along in the back of his mind he knew they were not coming back. On the way home he remembered the shopping bag and the gifts, but it was too late to turn around and go back for them. He thought of the furry slippers with a smiling Pooh Bear on the toes that he had bought for Lola, and he had a sudden deep ache for the child; he had to pull over to the side of the motorway because he couldn't see to drive anymore.

When he got back to the rectory he called Santa Barbara even though it was one o'clock in the morning. He got the answering machine and this fuelled his anger, because they must have known he would call. He wondered if she had planned this all along, and he wondered how the woman he had loved and married could behave in such a despicable manner.

The rest of the day he tried to keep busy, but his mind was in a fog and he couldn't concentrate. Whoever asked about Phoebe and the kids were told they'd been delayed, and he sounded so vague that people started wondering, because they could tell that something was wrong. He called Santa Barbara every hour, but no one answered the telephone. He was still calling at midnight. It was three o'clock in the afternoon in California, and still no one answered.

Finally, in an act of desperation, he called Air France. There was a seat available on a direct flight to Los Angeles the next morning. The fare was exorbitant. He paid for the ticket over the telephone with a credit card he had saved for emergencies. A number of times he had been tempted to use it for one thing or another, but he had resisted. He'd kept telling himself that it had to be something truly critical, when money really would make a difference. He figured this was one of those occasions.

* * *

It was a day flight and very long, and although there was plenty of room to stretch out he wasn't able to sleep. By the time he picked up his rental car at Los Angeles International, he was feeling like he'd been drugged, and he stopped at a gas station to get some coffee but it wasn't strong enough to do any good. The coast smelled the way it always did, a novel blend of salt air and exhaust and desert in bloom that roused his senses, and the change was enough to keep him awake for a while. A little south of Malibu he stopped at a roadside Dairy Queen. The girl at the order window wore a faded black T-shirt and a seashell necklace. She smiled and leaned on the counter on her elbows, winding one of her pigtails around a finger while he looked at the menu, and when he ordered a hamburger and a chocolate milkshake she winked and said, 'Good choice.' He laughed and so did she, and it felt good to be back in America. He sat at a picnic table which was sticky with spilled Coke and ate his hamburger and watched the sun sink into the ocean. He liked visiting California. He didn't want to live there but he liked to visit the place, and he liked the people who were so very serious about not taking themselves seriously.

Santa Barbara was a beautiful town. It was a particularly nice place for rich people, with Spanish *paseos* for walking and Moorish arches and thatched palms and orange trees and flowering *bromeliads*. The Spanish and Mexican past was genuine; adobes from the nineteenth century had been preserved, and there were families with blood ties to the old *dons* and *doñas* of the Spanish colonial era.

It was dark when Crispin arrived in the town and he drove straight up into the hills to the Darr's home. The property was hidden behind high white walls and you had to park at the gate and get out and press the buzzer. Hilary, Phoebe's mother, answered the intercom. If she was surprised at his unannounced arrival, she hid it well. She said for him to come in, but he had to wait for several minutes before the gates opened and he figured she had gone to tell Phoebe he was there.

A regiment of perfect foxtail palms, as refined as Greek columns, lined the reflecting pool that led to the pool house arcade. She was waiting for him there. He came up the path and she heard him and lit up a cigarette in the dark. He saw her and stopped at the far end of the narrow pool. She wore shorts and a scoop-necked sleeveless shirt and she was very brown.

She was contrite, but only just. 'Obviously you got my letter.'

He waited for her to go on, to explain herself, but she just stood there with her arms folded across her chest and the cigarette glowing in the dark. He didn't know where to start. He was angry and wanted to kick something but he paced instead. 'What is this all about?'

It was quiet in the garden and his voice carried on the night air.

'Keep your voice down, Crispin, please.'

He answered just a shade lower, but you could still hear the anger.

'Look, I flew nearly halfway around the world, you can damn well walk the length of this pool to meet me.'

She came sulkily towards him. It was a walk he had found sexy at one time, but not now.

'Come with me,' she said, and he followed her down a gravel path with more palms. He could smell lavender somewhere. She kept walking until finally he stopped her.

'I just wanted to get away from the house,' she said, turning to face him. 'So they wouldn't hear us.'

'What did you tell them?'

She tried to look him in the face but she couldn't. 'I told them the truth.'

'What truth?'

'The reason why we're not going back to Paris.'

'Which is?'

'You know why.'

'Phoebe, I flew all the way over here to talk to you face to face because you didn't have the decency to come back home. Now talk to me! Tell me what this is all about!'

'Don't yell at me, Crispin!' she said.

'What do you expect me to do? Roll over and play dead?'

'How do you think I felt? Getting that awful call from Gerry telling me you'd gone to spend a weekend with Julia? Do you have any idea how that made me feel?'

'Gerry called to tell you that?'

'As soon as we were gone, you went to see her, didn't you?'

'You make it sound like it was a planned tryst,' he sputtered, desperately trying to control his rage. 'Like I was just waiting for you to leave . . .'

'Weren't you?'

'Oh, Phoebe!' he burst out in exasperation. 'How could you possibly think that?'

'Then tell me. Explain yourself.'

'Her publicist in New York called and asked me if I'd go to see her.'

'Why you?'

'Because I'm a priest.'

'Doesn't England have any priests? Do they have to import them from Paris? Why are you so special?'

There was a pause, and then he answered quietly, 'Some people think I am. Apparently you don't.'

She looked down, knowing she had hurt him, and she flicked the cigarette onto the gravel and crushed it with her sandal.

'Everybody thinks you're having an affair with her.'

'They were saying that way back at the beginning. You didn't believe it then.'

She fixed him with a probing look. 'Where did you stay when you were there?'

'At Heather Cottage. Where she was staying.'

'That looks real good,' she quipped.

'They made the arrangements. I didn't.'

'Who's they?'

'Her publicist, and the director.' He didn't want to say more, but felt he had to. 'They were afraid she might do something . . .' He faltered. 'For heaven's sake, this isn't the first time I've intervened in a crisis like this.'

'Why didn't you tell me?'

'I would have if you'd returned my calls.'

'I did return your calls!' she flung back. It was a bold lie, but Crispin ignored it.

'Phoebe, you and I both know that Julia has nothing to do with this.'

'Well, it just pushed me over the edge. And it was a pretty big shove.'

'I think you had this planned all along. You wanted to get away and then never come back.'

'That's not true!'

'Not once has the word divorce been mentioned in our home.'

'That doesn't mean I haven't been thinking about it.'

'There are stages to this kind of thing. You don't just break up a family overnight . . .'

'*You* broke it up!' she snapped. 'You! Not me.'

He stared at her long and hard. What she was doing was incomprehensible. He couldn't get inside her head to figure it out.

All of a sudden, he wasn't sure that he wanted to figure it out any more.

Hardened, he said, 'You're going to believe what you want to. You always have. You never could think rationally.'

She slapped him then, and he grabbed her wrist and squeezed it so hard that she winced, 'You do what you want, but don't you dare take my girls away from me.'

He flung her hand away and she rubbed her wrist. 'That hurt,' she said, looking at him warily.

'That's nothing compared to what you're doing to me.'

He was angry with her like he'd never been in his life, and he wanted to get away from her, but there were the girls to think of and he glanced towards the house.

'I want to see them.'

'You can see them tomorrow.'

'That's fine. It'll give me time to cool off a bit.'

'Come around four o'clock. They'll be back from school then.'

Crispin was stunned. It made it all sound so permanent. 'You enrolled them in school over here?'

'Of course. I didn't want them to get behind.'

After he had gone, Phoebe sat outside and smoked cigarettes and cried. Crispin sat up most of the night in his motel room, flipping through television stations. Neither one of them had expected it to go the way it did. She had expected him to put up more of a fight. He had expected to feel differently. Both of them had wanted something else out of the encounter, something other than what they got.

The next day, they decided that Phoebe would send the girls down one by one to meet their father on the terrace behind the reflecting pool. This had been where Phoebe and Crispin used to sip margaritas and watch sunsets when they were first married and visiting her parents. They had even made love there, and it was a bitter reminder to both of them. But it was also a secluded place, removed from the main house, and Crispin insisted on seclusion.

He wanted to see Lola first. She came skipping barefoot down the steps in white shorts, with her legs all brown from the sun, and she jumped up into his arms and wrapped her-self around him like a little tree frog. It was tough on him, and a sob broke from his chest, involuntarily, but he hid it with a whoop of laughter.

To shield Lola from the truth, Phoebe had told her their father would be coming to join them in California. Even Caitlin and Megan had proved themselves fiercely protective of the child's innocence. Lola had always been a quiet, deliberating child, but she struck him as happy like he'd never seen her before. You could see it in her eyes. The way they sparkled and her mouth twitched with a repressed smile.

'I'll bet you had a good time at school, didn't you?' Crispin asked.

She nodded warily, looking to him for the right answer, taking her cues from him.

'School's fun here, isn't it?' he said.

Her face exploded into a big smile. And she went on to tell him about her first days in an American school. He loved the way Lola saw the world. She observed things closely and pegged people quickly, and he was praying that she wouldn't see through their lies. She didn't seem to, and this relieved him; watching her, he could see she was different here and happy in a way she had not been back in Paris.

What really hurt was that Cat refused to see him. Megan came down, and they talked a little. He could tell she'd been crying. She didn't want to talk about herself, but about Cat.

'She said she saw you and Julia in the cathedral way back last autumn, and she said you two had been kissing.'

'She said what?' Crispin exclaimed.

'Well, something like that. Kissing or almost.'

'That time in the cathedral was the first time Julia and I had seen each other in . . . I don't know how many years. Since I was seventeen. It was a pretty emotional thing.'

'She said you were touching.'

'If we were, it was appropriate. The way old friends touch when they meet.'

She was sitting back in the patio chair, her eyes fixed on the floor, legs stretched out before her, scratching at the metal armrest with a fingernail. He was surprised at her. She seemed mellow and contemplative, not at all as he had expected her to be.

'And then,' she went on, still not daring to look up, 'Cat said there was a time after that big fundraiser when all the girls at church started talking about the two of you.'

'Did they say anything directly to you?'

She gave him a fiery look from beneath her long lashes. 'They wouldn't dare,' she snapped, divulging an instinctive sense of protection that was as much for Crispin as for her mother. 'Cat's so gullible. She believes anything you tell her.'

'The rumours aren't true. I've never been unfaithful to your mother. And I don't want a divorce.'

She sat there for a moment, refusing to meet his look, a tear rolling down her cheek. She brushed it away, and he wanted badly to reach out and hug her, but that would be too much. So he took her hand, and she responded by squeezing it tightly; it was the only way she could tell him she loved him. Abruptly, she shoved out of the chair and shot past him up the stone steps.

25

He ate dinner alone that evening, at a very plain Mexican restaurant recommended by the locals, and when he returned to his motel he found a message from Phoebe asking him to meet her at the patio bar of a beachfront restaurant.

She slid up onto the bar stool he'd been saving for her. She wore a hooded sweatshirt over her shorts and her hair was tangled and windswept. She'd been walking on the beach.

'I've reconsidered,' she said. She had ordered a Perrier water but wasn't drinking it.

Crispin was tired and could hardly stay awake, and he wasn't prepared for this.

'You're right, Cris,' she confessed, fingering the bottle. 'There was a lot more to it than Julia.'

'I'm not having an affair with her.'

'I believe you.'

He took a drink of warm Scotch, then turned away to watch a wave break over the shore. He wasn't sure where to go with this now. He wasn't even sure if he cared. But there were the girls to consider.

He said, 'Then let's cut straight to the heart of it all. I haven't taken any vows of poverty, but I'm a priest, and I'm sure not about to get rich. I thought you could adjust. You certainly made me believe you could—'

'I did think . . .' she interrupted, but he raised his hand and she fell silent.

'Let me finish, please.' He turned towards her with a clear

gaze, and he was detached in a way he had never been before. 'If you decide to stick it out, and for the sake of our daughters I hope you do, let me warn you, it'll probably get worse before it gets better. I mean financially. But the deanship is something . . .' All of a sudden his eyes burned and he dropped his gaze to his glass because he didn't want her to see him get emotional about it. 'The deanship of St John's Cathedral . . . that's an incredible honour. And you're my wife, and that's something to be proud of. There's a certain status in that, Phoebe. If that's any help. The money won't make that much difference. But there are other benefits.'

'Such as the Noonan's apartment,' she teased.

'That too,' he said and returned her smile. The lightness should have been a sign of encouragement, but he couldn't be sure. He was trying to negotiate his future with a partner he no longer trusted.

She brushed a tangled wisp of hair out of her face.

'Okay,' she said. 'I'll call Dad's travel agent. See if she can get us on a flight within the next few days.'

Crispin had spent enough time in California to experience several earthquakes, and it felt a little like that now. He knew there would be aftershocks, but he didn't know when they would come. He would try to get on with his life, but he would be vigilant and on edge.

The first thing he did upon his return to Paris, even before a shower and shave, was to track down Tom Noonan. The Dean was in his office leafing through a catalogue of liturgical wear.

'Crispin. Come in,' he said. He stuck a Post-It to a page featuring a very nice bishop's mitre that he wanted to order, then he laid down the magazine and leaned back in his chair, clasping his spindle-thin fingers together over his stomach.

'We need to talk,' Crispin said as he stepped inside and started to close the door.

'Yes. We do. But I don't have time right now.' He glanced at his watch and said, 'Got an appointment to get my hair cut in a few minutes.' He rose from his desk. 'How about this afternoon?'

But Crispin closed the door anyway. 'This can't wait, Tom,' he said. 'Sit down. Please.'

Tom smiled pleasantly, but he was a little peeved. He sat down all the same. His smile sagged like a limp sail.

Crispin pulled up a chair to face his desk and said, 'We've got to put an end to these rumours.'

'If you're talking about yourself and Ms Kramer . . .'

'They're slanderous and they're false.'

Tom disowned any responsibility with a graceful gesture of his long hands, lifting them into the air in much the same way he blessed the chalice on Sunday mornings.

'I certainly never believed them myself. But it's what our parishioners believe that counts. They're the ones you minister to. You've lost their trust.'

'Because of this?'

'Adultery is no light matter.'

'The rumours are false.'

'Appearances matter in these things.'

'Appearances are what you make of them.'

'What are we supposed to make of your wife leaving you?'

'Who said she's left me?'

Tom's expression curdled. He reached into his pocket and drew out a box of mints.

'Who said she's left me?' Crispin repeated while Tom picked a mint from the box and popped it into his mouth.

'The sources are many.'

'The sources are misinformed. Intentionally so.'

Tom caught the implication. He stiffened a little. 'I certainly hope you're not implying that I had anything to do with it.'

'Phoebe and the girls will be back next Monday.'

There was a taut silence, and then Tom foiled with a dazzling smile.

'I'm very glad to hear that, Crispin. I hope you've got things ironed out.' He rose to signal the end of their conversation, but Crispin remained seated.

Crispin said, 'Another thing you need to understand, Tom. Julia Kramer cares very much about my family. I don't want her to think she's the source of any of my problems. She's gone through enough tragedy as it is. If she should decide to seek consolation here in our cathedral, I trust she'll be welcomed – by all of us.'

Crispin rose and strode deliberately out of the office.

Julia called that evening. Just the sound of her voice lifted his spirits.

'Hold on,' he said, groping for the remote control underneath the sofa cushions. 'Let me turn this thing down.' He muted the television and sat up. 'Hey. What's up?'

'I'm finished!'

'Already?'

'It's over! I got through it! Shot my last scene today!'

She was bubbling and he thought how good it felt to hear her voice, and suddenly he wondered if this was right, that she should make him feel so good.

'Congratulations,' he said.

'I couldn't have done it without you.'

'Yes you could.'

'You gave me hope.'

'You found it in yourself.'

'You can take a little credit.'

'You need to start taking credit yourself, for what you've accomplished. Without Jona. Without me.'

He came off a shade churlish, and in the silence that followed, he could hear her bewilderment. He wanted to blurt out an apology, but he didn't. He had crushed her enthusiasm, and when she spoke again her voice had lost the bounce.

'I think we've made a beautiful film. I don't know if anyone will go to see it, but it's a beautiful film. And my work is good.'

'You made the right choice, didn't you? To make it.'

'I guess I did.'

'The house is waiting for you.'

'Your offer's still good?'

'Of course it is.'

'Is tomorrow too soon?'

'I can get away around noon. I'll meet you up there. Go through the place with you. It's one of those quirky old houses where nothing works the way it should.'

'Like your umbrella?'

'Exactly.'

'Crispin, remember, if Phoebe and the girls or anyone else wants to come up for a weekend, I can move into a hotel.'

'Hey, there are plenty of rooms. Having friends and family around is what that place is all about.'

'I'm really sorry they never got the opportunity to visit the set.'

'They'll be other films.'

'But they were so looking forward to it. You'll tell them for me, won't you? Tell them I'll make it up to them?'

'Of course I will. Now, you'll need directions . . .'

After they hung up, Crispin turned the television up and laid back on the sofa with his shoes off and tried to focus on the news, but he ached inside.

Julia took the train back to France. At Waterloo station there was a moment when she was afraid she wouldn't be able to go through with it, but Michael Langham had accompanied her and brought along a burly chauffeur who carted her bags to the *quai* and loaded them into her compartment. They kept a constant watch on her, like guards transporting a convict, waiting until the train pulled out of the station to make sure she didn't jump off and make a run for it. She would have found it funny if she hadn't been so sick, and for the first fifteen minutes of the train ride she locked herself in the bathroom and sat on the stool shivering through a horrendous panic attack. When it had passed she dragged herself back to her seat and fell into a hard sleep and dreamt of the Norman landscape and the beach and a house she had never seen. Crispin was in the dream, not his face but the feel of him. The man in her dream had another face altogether, but she knew it was Crispin because of the love coming from him, and the way he made her feel happy and safe. When she awoke they were already through the tunnel and arriving in Calais.

She hired a taxi to take her all the way to the village of St Yvi. The driver had to get out and enquire at a *tabac* because they couldn't find the house, but eventually they found it off a narrow street up the hill from the priory. It was much larger than she had imagined. It was composed of a generous two-storey stone central structure with a half-timber wing on one side and a barn on the other. Built in the nineteenth century in the Norman Revival style, it was not old by French standards, but it had languished for decades due to a long family estate dispute. The roof over the barn had collapsed and there were broken panes in the dormer windows of the half-timber wing. Nature had reclaimed the place; gulls and ospreys nested in the chimneys, and deep crimson creeping vines had overrun the barn.

Julia found bicycles in the barn, and while she waited for Crispin to arrive she rode a bike around the courtyard, and then finally summoned the courage to press on into the village. If she had succeeded in taking the train all the way from

London, then she could darn well make it into the village centre. The sun was warm and the breeze sweet, and she felt brave and good about life. The local bakery was open, so she went in and bought some bread. On the way back she passed a lilac tree, and she broke off some blooms and put them in the basket and raced back to the house before anyone could catch her. She was so pleased with herself that she wheeled around the courtyard singing loudly and doing fancy figures of eight. This was the way that Crispin and Maddy found her when they pulled in.

Crispin had asked Maddy to come up with him.

'I need to open up the house for her,' he had explained. 'And I don't think it would be wise to go up there alone.'

'So you want a chaperone, is that it?' she asked.

He answered, 'No. An eyewitness.'

When they pulled into the drive, Julia came wobbling towards them, guiding the bike with her knees, arms outstretched with the wind, the lilacs and a half-eaten baguette crammed into the basket on the handlebars. She had lost weight since Jona's death and her arms were thin, her brown hair had been cut, and she looked very young and artless, like a gamine. She pedalled up alongside the car and grabbed the rear-view mirror to steady herself. As Crispin rolled down his window, Maddy watched them together. There was unguarded joy on his face even though he didn't say much and tried to repress a smile. If he was in love, he didn't know it or wouldn't believe it; Maddy was sure about that.

Julia and Maddy had met briefly at the fundraiser and once Maddy had dropped by the rectory when Julia was there, but they had never had an opportunity to get to know one another. Julia, who loved dogs, made much ado about Piaf. She nestled the dog into the bicycle basket amid the lilacs and took her for a spin around the courtyard while Crispin unloaded their bags from the boot of the car.

This house was special to Crispin. It was the only piece of property he owned, and he had wanted it to be special to his family too. He wanted a family retreat for their holidays, a place they could make their own and return to year after year. Its renovation had been a family affair. When they came to Normandy, if the weather was too cold or rainy to go to the beach, Crispin always put them to work with a paintbrush or spade. In exchange for their labour the girls had the right to choose their room (there were seven bedrooms) and they were given free rein in decorating it. Megan splashed pink on the walls and then pasted together fashion ads to make a ceiling-to-floor collage; Cat chose a more subdued effect with glow-in-the-dark stars upon a midnight blue ceiling and posters of unicorns and magical beasts. Lola, who had just turned three when they bought the house, had been too frightened to sleep in a room by herself. Then one day Crispin came home with an antique armoire. On the inside back panel he painted a winter landscape, and he lit it from within so that when the doors were opened it appeared as if you were entering Narnia. The effect was magical. He positioned the armoire against the wall at the foot of her bed, and Lola would lay there and gaze into the wardrobe and dream her way to sleep.

Over the three years that they had owned the house, they had worked hard to make it comfortable and inviting. They ordered new mattresses and appliances, but the rest of the furnishings came from the *brocantes* in the area. Once, in an unusual display of humour, Phoebe had walked in, dropped her bag onto the scarred hardwood floor, glanced around the house and pronounced it 'butt ugly' and they had all roared with laughter.

And yet, for all their work, it had never become what Crispin had wanted it to become. If it had fallen short of his expectations, it was not because the house itself was lacking. After the first year their visits had become fewer and shorter in duration, and every year as soon as school was out, Phoebe took the girls back to California for the summer. Crispin would go up to Normandy by himself during the months that they were away, driving up alone on Sunday after service and returning early on Tuesday morning. Often friends came to visit, and he enjoyed this, but he enjoyed being alone too. But he had wanted someone to attach themselves to it the way he had done, and that had not happened.

Now, the idea that Julia would be staying there made him a little self-conscious. He hesitated in the doorway with Maddy's bag in his hand, seeing it with a freshly critical eye, but then Maddy nudged past him with Piaf's bed under her arm and trudged up the stairs. Crispin didn't notice Julia step up behind him. He was lost in his thoughts for a moment and then she prodded him with the baguette.

'May I come in?'

He moved aside and she swept past, bringing the smell of dog and lilacs with her.

'I love it!' she cried. She set Piaf down and stood in the hall with the flowers dangling from one hand.

'Can't see a thing until we get some light in here,' he said and he stepped past her into the sitting room. She followed him and watched as he opened the double doors and folded back the louvred shutters, and light flooded into the room.

'Do I really get to live here?' she said.

Crispin gave her a wary glance. 'It's not the standard you're used to . . .'

'But I love it! Nothing matches!'

'You're pulling my leg.'

'Absolutely not. I'm so fed up with places done by decorators.'

'Well then, you'll feel at home here.'

'I already do,' she said, and while he went around the dining room throwing back the shutters, she rummaged through a cupboard and found a vase and took it into the kitchen to fill with water. When he came into the kitchen, she glanced up from arranging the lilacs and said, 'You know, I was so worried. I was wondering how I'd manage. But I'll be fine. I can tell.'

'I'm worried about your being too isolated.'

'I'll get along.'

'The neighbours are good people. Madame Cristophani's husband has Alzheimer's so you won't see her out much, but she loves to talk to you from her window. Now the old peasant up there on the hill with the horses, he's another story. He shot the Mège's poodle last spring. The dog was chasing rabbits out of his vegetable patch, doing the old man a favour. But he shot him anyway.'

'Oh good grief,' Julia said, and then Maddy burst in on them to suggest they drive in to Deauville for dinner. Crispin made excuses, said he thought it might be nice having dinner there at home. He and Maddy could drive into town to pick up some fish at the market, and if the weather held they could eat outdoors.

Julia could see that Maddy was a little disappointed. She turned to her and said, 'Maddy, if Crispin doesn't want to go out to eat, it's because of me. He knows I have panic attacks in public places. I'm agoraphobic.'

No one knew quite what to say after that. Julia seemed suddenly embarrassed, and she gave Maddy an apologetic smile and left the room with the vase of flowers.

Maddy stood mouth agape. 'She's agoraphobic?'

Crispin nodded. 'At times she's completely debilitated by it.'

'So that's why you went to England.'

'She wasn't able to work. She was afraid she couldn't finish the film.'

'Oh goodness gracious,' Maddy muttered, and she pulled out a chair from the kitchen table and lowered herself into it. 'How's she going to manage up here all alone?'

'She thinks she'll be okay.'

'Do people know about this?'

'Only a few. Me. Her publicist. Jona did, of course.'

'Phoebe?'

Crispin shook his head. 'It can't get around.'

'I understand.'

'Obviously, she trusts you, Maddy.'

Maddy thought about how so many people had been wrong about Julia, and the injustice of it all struck her hard.

'I'm glad she trusts me,' she said, putting a reassuring hand on Crispin's arm.

Crispin lowered his voice and said, 'Something else you should know. I've never said a word about the problems Phoebe and I have been having. I don't confide in her like that. She thinks . . .' He hesitated. 'She thinks my marriage is doing just fine. And if she knew people thought we were having an affair . . .' He took a long breath. 'She wouldn't see me again. She'd never come around to the cathedral, and she needs that. She wouldn't even stay here. And she doesn't have anywhere else to go.' He levelled a tough gaze on Maddy. 'She needs me, Maddy. She needs you. She needs all the stability she can get.'

When Maddy and Crispin returned from Deauville, Julia had set the table with their mismatched dishes, a few half-burned candles and the vase of lilacs. Crispin had bought champagne to celebrate Julia's successful completion of her film, but he felt like celebrating anyway. It was an evening where everything was good. Maddy did the fish very simply but it was fresh and tasty and they had good wine. It grew cool, and Crispin went inside and brought out sweaters for all of them.

As the night closed in around them, they could smell the heavy greenness of spring sitting on the earth. They drank coffee and talked late into the evening. When they finally went inside, Crispin lit a fire, and Maddy and Julia sat together on the sofa while Crispin poked at the burning logs. After a while Maddy went off to bed, but Julia stayed.

She smiled at him and said, 'You know, it looks like my career's taking off again. The word's out that the film is good, and I'm getting some offers.'

'That's wonderful.'

'It's exciting.'

'How are you getting along?'

She gazed into the fire, gave it some thought and then said, 'The worst thing is the confusion. I'm either aching for him to come back or wanting to kill him. If I just knew what I was supposed to be feeling, it might help a little.'

'I have a little more information for you.'

'About the woman?'

'She was a journalist in Moscow. She wrote for a Russian economic review. Apparently, they met when she interviewed him.'

'When was that?'

'The first time was in December, about three years ago.'

She let out a soft cry. 'Three years? That long?'

Julia curled up into a ball in the corner of the sofa and stared sadly into the fire. He hated to see her hurt like that, and he wished then he hadn't brought it up. Suddenly he felt very angry, and he wished he could drag the bastard up from the pits of hell and beat him senseless. Not since his teenage years had he felt such a blinding urge to hurt another man.

'We don't have to talk about this right now. It's all in a memo. I brought you a copy.'

'That's all right. I'm okay.'

'Shall I go on?'

'Yes.'

'She's forty-one. Born and raised in Leningrad. Studied at the London School of Economics then went back to Moscow to teach at the university. Got married to a mathematics professor. They got divorced and he emigrated to Israel. No kids. After the Soviet collapse she went to work for Tarazov's television station.'

'So she was Jewish?'

'It looks like Jona pulled strings to get her a green card. She moved to New York and they were married last summer.' He hesitated, then added, 'In a synagogue.'

'And the baby?'

'He was born in September. Jona's name is on the birth certificate.'

'Wow,' she said with a sad smile. 'Can't beat that for legitimacy, can you?'

'Rhoderic thinks you should fight it in court.'

'For what? What am I going to win? His estate? That's nearly worthless. What's left? His loyalty? His love? I sure can't contest that now, can I?'

She sat up and brushed her hair back with a tired gesture. 'I have to reconstruct myself. And I don't want to do it with his rotten money. I'll do it with my own.'

Crispin said, 'Hey, that's the spunky kid I used to know.'

Julia smiled a little shyly, but you could see how much his approval meant to her.

'Remember when you were in ninth grade and you were on the Wendy's float at the state fair?' he recalled.

She groaned. 'That was awful. My mother made me do that.'

'You were supposed to throw candy to the kids, but you were trying to hit them.'

'I was not!'

'Yes, you were.'

'I didn't do that.'

'You told me so yourself. It was completely premeditated. You told me ahead of time you were going to do it. I was walking behind the float watching, laughing my head off. You were a darn good aim.'

'I'd forgotten.'

'You could be so rebellious. I liked that about you.'

She turned to him and an easy smile passed between them, and neither of them wanted to let it go.

'Are you sure you're going to be okay here?'

'I'm going to be fine here. There isn't anywhere else I'd rather be.'

'In the morning I'll do some shopping before we go. You can make me a list. I'll get what you need.'

'No. You let me take care of that. I need to handle this. I need to take my life back.'

She checked her watch and saw it was late, and she rose. She was thinking about giving him a goodnight kiss, but decided against it.

26

A little before eight o'clock in the morning, Crispin was awakened by Julia pounding on his door. He was stumbling blindly into his jeans when the door flew open and Julia barged in. She was wearing the baggy sweater he had lent her the night before over flannel pyjamas, and she didn't seem to mind that he was zipping up his fly. She waved a tabloid newspaper under his nose.

'*Look at this! Look at this! I cannot believe them . . .*'

'Okay, hold on. Just a minute . . .'

Crispin was still muddled of thought and didn't know if he should put on a shirt. He had been sound asleep and dreaming something very pleasant. He sat back down on the edge of the bed and tried to remember what he was looking for.

Then Maddy appeared at the door looking as sleep-rumpled as Crispin and asking what on earth had happened.

'*Look!*' Julia cried, and she spun around and held the tabloid open for Maddy.

Maddy took the newspaper from her and Julia pointed to the headline: 'JULIA KRAMER'S REAL LIFE LOVER-PRIEST'. Below it was a photograph of Crispin herding Julia down Main Street in Haworth with a protective arm around her shoulders – Julia in a hooded cloak, attempting to hide her face from the gawking tourists, Crispin wearing the Victorian overcoat she had loaned him, his white priest's collar starkly visible at his neck. Next to this picture was juxtaposed another photograph revealing Julia in costume embracing a man dressed in the same overcoat. The hood of her cloak had been thrown back and her hair was loose, and you saw on her face a look of absolute abandon, the look of a woman's resolve overthrown by passion. But the man's face was obscured by the brim of his hat. Only his hand cradling her head was visible.

Finally Crispin found his shirt, and he buttoned it up while peering over Julia's shoulder.

'What's this all about?'

But then he saw the photographs, and before Maddy had a chance to read the article, Crispin snatched it out of her hands.

'What on earth is this?!'

'That's not you,' Julia said to him.

'I know it's not'

'That's Heath McEwan.'

'That's the same coat I wore the day we went up to Top Withens,' Crispin recollected.

'Heath left it in my cottage,' Julia explained to Maddy. 'That's where we always rehearsed. I loaned it to Crispin the day we went out for a walk.'

'Where'd you get this?' Crispin asked.

'Heath sent it to me. He called and said he was sending me something very amusing. I didn't bother opening it until this morning.'

Crispin passed the paper back to Maddy, who couldn't help but notice the troubled look on his face. 'At least it wasn't front page,' she interjected.

'No one's going to believe it,' Julia said.

'Let's hope so,' he replied, ignoring the quick look Maddy gave him.

'You should tell Phoebe anyway,' Julia said. 'I learned that with Jona. These tabloids splash around such trash. You need to explain what they did.'

Maddy looked up. 'She's right. You should do that.'

'Nobody's going to believe it,' Julia repeated. 'Phoebe won't believe it. She knows you too well.'

There was such assurance in her voice, and Maddy noticed it. It seemed that Julia believed in his marriage more than Crispin did himself, and Maddy's heart sank at her innocence. There was a beautiful earnestness in Julia's face, a true love and concern for Crispin. No guilt, nothing to conceal. There on her face was the gospel truth.

Julia was looking over Maddy's shoulder at the photograph of herself and Heath McEwan, and she said to Crispin, 'But his hands do look a little like yours.'

He broke away from them and headed downstairs. 'I need some coffee,' he mumbled.

Maddy called to him, 'Make some for me too. I'll be down in a minute.' She passed the newspaper back to Julia and headed to her room but Julia followed her.

'You don't think Phoebe will believe this, do you?'

Maddy stopped at her door and turned, trying to avoid Julia's probing look. 'I don't know. But I do know that a scandal like this could ruin his chances for the deanship.'

'But it's just not true.'

'I know that.'

She saw the devastation on Julia's face and she reached for Julia and gave her a big hug.

Julia seemed to melt, and Maddy thought how lonely and hungry for affection she must be, and she remembered how she had felt after she had lost her own husband. 'I believe you,' she repeated.

'Oh I hope you do,' Julia said with conviction. 'He's such a good man.'

Maddy attempted an encouraging smile. 'Let's just hope the French tabloids don't carry it.'

Julia found Crispin downstairs in the kitchen where he was opening a box of coffee filters. She wanted to talk about it but wasn't sure what to say. She went to the window and opened it, then threw back the shutters. The sky had that scrubbed look, blue and cloudless and clean, and she paused there with her face raised to the morning light. Crispin looked up from measuring coffee and his heart stopped because he was beginning to realise how much she really meant to him. He just watched her and said a short prayer, part plea, part thanks. She was a blessing to him even though she didn't know it, and even though he wasn't sure how he would live without her now.

'What a gorgeous morning,' she said.

'Often is this time of year, but then the clouds come in just before noon.'

She found the coffee cups and set them on the table with spoons.

'Maddy said it could ruin your career.'

'It won't,' he said, dismissing the idea with a shake of his head. 'No one will even see it.'

'Phoebe knows better than to believe that trash, doesn't she?'

'Of course she does.'

'I would hate it if she ever saw me as an adversary. I couldn't live with myself if I thought I'd ever given her any reason to doubt you.'

He glanced up and saw those earnest, limpid eyes boring into him, and he couldn't help but smile at her.

'She doesn't. Don't you worry.'

'That's good.' Her eyes followed his hands as he poured milk into a saucepan. She said, 'Sometimes it sort of gets sticky. Men and women being what we are – which is men and women. But in the end it's what you do with it. It's not what you feel, but how you act on those feelings.' She lifted her gaze and held him in a direct look. 'Don't you think?'

'Took the words right out of my mouth.'

'Good,' she said with finality. 'I'll go get dressed.'

'Don't be long. Breakfast is almost ready.'

What really worried Crispin was the way he had felt when he saw the photograph of Julia and Heath McEwan captured in an intimate moment. He had never seen her look like that before. It was the face of a woman in love, passionate and surrendering. It struck him then what a formidable actress she was. He knew she felt nothing for Heath, had not even par-ticularly liked the man. And yet there was that look, and Crispin was jealous.

Crispin and Maddy drove away just before lunch, leaving Julia waving to them from the courtyard. They were quiet on the way out of Deauville, and then Maddy turned to him and said, 'You really try to protect her, don't you?'

'Yeah.'

'Does she have any idea how volatile this whole situation is?'

'I don't think so. But that's fine with me.'

'Having her living in your home doesn't help things.'

'She doesn't have anywhere else to go.'

'Of course she does. She lived in London for a long time. She must have friends there.'

'Maddy, from what I understand about the film business, the friendships you make there are pretty short-lived. Jona's friends were the only constant in their lives. And she doesn't want to have anything to do with them any more.'

'She's going to get terribly lonely. Especially if she's afraid to get out and do things. I offered to have her come and stay with me.'

'What'd she say?'

'She said she liked your place. She said she felt at home there.'

That she felt this way made him smile inside, but he kept this to himself. He sounded detached when he said, 'You might want to invite yourself up to visit from time to time. She'd like that. I know she would.' Crispin glanced at Piaf. 'I've been thinking about getting her a dog.'

'A dog?'

'She's always wanted one. Be a good companion for her.'

'That they are,' Maddy said, caressing the sleeping terrier.

'I thought it might give her a little practice at taking care of something.'

Maddy asked in an offhand way, 'So she's planning on staying there for a while?'

'We just sort of left it up in the air.'

Maddy went silent, still stroking the dog in her lap. Then she asked, 'And I suppose you're planning on visiting her from time to time?'

'I expect so.'

'You need to realize, even after you're dean, this thing could still be a problem. People just won't understand.'

Crispin was quiet after that. But the silence indicated neither consent nor defeat.

Too many things had piled up over the past few weeks, and when Crispin returned to the cathedral that Monday afternoon, he closed himself in his office and reviewed his agenda. To his horror he had forgotten an appointment with the mission and outreach president that morning, and he had not yet read the book assigned for the monthly book study group he was to lead the following evening. There were messages and mail piled high on his desk that needed his attention, and seeing all of this, he became fully aware of how he had neglected his duties in the past month. It shook him up, to think that things had gotten so far out of control. He wasn't like this. He had always been able to handle everything anyone threw at him.

There were two voicemails and an urgent note that Irène Bourdin, the cathedral's finance director, had left for him. The first message was dated over a week ago, while he had been in Santa Barbara. He called the front desk and found she was in the building, and he thought he'd better find her and apologize for not returning her calls. On the way down the stairs he ran into Edward Ribbey.

'Crispin,' Edward said. 'Just coming up to find you. Tom would like to see you.'

Crispin followed him into Tom's office. Irène was there, perched on the edge of a chair in front of Tom's desk. She was an older woman, very no-nonsense and competent. Crispin had never seen her dressed in anything but Chanel, but it was the same wardrobe she'd been wearing for decades. She was frugal and meticulous, and watched over the cathedral's accounts as if her salvation depended upon it.

Crispin greeted her warmly, and she gave him a fond smile but quickly turned away. Edward closed the door behind them and stationed himself next to Tom like a centurion, his arms crossed over his chest, a solemn scowl on his face.

'How was Deauville?' Tom asked, addressing Crispin over the top of rimless reading glasses.

'Nice. Had some sun this morning.'

'Good.' Tom removed his glasses slowly, carefully folding the arms and laying them on top of a leather blotter. Then he rubbed his eyes. It was the meditative gesture of a man weighing his next words.

'Precisely how much did Julia Kramer donate to the restoration fund?'

The question took Crispin by surprise. He glanced warily towards Irène. 'Twenty-five thousand,' he answered, turning back to Tom. 'Why? What's up?'

Edward spoke up. 'The cheque was made out to you, is that right?'

'Yes,' Crispin answered.

Tom asked, 'Was part of it intended as a personal gift?'

'Absolutely not. It was all for the renovation. Why?'

'Why did she make the cheque out to you?'

Irène interrupted. 'I told you about that.'

But Edward cut her off. 'Irène, we know how it was handled, but we thought it might help if Crispin explained why she made it out to him in the first place.'

The 'we' added a disturbing note to what was already sounding like an inquisition.

Crispin would not give Edward the satisfaction of recognition. He addressed his reply directly to Tom, without so much as a glance at Ribbey.

'Julia wanted to make sure it went to the renovation,' Crispin explained. 'She knew I'd channel the money where she wanted.'

'And can you explain exactly how the money was passed on to the church?' Tom asked.

'Irène and I discussed how to clear the cheque. Instead of my endorsing it over to the cathedral and putting it in the French account, then waiting a month to six weeks for it to clear, I deposited it into my savings account in Chicago and gave instructions to have the money cabled back here as soon as the cheque cleared.'

'And how long did that take?'

'I don't know for sure.' He looked at Irène. 'What did it take? A week? Ten days?'

'About that.'

Edward asked, 'You never asked about the money after that?'

Finally, Crispin turned in his chair to face him. 'No. I had no need to. I never use that account. I leave just enough in it to keep it open.'

'So you didn't verify the transaction?'

'Like I said, I gave very precise instructions to the bank. I faxed them.' He turned to Irène. 'You've got a copy of the fax.'

'Yes,' she confirmed. 'I have it in the file.'

'Irène, what was the exact balance that was transferred back to us?'

Irène slipped on the reading glasses hanging from a chain around her neck. Her hands shook ever so slightly as she opened the file in her lap and read from a bank statement. 'Eighteen thousand, seven hundred and twelve dollars and thirty one cents.'

Crispin looked puzzled. 'What?'

'That's not twenty-five,' Edward piped in.

Crispin reached for the file. 'May I see that?'

She eagerly passed him the statement. Her tone was apologetic. 'That's all we ever got.'

Crispin examined the statement. He looked up at Irène, baffled. 'Why didn't you tell me?'

'It was your money coming from your account, and Ms Kramer was your friend. I just thought . . .'

'That I'd skimmed a little off for myself?'

The look he gave her shamed her into blushing.

'You know me better than that,' he said gently. And then she threw him a furtive, pleading look, and he knew by that look that she was a pawn in their game.

Attempting an avuncular, caring tone which came out strained since it was not at all in line with his character, Tom added, 'Crispin, it's no secret that you've been having financial problems.'

'You're accusing me of embezzlement!' Crispin countered hotly, and Tom leaned forward with his hands folded on his desk.

'No, Crispin, we're not. We just want to know where the rest of the money went.'

And then it occurred to Crispin that Phoebe had access to that account, and he grew bright red at the thought of it.

He asked Irène, 'Did you talk to anyone at the bank about this?'

'I did, but they wouldn't give me any transaction history. They just said they were following your instructions.'

Edward started to speak again, but Tom shot him down with a sharp look, and then he said to Crispin, 'You haven't checked your own account balance?'

'Like I said, I don't use that account. I called to make sure they had received the cheque. The rest I left up to the bank and Irène.'

Crispin thought of the unopened mail piled in the corner of his desk, all the unpleasant business he always shelved until he could stomach dealing with it. Sometimes, when he couldn't sleep for worrying about it, he'd get up in the middle of the night and go downstairs and sit at his desk in his pyjamas ripping open the envelopes and sorting it all, putting enough order into things so that he could return to bed and sleep.

'Let me look into this,' Crispin said, rising from his chair with the file in his hand and marching solemnly from the room.

Irène caught up with him in the cloister as he was returning to the rectory.

'I have been trying to speak to you about this for weeks, Father. I left several messages,' she explained.

'It's okay. It's my fault. I should have gotten back to you.'

'I really didn't think it was urgent, and then Edward, Monsieur Snoopdog, he comes and puts his nose in my books. He says he is doing an internal audit. *Quel farceur celui-là*,' she fumed, her chin lifted in typical Gaulish disdain. 'I knew what he was up to. But I couldn't hide the facts.'

'I didn't expect you to.'

'I'm very sorry.'

'You've done your job well, Irène,' he said, trying to absolve her with a reassuring smile.

He returned to the rectory, and his heart knocked into his

chest like a battering ram as he sat down at his desk and switched on the lamp. The bank statements were buried somewhere among all of his papers. He found the one from the Chicago bank and slit it open. When he unfolded the statement, a wire transfer notice slid out, sending waves of sickness through his stomach. Phoebe had cabled money directly to PADD, the equestrian outfitter where she bought Megan's tack and the expensive riding gear she needed to participate in the horse shows. The cable was dated one day before the remaining balance was transferred out to the cathedral.

It was rush hour and he had an awful time in the traffic, and by the time he got to The Cricketer he was feeling very unpriestly and like he could punch someone. There was a good, healthy crowd at The Cricketer, and the place hummed with pleasant conversation and the smoke wasn't too bad. There was enough laughter and women to make it all a very good place to be. He slung his helmet on the rack and unzipped his leather jacket, and the barman greeted him by name. He ordered a beer, and looked up to see Rhoderic blow in.

'Am I off a day?' Rhoderic quipped as he set his briefcase on the floor and loosened his tie. 'Is this Tuesday?'

'Phoebe's still in California. I'm a free man. Until tomorrow night.'

'You're not wearing your priest's collar,' Rhoderic commented after they had ordered.

'Nope,' Crispin replied, watching the barman pulling their beers. The beer looked good set before him, and he drank into the foam and felt better because there were ordinary men around him, and no one expected anything of him dressed the way he was.

Rhoderic pried a little which was inevitable given the mood Crispin was in, and Crispin told him about the money Phoebe had taken.

'What I can't figure out is how on earth she managed to find out it was there and spend it.' He shook his head in utter disbelief and took another deep drink.

'Radar,' Rhoderic pronounced.

Crispin wiped his mouth. 'She knew about Julia donating that money, but she didn't know where I was depositing it.'

'My wife's right over my shoulder every time some money comes in.'

'But your wife has the common sense to pay your phone bill with it, not go out and buy extravagant things for stupid horses.'

Rhoderic gave a sympathetic grunt.

Crispin looked up and caught a glimpse of himself in the mirror behind the bar. His unruly hair was looking distinctly shaggy, and he hadn't shaved this morning. He looked like someone he would minister to on the streets.

'I'm in deep trouble,' Crispin said wearily.

'You'll pay it back,' Rhoderic said.

'I can't. I don't have it. It's embezzlement.'

'A judge wouldn't think so. It wasn't intentional.'

'I can't be sure of that.'

'You don't think Phoebe knew it was the cathedral's money, do you?'

'I don't know. Maybe she did.'

'Well, ask her.'

'Ask Phoebe?'

'Absolutely.'

'I can't do that.'

'Why not?'

It was painful for him, but finally he confessed. He told Rhoderic everything, about Phoebe's desertion and her accusations, and the rumours about Julia. It was going to be a week from hell, he said. Phoebe was due back the next morning and the vestry would be meeting the following Sunday to vote for the next dean, and he was just trying to keep a lid on the thing until after the vote.

Rhoderic listened, and grimaced and groaned in all the right places, and Crispin felt a lot better when he'd finished. That's why Crispin went to The Cricketer, to lay his troubles at the feet of ordinary men and feel himself relieved of the paralyzing burden of priestliness, of holy actions and holy thoughts.

Rhoderic drained his glass and said, 'That's bloody awful. Being innocent of something most men out there would love to be guilty of.'

Crispin had not thought of it in quite that light, and he concurred that the dilemma was not without humour. He smiled for the first time since he had waved goodbye to Julia.

27

Julia was the one person who would have offered Crispin the support he desperately needed that week, but he didn't dare call her. Nor did she think it wise to call him. She sensed that Crispin was more concerned about the tabloid photos than he had let on, and – contrary to what he thought – she suspected all was not well with his marriage. It was hard not to think of him as she shuffled around the cold stone floor dressed in one of his old sweaters, reading her scripts and chasing away the ghosts. At night everything got thrown together in the great cauldron of her subconscious, where Jona looked like Crispin and Crispin was dead and Jona was standing at an altar blessing her in Russian.

Crispin had tried so hard to save her from despair, and to succumb would be every bit as much his failure as hers. For his sake as much as her own, she used every available means to connect herself to the outside world. She made calls to her agent and producers, and spoke daily to her publicist in New York. Even the Fedex man was a welcome sight. On her second day there she made a *fondant chocolat* from scratch and took it across the street to Madame Cristophani. For twenty minutes she listened while the old woman proudly recounted how her husband had fought alongside the Americans in North Africa in World War II, and how they used to visit the American cemetery every year but they didn't any more because he could no longer remember the war.

She rode her bike around the village where wisteria cascaded over stone walls and yellow tulips sprang up bright and gay, and lilac trees sweetened the air. Each day, sun or rain, she forced herself further down the hillside towards Deauville, and the sheer beauty of the Normandy spring reduced her anxieties to mere twitches of discomfort.

Julia wanted more than to just survive Jona's death and despicable betrayal; she wanted to claw her way back into the world of normality, to take joy in places and people, to experience the unknown without fear. There were moments in the evening when she cried and sometimes at night she would awake with tears in her eyes, and she was sometimes lonely, but there was no other place where she would feel as safe as she did in Crispin's home. Often in the evening when she grew tired of French television, she would go through the bookshelves. She discovered some Steinbeck he had held on to from his high school days (his name was scrawled inside), and she laughed out loud thinking what a hoarder he was. But then she would go and do something insanely sentimental and equally laughable, like taking one of those old books to bed with her and clutching it to her breast so she would fall asleep with him close to her heart.

Crispin didn't know what to expect when Phoebe and the girls returned. He did expect awkwardness and there was plenty of that on the drive from the airport back to Paris, but then they all went to bed and slept through the day. He cooked dinner himself that night, made the girls' favourite tuna casserole from his mother's recipe; it was the only thing he could make that tasted as good as when Phoebe made it. He woke the girls so that they could eat, but he let Phoebe sleep on. He was glad to have them to himself for a change.

At the beginning of the meal Cat was sullen, but the tuna casserole softened her up and by the second helping she was talking about her classes and looking forward to going back to their school. The idea of returning to the French *lycée* had Megan totally depressed, and she sat at the table with the calendar counting the number of days until they would return to Santa Barbara.

'Is it true we might move back to California?' she asked her father, forking aside a chunk of celery that was thicker than the accepted norm.

Crispin was cutting Lola's noodles. He handed the fork over to the child and sat back. Cat was watching him with troubled eyes.

'I'll tell you something. You all know I'm hoping to be elected Dean of St John's. That's a position I'd really like.'

Lola had stopped chewing, but her mouth was full like her eyes, and Crispin smiled at her and said, 'Lola, honey, swallow your food before you choke.' Then he went on. 'But if that doesn't happen, then who knows? Maybe I'll stay on here, maybe not. But one thing's certain, wherever we go, we go together. As a family. And whatever decision we make, we make it for the family. Just like we did when we came here.'

'Well, what about Santa Barbara?' Megan pressed.

'I don't have a job there, Megan. I have to go where the job is.'

Twirling her noodles around her fork, Cat said softly, 'I think it'd be cool.'

'Moving back to Santa Barbara?' he asked.

'No. I mean you being dean. I think that'd be cool.' She didn't look him in the eye, and you knew she was still hurting and feeling betrayed, but there was forgiveness there too.

'Thanks, honey,' Crispin said.

Phoebe used jet lag as a way of avoiding a confrontation with Crispin, sleeping until noon and coming to bed late when he was sound asleep. As for Crispin, his pastoral duties that week kept him away most evenings, and when he was at home he kept to his study. He had decided not to confront Phoebe about the money she had misappropriated from their Chicago account, but he gave a full account of the situation, in writing, to Tom Noonan, with a copy to Irène and Maddy, along with a proposal to repay the money according to a detailed schedule of payments over the next six months. That was the best he could do. His proposal drew no comment from Tom, but Maddy found it perfectly workable and honourable. She said the fact that Noonan had not responded to it meant that there was nothing more to say. She felt confident the situation had been defused.

But at home, the silences between husband and wife were indicative of strain and confusion. There were times when Phoebe warmed to Crispin, and he sensed that she regretted the Santa Barbara fiasco. But the marriage seemed to have undergone a subtle shift in power. Throughout all their years together, even after joining the priesthood, Crispin had always done whatever had to be done to give Phoebe what she wanted. But that wasn't the case any more. Crispin was emerging from the crisis toughened rather than weakened, and Phoebe found this unsettling.

On Thursday, Phoebe lunched with Gerry Noonan and their circle of friends, and she got back late in the afternoon when Crispin was already home. She opened the door of his study and stood quietly waiting for him to look up, and Crispin was thinking, 'This is it. She's seen that miserable photo.' But then he looked up and she smiled, and astonished him by telling him how she had come to his defence that afternoon when all her friends were urging her to play the role of the innocent wife wronged by her cheating husband.

'I told them there was absolutely nothing going on between you and Julia,' she said.

'Good.'

'I could tell Gerry didn't believe me, though,' she said, reaching down to take off her shoes.

'It's a political thing. You know that.'

'I think they want to see you fail.'

'Of course they do.'

She stared at the floor for a moment, and then asked, 'Are you sure you really want this?'

'You mean the deanship?'

She nodded.

He gave her a long hard look of utter disbelief. 'You mean you don't know?'

'I just thought . . .' But she didn't finish her sentence. She walked out with her shoes in her hand, closing the door behind her.

Phoebe's support, wavering though it might be, had sufficient impact to silence the rumours of infidelity, thus avoiding a full-blown scandal. On Sunday after the Eucharist service, the names of the final candidates evaluated and interviewed by the search committee would be set before the cathedral vestry for a vote. Crispin was utterly adamant that the entire family attend the ten-thirty service that day. This meant Megan was forced to drop out of a regional dressage event, and for once Phoebe sided with her husband. Throughout the coffee hour after the service, Phoebe stood resolutely by her husband's side; it was awkward between them, but no one noticed except Crispin. After coffee, they went to the Chinese buffet across the street to wait for the election results. They hadn't made reservations so they ate up in the lounge and watched Fashion TV on the overhead monitor. Crispin drank Chinese beer and was glad for Fashion TV because they were all absorbed by it and he didn't have to talk. Around one-thirty, Maddy came to report the results. Crispin saw her coming through the door but she was backlit and the lounge was dark, so he couldn't read her face until she got closer, and then he saw it was a smile.

'Congratulations, Dean Wakefield,' she said. The girls

squealed and Phoebe reached for his hand, looking honestly moved and very proud. Cat jumped to her feet and hugged her father so hard she knocked him back into the lounge chair, and Lola crawled up on top of him and hung around his neck. Megan's pout was eclipsed by that stunning smile of hers. Crispin was glad for all the enthusiasm because he really wanted to cry.

Afterwards they went back home and everyone had something to do, and for the first time in months it seemed like an ordinary Sunday afternoon. He made a few calls to spread the good news – first to Rhoderic, and then to Julia. Julia was ecstatic and very relieved. After that, Crispin just went to bed.

He was exhausted, but it took him a while to get to sleep. The phone was ringing and there was music from the girls' rooms, and the sound of feet tramping up and down the stairs.

Finally, the house grew quiet. Phoebe had taken Cat and Lola to the cinema, and Megan was in her room. Eventually, Crispin fell asleep.

When he awoke, it was slowly, and he had the feeling that there was someone in the room with him. As he rolled over, he felt a sheet of paper crackle underneath his shoulder. He brushed it onto the floor without opening his eyes.

'Look at it,' Phoebe said.

He knew by her voice, in that one split second, what it was about.

He sat up and swung his legs over the side of the bed and yawned.

'Hold on,' he said, shaking his head. 'Let me wake up here.'

She jumped up from the armchair, picked up the paper and flung it at him. 'Look at this!' she cried.

The paper floated to the floor.

'I've seen it,' he said calmly.

'You've seen it?'

'It's faked.'

'You lying bastard.'

'Call the tabloid and ask them. That's not me.'

Phoebe was stung. It was hitting her a lot harder this time than it did before, because now she was believing it.

Crispin retrieved the sheet of printer paper; it had been printed from the tabloid's website.

'How'd you get this?'

'Megan pulled it up. Florence Ribbey saw it on the Internet and emailed it to her.'

That's what had worried him more than anything else, that one of the girls would hear about it.

'Have Megan come in here,' he said firmly.

'I will not!'

'She needs to hear the truth. That's the actor who plays opposite Julia in the Brontë film.' He held it out for her to examine. 'Come on, Phoebe, look at it closely. You can't see his face.'

'That's your hand. I'd recognize your hands anywhere.'

'That's not my hand. That hand belongs to Heath McEwan.'

'How do you know about it?'

'Julia showed it to us when Maddy and I were up in Normandy.'

'Julia's seen this?'

'I told you. She brought it in and showed it to Maddy and me. She was worried. She even encouraged me to tell you about it. But I didn't. Because I was afraid you wouldn't believe me.'

'You're a liar.'

'I'm not a liar,' he said. All this defending himself was making him tired.

'And she's a husband-stealing bitch!'

He sat there on the edge of the bed in his T-shirt and trousers, staring down at his socks and weighing up his next words. There was so much he could say, and it all depended on what he wanted in the end.

'Don't say anything else like that, Phoebe. It's not right.'

She had started to cry. '*Right?*' she screamed.

Crispin rose from the bed. She was doubled over in the chair with her head in her hands, and he kneeled in front of her and tried to pry her hands away from her face but she shook him off.

'Don't touch me, you bastard!'

'That's not me in that photograph, and if I have to, I'll get Julia to get Heath McEwan on the phone and he'll tell you it's him.'

'Of course he'll say it, because Julia will tell him to, and she'll do anything to get you away from me!'

'Phoebe, Julia doesn't want me,' he said gently. 'She wants a man who's dead and who's never going to come back.'

Phoebe grew very still, and the hot tears cooled to a look that was more menacing than threats and screams.

'You're going to lose everything, Crispin. You just wait. You'll lose me, and the girls, and your job, and I won't be sorry one damn bit!'

She gave him a shove and bolted to the armoire, where she began ripping his clothes off the hangers and flinging them onto the floor.

'Stop it, Phoebe.'

'I want you out of here tonight. I don't give a damn where you go. You can go up to Normandy, live with your little actress whore.'

'Don't talk like that.'

'I'm taking the girls back to Santa Barbara.'

Then he stopped her. He took her by the arm and stopped her in mid-stride and she squirmed to get out of his grasp.

'Don't you dare take my daughters away from me. I told you that in Santa Barbara.'

253

'I'm getting out of here. I'm not staying here one day longer than I have to.' She pointed to the crumpled paper on the floor. 'That'll be all over the cathedral tomorrow. You think I can bear to show my face around here after what I've been through these past few weeks?'

'We've all been through it. Not just you.'

'Yeah. And you've made me out to look like a stupid fool!'

'Not if you stand by me like you did this week.'

'The next time I stand by you, it'll be in a court of law!'

She was pulling down suitcases now. 'I'm leaving. I'll take the girls and we'll move into a hotel.'

'I can't afford to pay for a hotel.'

'*Screw you!*'

'Phoebe . . .'

She was so rattled, tearing around the bedroom from drawer to armoire, that Crispin felt a wave of honest pity for her.

'Phoebe, take it easy. Just calm down.'

'I just have to get away from you.'

'At least let the girls finish their school year here. You can't move them again.'

'I hate it here! I hate this place! This damn cathedral! Everything around here reminds me of you and your tightwad . . .' She knew she had already said too much, said things she could never take back, but she couldn't control herself anymore. 'You don't deserve me, Crispin! You never did! I deserve somebody who can give me what I need. I'm still young and beautiful and I'm not about to waste my last good years counting every penny and not being able to pay for pretty things and living in homes that'll never be mine, with this God-awful furniture . . .'

Sobbing, she collapsed to her knees in the middle of the mess of clothes strewn on the floor. Crispin stepped over a wool jacket and stooped down and pulled her to her feet. As awful as it had been, all he could feel was pity. She looked pathetic and hopelessly miserable, so he took her in his arms and held her while she cried. She lifted her tear-streaked face to him and whispered, 'Don't think I never loved you. I did. But I can't be your wife any more.'

28

Even as he comforted her, he knew it was the end. Phoebe didn't know it herself until those words spilled out, bringing the truth along with them. Even up until their final moments together, Crispin was remarkably decent towards Phoebe. Some people read it as remorse and proof of his guilt, but it wasn't that at all. It was simply the way he dealt with the brutal gods that sought to destroy his belief in goodness.

The saddest thing was that there was no one there for him, not really. Not the way Julia would have been, if he could have turned to her. He had stalwart friends at the cathedral who believed in his innocence, but even those who were very fond of him had heard too much for their liking. In the end, Tom Noonan's subtle campaign succeeded in undermining Crispin's bedrock popularity; one final rumble and a crater remained where there had once been a mountain.

Although the vestry had voted, there still remained the Bishop's final approval of their recommendation before Crispin could be confirmed as Dean of St John's. In a telephone call early on Monday, Crispin requested an urgent meeting with him, and by the time they met that afternoon in the Bishop's home on the Avenue Maréchal Lyautey, the Bishop had already seen the damning evidence on the Internet.

It was one of those sweet spring days that makes you forgive Paris all its transgressions of the winter, and Crispin found Bishop Stroup out on his balcony elbow-deep in potting soil.

'Hope you don't mind if I continue with this while we talk,' the Bishop said.

'Not at all.'

'Should have finished it yesterday.' The Bishop poked a red geranium down into the window box and patted dirt around it. He looked up at Crispin. 'I suppose you've come here to offer me your resignation.'

'Yes.'

'I've spent a lot of time in thought and prayer about all that's gone on.'

'None of it's true.'

'I know that.'

'I suppose I contributed to the rumours myself. I didn't think people would see my friendship with her in that light.'

'A lot of people love dirt, Father,' the Bishop said, removing his gardening gloves. 'In one form or another.'

'This is breaking my heart, you know.'

It was such a disarmingly honest thing to say for a man who appeared so reserved and collected, standing there with his hands thrust deep in his pockets, admiring the green meadows of Auteuil and the woods behind.

'It's a grave injustice they're doing you. You have a right to be angry.'

'Even if you went ahead and confirmed me, I couldn't stay. I couldn't put an ocean between me and my children.'

'What do you plan on doing?'

'I'll look for a parish in California, not too far from Santa Barbara. That's where the girls will be living.'

'So you're divorcing.'

'I'm afraid so. Phoebe's agreed to do it amicably.'

'Let's hope it continues like that.'

He said it as if he knew Phoebe well, and Crispin couldn't refrain from smiling. 'I could use your prayers on that one.'

'You'll have them. Every day. Even when you're far away

in some thriving California parish and have forgotten all about us.'

'I could never forget this place.'

Crispin insisted that he and Phoebe confront the girls together, and on Monday evening, after Crispin had formally withdrawn his candidacy for the deanship, he and Phoebe sat the girls down in the living room and told them they had decided to separate. From the very beginning, Crispin set the tone, and it was gentle and non-confrontational. He took Lola on to his lap and talked about mothers and fathers and husbands and wives in a language he hoped she could understand, and Cat and Megan listened to their father with raw, red-rimmed eyes full of disbelief. He explained that this had nothing to do with Julia, and once again affirmed Julia's and his own innocence. He talked to them about tabloids and the things they did to sell their papers, and how the stories implied falsehoods through trickery and deceit. Then he gave them the choice – to finish the school year in Paris or to return immediately to Santa Barbara. But at that point the whole thing broke down because Cat jumped up and ran sobbing to her room and slammed the door, and Lola buried her face in her father's chest and covered her ears with both hands. Megan sat on the edge of the sofa with her hands wedged between her knees, tears flowing from her cheeks. Phoebe moved over and sat down next to her and tried to take her in her arms, but to Crispin's astonishment she wrenched free of her mother's embrace.

'I'd rather just go back to Santa Barbara. I don't want to face anybody here. They're already making fun of us. Florence told me this evening that they were firing you.'

'I've given my resignation. I'm resigning so that I can go back to California to be near all of you.'

This took her by surprise, and she met his gaze with a curious look.

'You'd do that?'

'Of course I would.'

'But you love it here.'

'I love you more.'

She grew a little calmer then, and asked, 'So you'll be in Santa Barbara too?'

'As close as I can.'

So it was agreed that the girls would return immediately to Santa Barbara to Phoebe's parents' home to finish out the school year in California, and Phoebe would join them as soon as she had packed up their things for the movers.

It was distressing for them all, particularly for Lola who cried so pitifully at the airport that Crispin had to board the aeroplane with her; even the pilot came out from the cockpit and tried to reassure her. Megan and Cat were so moved by her distress that they forgot their own embarrassment and did their best to distract her until the plane took off.

Phoebe's last week was spent sorting through their furnishings and their clothing for the movers, and she slipped in quite a few lunches with her friends, but she was generally subdued and made no demands on Crispin. Crispin slept downstairs in Megan's room which was a good thing. He didn't want to go soft on her at the last minute, and it was just the kind of thing he would do.

The night before her departure, Crispin went up to their bedroom. She was packing her suitcase, and she looked up at him in sweet bewilderment, thinking perhaps he had come to offer some gesture of affection.

'We need to get a few things clear before you leave,' he said, noticing the bareness of the room without her things.

She put down the cosmetic bag and sat on the bed to listen.

'I know how lawyers can be,' he said. 'They feel like they've got to get the best possible deal for their client, and the only thing I have left to lose are my kids.'

'I'm not going to take the girls away from you.'

'You did it once. I don't trust you.'

'This is different.'

'I suggest you come to full disclosure with your lawyer before you put him up to anything.'

'What do you mean?'

'I'm talking about Lola.'

It was like he had slapped her. For a few seconds she even stopped breathing.

'If you make it hard for me, I swear, I'll ask for a paternity test.'

Her jaw went slack with astonishment. 'You what?'

'Just remember that.'

'You wouldn't . . .'

'Lola's my child because I've raised her. And I'd cut off both hands before I'd tell her any different. But your lawyer might be a little more flexible if he knew the truth.'

They didn't talk much after that. He took her to the airport and helped with all the luggage. He even waited until she had checked in, and then he walked her to the concourse. But he resented the way she turned to him with watering eyes, as if there was still some lingering regret, and it sickened him so much that he couldn't even kiss her goodbye. He set down her bag and wished her a good flight, and then strode away without looking back.

Even after Phoebe left and the movers took away most of their belongings, and he was alone, he still would not call Julia. It became a kind of grim mental exercise in will. He'd be queuing in the supermarket, reluctant to go home, and he'd have this sudden urge to pull out his mobile phone and give her a call, but then he'd restrain himself. If he had made errors in judgement before, he would not make them now. His silence was a way of defending her honour and his, and his honour as a priest and husband and father had become his standard. The silence was a wall he erected around his heart; it was punishment, self-inflicted. He was in love with her and he knew it but he would not allow himself to take one moment's pleasure in it.

There was the same sense of guilt towards his parishioners, and in order to avoid offending those who were sensitive to his alleged transgression, Crispin thought it best that he no longer officiate at *matins* or Sunday Eucharist, nor did he perform weddings during his final weeks as canon. There was much wailing and wringing of hands as they rushed around to find a respected member of the Episcopal clergy to whom they could entrust their spiritual leadership during this period of upheaval. The cathedral was losing both its canon and its dean, and there was much name-calling, and accusations were tossed about, but most of all there was a sense of great loss.

Now that Crispin was going, there were many who began to see him in the light of a martyr. He cleared out his office and performed his functions from his study in the rectory, and if anyone went to him for spiritual guidance he was there for them, but now there was no one to shoulder his many responsibilities, no one to provide clarity of vision and purpose, no inspiration. Many people felt his absence deeply, and believed, as did their bishop, that a great injustice had been done to a remarkable man.

He'd been terribly busy and exhausted by all that had to be done on such short notice – not the least of which was finding a new parish – and there were many goodbyes to be said. Maddy hosted a party at her home one evening, and Crispin left that night fighting back tears, overwhelmed by the generosity and warm wishes of those who had seen him through to the end.

Then there was the tedious job of packing up all of his personal belongings. What disturbed him most was not the things

Phoebe had taken, but what she had chosen to leave behind. Small things he thought might hold some sentimental value had been passed over, so Crispin wrapped them up in packing paper and stuffed them into boxes. Stacks of boxes grew up around the house like cubicles of his past to be stored away and forgotten. He had nowhere to take them, except to Normandy. He had decided to keep the house in Normandy. No matter how tough things got for him.

On the morning of his departure, he made one last visit to the cathedral. Here was a vivid testimony of man's search for eternal things in the order of numbers, in vaults and domes and frescoes, and sacred enclosures. But most importantly, it was an orderly and peaceful island within a deeply confused society. Here was where he had rested the taut fibres of his existence, where he was put back in tune. Here he had taken refuge from the man society doggedly insisted he be, a man he believed to be misshapen.

As he walked through the aisles he felt himself already detached from it. He had loved it with all his heart, but it was already slipping into the past. He closed the door, strode through the cloister and outside to his car, and drove quietly away.

29

He always loved the stretch of road north-west to the sea; it passed through countryside where the remains of once great forests rose on distant hills, and in the spring the orchards burst forth pink with apple blossom. He loved the drive even in the rain when the green windbreaks of beech trees and high hedges, and pretty brown-and-white patch-eyed cows muzzle-deep in fat grass were all softened by a pale grey drizzle. But this morning, after weeks of waiting, Crispin drove with reckless speed, ignoring the beauty. His mind was already there. He even timed himself, and arrived at the village one hour and fifty-three minutes from the time he sped away from the cathedral.

When he pulled into the courtyard it was early and the shutters were all closed. He noticed that Julia had set terracotta pots of pink geraniums around the perimeter of the courtyard and the debris beside the shed had been cleared away. He thought she would still be sleeping, and he imagined what it would be like to see her come down the stairs in the morning. He shut off the engine and sat for a moment, bowed over the steering wheel. He had not called to tell her that he was coming. He hadn't even made up his mind until last night. He had a few days before his plane left, and he had wanted to take a little time to himself, to visit a few places he had never seen. But he wasn't sure how to handle saying goodbye to Julia.

The day after his visit with Bishop Stroup, he had sent her an email to say that he was turning down the deanship and returning to the States. He had been deliberately vague, saying only that it was the best solution for the family, and he hadn't mentioned a word about his separation from Phoebe. He thanked Julia for her support and encouragement. He knew she would be stunned, and disappointed, he said, but he felt that he was doing the right thing, painful as it was for him and so many others. He explained he was keeping the house in Normandy, and assured her she would be welcome to stay as long as she wished.

Now, sitting in the car in the early morning while the mist still hung over the village, looking up at the window of the room where she slept, he wondered if it wouldn't be better if he just drove away without ever seeing her again.

There was no longer any doubt in his mind that he was in love with her, but he had buried it deep in a solid and well fortified heart. He would never know for sure if Julia shared the same feelings; if she had responded to him so tenderly in Haworth, it was because he had been acting in the rôle of friend and priest. If it was something more, he didn't want to know. He had sworn their innocence to his wife and his daughters as well as his many friends and supporters at the cathedral. It was their innocence that had helped him bear the unjust accusations. To give in to his feelings for Julia would make a mockery out of his denial.

Crispin had never ceased examining his conscience throughout this entire ordeal. And even though he had lost the things he had prized so greatly, his integrity remained whole and intact. His stubborn loyalty to Julia was inextricably linked to who he was, to how he saw himself in relationship to man and God. He believed in the necessity, if not the triumph, of goodness. He believed that somewhere on the cusp of the universe there existed a well of love, and he hoped that some small part of his life was a reflection of this.

* * *

It was quiet in the house, and he started coffee brewing while he stored his boxes in the basement, and when he went back up to the kitchen, he startled a big, scruffy-looking man in a woollen bathrobe pouring himself a cup.

'I heard someone drive up. I assume you're Crispin,' he said as he extended his hand. 'Michael Langham. Julia's director.'

'Yes. Sorry about the intrusion,' Crispin replied, trying his best to conceal his astonishment at having a strange man in his house. He had to remind himself that it was Julia's home now.

'You're the bloke who bloody well saved my film,' Michael said.

'I'm glad I could help.'

Crispin poured himself some of the coffee and eyed Michael warily over the rim of his mug, while Michael rambled on about his film and how Julia had given such an astonishing performance. Crispin wasn't paying much attention. He was too busy wondering if Michael Langham had just crawled out of Julia's bed.

'Are you two talking about me?'

Julia stood in the doorway in white socks, tying a rumpled floral-print robe around her waist. Her eyes were puffy, and she was smiling at Crispin.

'You sneaky thing,' she said, coming up to him and bending over to hug him. He could feel the curves of her warm breasts through the light robe.

'Sorry,' he said in a low voice. 'I should have called first.'

'I was so afraid you'd leave without coming to see me,' she whispered, lingering over him.

'I wouldn't do that,' he smiled back.

Just then a stunning Medusa-like creature with black hair snaking down her shoulders in crisp tight curls bounced into the kitchen in black jogging pants and running shoes.

'Is this the morning-after party?' she asked.

'Susannah, this is Crispin,' Julia announced proudly with her hand on his shoulder, as if he were some myth.

'Oh, my goodness,' Susannah exclaimed. 'So you're Crispin!' She leaned down and gave him a hug, burying him in a cascade of curls.

'This is my publicist, Susannah Rich,' Julia said. 'From New York. You spoke to her on the phone.'

'Of course,' Crispin said. 'I remember.'

'I'm so pleased to meet you. That was so marvellous, what you did for Julia. Actually, for all of us.'

Crispin mumbled an acknowledgement, but he was more interested in the way Susannah had slipped her arm over Michael's shoulder, and the way he slid his hand along her hip. She bent down and they kissed briefly, and it was sexual.

Relief flooded through Crispin.

It seemed they had already made plans to go into Deauville that morning to the open-air market and shop for dinner, but now Julia insisted the dinner be in honour of Crispin, something very special, a thank-you and going-away celebration all in one.

After breakfast Crispin drove them into Deauville, and while Susannah and Michael worked their way along the chain of stalls, Crispin and Julia finally had a moment to themselves.

'Are you okay with this?' he asked, gesturing to the crowd.

'I'm always more courageous with you around.' She said it lightly, like a child brandishing a toy sword, and she laughed and linked her arm through his. 'I know you don't like me to say it. You don't want to be a crutch . . .'

'It's not that.'

'But you're right. I've been using you like that.' Then she caught herself and said, 'That didn't come out quite right. That wasn't what I meant.'

'I know,' Crispin assured her, but he wondered if maybe

there was truth in it, that this was the extent of her affection. There was no way of knowing. And there was no point in it anyway.

They came upon Michael at the fish stall where he was stumbling through a conversation with the fishmonger about recipes for monkfish, and Susannah was over in the cheeses, and so Julia stopped Crispin in front of a vegetable vendor and said, 'So, you're moving back to California.'

He nodded.

'You gave it up?'

'It's best. For all of us.'

He stuffed his hands into his pockets, and there between the cucumbers and the Boston lettuces he felt the impact of it all. It was because he had let it go, and because Julia was there and he could admit to himself how much it had meant.

Julia could read the look on his face. 'Oh Crispin,' she whispered, and she reached out for his hand and squeezed it.

'It just wasn't going to work out. I was getting carried away with my ambitions, and ignoring everyone else.'

'Don't you think it's okay to do that sometimes?' She said it gently, and it was truly a question, not just a point of view.

'You have to make decisions for the family. Sometimes it means no one really gets what they want, but the family as a whole is better off for it.'

'I know,' she said, a shade apologetically, and she gave his hand another tender squeeze, 'I've always lived such a self-absorbed life. I don't have any experience with making those kinds of decisions. But it must be the right thing, if that's what you've decided to do.'

'I think it is.'

'Oh, goodness,' she said, 'that means there will be a whole ocean and a continent between us.' She tried to make it sound carefree and teasing, but she couldn't hide the sadness in her voice.

'The house is your home as long as you want it. And I'm hoping that maybe at some point the girls will want to come back for a holiday.'

She smiled, trying to sound happy. 'Then we won't be completely out of touch.'

He wanted to say something then, say something that would let her know how he felt, but there was no point in it.

'You're scowling,' she said.

'I am?'

'Crispin,' she whispered, and amid the blur of vendors and shoppers with their bags and wicker baskets, amid the crates of fat creamy cauliflowers and beds of spinach, she locked her eyes on his and said, 'You're hiding something, and I don't know what.'

'I'm not . . .' he started to deny, but then he stopped, and looked down into her sweet eyes. 'I'm worried about you. I truly am. I don't want anything to happen to you. I feel like I've let you down.'

'You haven't let me down,' she assured him. 'You've helped me through the most difficult time of my life.' She caught herself and said, with a quick grin, 'Actually, you've done it twice. You've taught me so much, just being here in my life and being a part of my tiny little circumscribed world. You've reminded me of all the things that are important.'

'Oh, Julia,' he smiled, full of gratitude.

'I'll get along fine, I promise. I won't let you down. I won't fail you.'

'Fail me?'

She nodded emphatically, and said, 'I don't know what brought us together again. It was so incredible, the way our lives intersected again, and I don't know if there is some great cosmic reason for it, but I do know that after all that's happened, a lot of good has come out of it. At least for me. And I hope it's been the same for you.'

He hadn't been able to tear himself away from her eyes, and when she said that, he took her face between his hands. The gesture was almost ferocious, and so full of passion it took her by surprise. She gasped, and then he closed her mouth with a kiss.

It was a full kiss, not some light, timorous thing. Crispin meant that kiss with all his heart, and he gave it to her the way a drowning man succumbs after a long exhausting struggle. Her lips were soft and heavenly but that kiss scorched his soul.

She kept her eyes open. His were closed. When their lips parted, it seemed a violent thing, separating one breath into two. She let out a soft exclamation.

In the stunned silence that followed, the world pounded its way back into their consciousness, and they heard the clamour of vendors and the sounds of the market. There were tears in Julia's eyes, and he saw them before he looked away.

It was reassuring that he took her hand and held it as they searched the crowd for Susannah and Michael, but not long after that Julia began feeling lightheaded and anxious, so they completed their shopping and drove home.

Julia stayed in her room most of the afternoon while Crispin took care of things around the house, and even when Michael and Susannah went for a walk, Crispin would not go to her room, and she did not come down. He kept thinking about what she had said to him. 'A lot of good has come out of this,' she had said, and her innocence had left him burning with shame. If anyone had been deceived, it was Julia. He had led her to believe his marriage was strong and healthy. That he was returning to California, the Sunshine State, with his wife and children, where they would all be quite the happy family. It made him sick to think how monstrous had been his deception. He had told himself all along that he was misleading her in order to protect her, that he was putting on a front of family unity for the sake of Julia's mental stability. But it wasn't Julia who was the weak one; it was him. When he was away from her, he could somehow manage to keep their friendship locked into its narrow little chamber; but in her presence, he felt his will unravel. If Julia's feelings for him were anywhere as deep as his own, and as sexual, he would not be able to resist her. He would become a caricature of himself.

The kiss had been so unexpected, and it had confused Julia. For a long time she had been reluctant to try to sort out her feelings for Crispin for fear of what she might discover. Jona's murder and the revelations that had followed had left her dealing with a maelstrom of powerful emotions, and Crispin had always been there to settle her and keep her anchored to life. But ever since their days together in Haworth, there was never a doubt in her mind that he was much more to her than friend and priest. She lived in his home and every day she went into his room and sat on the bed; sometimes she napped there in the afternoon, although she would never sleep in his bed at night. She searched the house for things that bore his mark, wore his old sweaters and coats, and read his books. She became intimate with him in this way, furtively, because there was no danger in it.

His kiss had changed all that.

Julia didn't consider herself a strong woman. She thought herself easily deluded and unsure of her own judgement. She had no way of knowing what was good for her, but she knew what was best for Crispin. Regardless of his motives or intentions, any real involvement would destroy him. And if he should ever guess how she felt, it would make the burden all that more difficult for him to bear.

She stayed up in her room that afternoon, at times gazing out the window onto the courtyard and the lilac trees across the lane, at times curled on her bed with her face buried in her pillow to muffle her tears. She let her imagination wrap around thoughts of him. She recalled the way he had looked when he had kissed her, the warmth of his mouth, the touch of his hands on her neck. He excited her and she knew how easily it would be to respond to him, and she re-lived that kiss a hundred times.

When she came down and went into the kitchen to help Susannah with dinner, she appeared serene and untroubled. She had changed into more sophisticated clothes, and styled her hair and wore a little make-up. Julia knew her craft well. She knew it so well that Crispin didn't recognize it as craft at all. He mistook it for something real. She was light-hearted but distant, and when he tried to connect with a look, she returned a sweet, almost apologetic and purely dispassionate smile. She was at ease with him. She put on music and hummed a little to herself in the kitchen while they prepared dinner, and when Michael came down they opened the champagne. Susannah commented how much better she seemed and Julia answered that it was that old anxiety thing, and apologized for spoiling the morning for them.

They had dinner, and Julia was utterly charming, the way Crispin had often seen her, so natural and amusing and radiant. But there was not one indication of a desire for intimacy with him. He was beginning to think the kiss had been a foolish and very humbling mistake. She was the kind of woman any man would desire, and when you wanted a woman as badly as he wanted her, inevitably you would read things into her looks and her words and see things that weren't really there.

During dinner they talked about Crispin's decision to move to southern California, and Julia teased him about it. She warned him about the land of temptation, and predicted that he would leave the clergy and return to a secular vocation, make tons of money and live happily ever after. Her pre-science unsettled Crispin, and he felt dull and tongue-tied throughout the dinner.

'But, honestly, if that's what makes Phoebe and the girls

happy, then you should do it,' she urged, with a sincerely candid smile. 'Your family should come first. Always. You're so lucky to have them. But then you know that. I don't have to tell you that.' She went on, addressing Susannah and Michael. 'Crispin has the most incredible family,' she said. 'Phoebe is gorgeous and fun, and a very good mother to the three most entertaining girls I've ever met.'

She looked to Crispin for confirmation. Fortunately his mouth was full of monkfish and he got away with a tight smile and a nod. He didn't have her acting skills, and he covered his discomfort by reaching for the bottle of wine. He emptied the last of it into Susannah's glass, then went into the kitchen for another bottle. When he returned, the conversation had changed; it seemed Michael was urging Julia to move to Los Angeles for the sake of her film career.

'Crispin,' Michael said, 'what do you think?'

'I don't think I should try to influence her,' he answered, as he refilled Julia's glass.

Julia said, 'But I'd like to know what you think. Truly, I would.'

'I don't think you'd be happy there.'

For just a moment, her composure slipped. A wounded look flashed across her face, but Crispin was pouring wine for Michael and didn't notice.

Julia recovered, then turned to Michael and said, 'So, there. He knows me better than anyone else.'

'But sometimes our own personal happiness has to take a back seat,' Crispin added. 'You need to earn a living, and like Michael said, this film has put you out there. Made you visible. You need to seize the moment. You may not have another chance.'

Susannah jumped in. 'The man's wise, Julia. You should listen to him.'

'I suppose if you want to go back to London, you could do theatre,' Crispin said.

'You know I can't do theatre. I couldn't stand up on a stage in front of a live audience every night.'

'Then what will you do when you get older? Find another Jona?'

A stunned silence fell over them. Susannah shot Crispin a horrified look. Julia slowly lay down her fork and folded her hands in her lap, and when she looked up at him, there were tears in her eyes.

Crispin was furious with himself. It was the only time in his life that he had ever willingly caused her pain.

'I'm sorry,' he murmured. 'Forgive me.'

Susannah rose then and began to clear the table, and Michael followed her lead.

When they had gone into the kitchen, Crispin said again, 'I'm so sorry.'

Julia brushed away a tear and said softly, 'But you're right. I do have to think about these things.'

'You'll be okay. You'll find someone to take care of you.'

'*That's not what I want, damn it!*' she lashed out, flinging her napkin onto the table and rising from her chair. 'That's the very thing you've been warning me against! And I listen to what you say because you always get it right!'

'I don't always get it right. You make me out to be some kind of a saint. I'm no bloody saint, Julia!'

She gave him a wounded look and then marched up the stairs to her room.

Later, Susannah and Michael drove into Deauville, and Crispin sat by the fire, trying to concentrate on a book. For a long while he debated whether or not he should go up to her room. He would be leaving early the next morning, and it struck him that he might never see her again. For a while he heard her footsteps creaking on the old floorboards overhead. Then the house grew silent. Crispin put out the fire and went to bed.

In the morning he rose before dawn, and before he left the

273

house he went back upstairs and stood in front of her bedroom door with his heart pounding. Finally, he summoned
the courage to knock softly, and when there was no answer,
he opened the door and looked in.

She was awake, and she rolled over and sat up, and in the
deep shadows you could see only the faint outline of her head
and shoulders against the white pillows.

'Crispin?' she whispered.

'Did I wake you?'

'No. I've been awake. I was going to get up to see you off.'

'You don't have to.'

'Don't you want some coffee?'

'I'll stop in Deauville. Not to worry.'

'It's raining, isn't it?'

'Yes.'

'Drive safely.'

'I will.'

There was just a moment of silence while Crispin stood in
the doorway gripping his keys in his hand.

'I couldn't go without an apology,' he said. 'I'm sorry for
the way I spoke to you. I was suffering from wounded pride.
It's a guy thing.'

He wanted very badly then to stay and explain everything.
All it would take was a small gesture on her part, a tiny indication of what she felt for him, and all the barriers would
come down.

Julia looked at him, standing in the dark doorway with the
collar of his raincoat turned up around his ears, and the thought
of expelling him from her life terrified her. But she would
have to rise above her fears and love him the way he needed
to be loved.

'Could you come in?' she asked. 'For just a second?'

He approached the bed and she reached out and took him
by the hand. Her hand was warm.

274

'Sit down here,' she said, patting the edge of the bed.

He sat down next to her.

She spoke very quietly, but her voice was cool and controlled. 'You're a very special friend,' she began. 'My most special of friends. You always will be. And I'm so sorry if I ever led you to think I felt anything for you other than just deep affection.' She paused, and Crispin withdrew his hand. 'Sometimes when men and women are friends it's hard to keep it balanced. Sometimes we tilt a little towards the physical and the romantic. But that's not what I feel for you. Not really. And I don't want you leaving this morning thinking there may be something between us other than friendship. At least not for me.' She smiled, and then scolded gently, 'You took me a little by surprise, you know.'

'I'm sorry for that.'

'No, you shouldn't be. It was good. That way we got it out in the open. It's been haunting us a little, hasn't it?'

Crispin nodded, feeling a little like a chastised schoolboy.

'I will see you again, won't I?' she asked gently.

'Of course. Nothing's changed,' he said. It was such a bold-faced lie. It would never be the same between them again.

He drew her hand to his lips and kissed it.

'God bless you Julia.' He rose from her bed and went out and quietly closed the door behind him.

30

Crispin's warning about the future of her career had a harrowing impact on Julia's outlook, and she vowed to rebuild the infrastructure of her life. To work again, and as soon as possible, became a clear priority. Her old Hollywood agent, who had often been offended and frustrated by Jona's interference, was now succeeding in getting her considered for films Jona never would have agreed to. In June she flew to London to audition for a role in a Hollywood studio production with a big budget and a maniacal director, and the next day her agent called and announced she had the role. It was a major departure from anything she had done before – the story of a single mother who welds her own identity as she struggles to guide her teenage rock star daughter through the tumultuous corridors of early fame and wealth.

'I can't believe they wanted me!' she cried to Susannah over the phone.

'You underestimate yourself.'

'I thought the audition was dreadful.'

'If they cast you it's because they know you've got the emotional range to do it. Don't start doubting yourself.'

'It's a fabulous script. And doing this right on the heels of the Brontë film really breaks me out of the mould.'

'Look, Julia, I know this is delicate, and I don't want you to take it the wrong way. I know Jona's death was a tragedy for you, but he had you trussed up like a Thanksgiving turkey. And I think this is just the first glimmer of the silver lining in that cloud of yours. Now, having said my piece, tell me, where will they shoot it?'

'Los Angeles.'

'Good. Maybe this will be the kick in the butt you need to get you over there. Once you're there, maybe you'll stay. And Crispin's there, isn't he?'

'He's up in Santa Barbara.'

'Close enough. Are you still in love with him?'

Julia was struck silent.

'Aha,' Susannah teased. 'I hit a nerve, didn't I?'

'You're wrong,' Julia said in a controlled voice. 'I was never in love with him.'

'Ha!'

'We're friends. That's all.'

'That fight you two had at dinner that night was not the kind of fight friends have. That was a lovers' quarrel.'

'He's married, Susannah.'

'Yeah. And a priest. I suppose you're right to go into denial. You shouldn't mess with that combination.'

'He did me a favour that night. It was cruel, what he said, but it worked.'

'I've been trying to send you the same message for years. You just wouldn't listen. When Crispin talks, you listen.'

'Well, we don't talk much anymore.'

'That's too bad. Because you two sure had something extraordinary.'

Although determined, Julia had little experience in fending for herself, and she questioned her every decision, praying she was doing things for the right reasons. Behind every move she made was the hope that Crispin would approve, and beneath that was a constant struggle to free herself from the need for approbation. Confusion and indecision bogged her down at every turn, until finally she plunged in and signed a one-year lease on a bungalow apartment in the hills north of Sunset in west Los Angeles that her agent found for her.

In Crispin's absence, Maddy Cartwright had become caretaker of the house in Normandy. Although Julia and Maddy spoke occasionally over the telephone after Crispin's departure, there seemed to be a natural reticence on both sides to talk about him except in broad, guarded statements. But with Julia leaving, the house would be rented, and in July, Maddy drove up to take a look at the house, and together they went from room to room, discussing what should be done to ready the place for rental.

Maddy opened the door to Lola's room and poked her head in.

'Oh my goodness. He'll never be able to rent it like this.'

'I think it's absolutely fabulous!' Julia smiled. 'What little girl wouldn't love a room like this?'

'I don't know. I just hope we'll find someone so he can keep up the mortgage payments,' Maddy sighed.

Julia sank down on the bed. 'Sit down, Maddy,' she urged, sweeping aside a few old stuffed toys. 'Tell me about him. How's he doing? Has he found a new parish yet?'

Maddy lowered her heavy frame onto the squeaking bed. 'No,' she answered. 'He hasn't.'

'Why? He's such a marvellous priest.'

'Indeed he is. The best.'

'Then why won't anyone take him?'

Maddy fixed her with a steady gaze. 'He's been blackballed, at least that's what the Bishop told me.'

'Oh no,' Julia cried. 'Why?'

Maddy stretched out her legs and stared down at her swollen ankles. 'Phoebe left him back in April. Right after he was elected dean.'

'*What?*'

'He was essentially blackmailed. Tom Noonan took his

devotion to you and twisted it into something very lascivious and lurid, and did such a darn good job of it that just about everybody, including Phoebe, believed it.'

Julia's hand flew to her mouth, and she suddenly felt sick to her stomach. She jumped up from the bed and ran down the hall to the bathroom.

Maddy waited quietly, listening to Julia retching.

After a while, Julia returned. She was a little pale, and she sat down next to Maddy and Maddy reached out and patted her hands. They were wet and cold, and she was trembling a little.

Julia was focusing on the illusionary Narnia.

'Crispin did that,' she said softly. 'He is so very much in love with his children.'

'And you're in love with him, aren't you?'

Reluctantly, Julia nodded. Tears glistened in her eyes. 'But he doesn't know it. As a matter of fact, I told him just the opposite.'

'When was this?'

'The last time I saw him.'

'Phoebe had left him by then. She'd gone back to the States.'

'So they were already separated.'

'Yes.'

'I had no idea. He never told me.'

Julia reflected in silence for a long moment, and then she said, 'Even if he knew how I really felt, Maddy, nothing could ever happen between us.'

'Why do you say that?'

'Because it would prove them right. It would seem like we'd been having an affair all along.'

'It doesn't make any difference now. The damage is done.'

'Oh, no,' Julia contradicted. 'It would make all the difference in the world to his daughters. Those girls are the backbone of his soul. It's what they believe that matters to him.'

Julia took a deep breath and rose, then helped Maddy to her feet.

'What colour shall we have them paint this room?' Maddy asked.

'Something neutral,' Julia replied.

31

Phoebe had truly loved Crispin, but over the years, and since his calling, he had matured into a man with values starkly different from her own, and she returned to Santa Barbara resolved to find a new husband more suited to her material needs, if not her heart. Santa Barbara was the Promised Land for Megan who had always dreamed of living the California life. Lola missed her father too much to be happy, although he saw them every weekend. Perhaps Caitlin suffered most from the upheaval; she was like her father, a combination of sobriety and passion that had truly blossomed in a place as wonderful as Paris, and she had lived there at an impressionable age when attitudes and opinions are formed. She had always been proud to be the daughter of a priest, and her father had been canon pastor, and nearly dean, of that most beautiful cathedral, and she had hoped to grow up there. She deeply resented her parents' separation and the sweeping changes it had provoked, and as time went on she began to see more clearly the role her mother had played in the destruction of her father's life.

Phoebe urged Crispin to relocate to Santa Monica, a beach resort community on the west boundary of Los Angeles and reasonably close to Santa Barbara. Crispin acquiesced, although he felt pretty much a misfit. Santa Monica's population was comprised primarily of hardcore high-achievers with sophisticated needs and tastes. It was a hard place to be ordinary or humble.

But Crispin kept himself focused on the one thing that brought him joy: his children. He took Phoebe's advice and – swallowing his pride – accepted a generous loan from her parents to enable him to sign a lease on a two bedroom apartment overlooking the ocean. It was furnished in taupe leather and chrome and glass with soothing neutral colours throughout. The girls loved it because it was thoroughly modern, although Crispin found it impersonal and was very lonely there during the week when the girls were away.

Numerous churches had initially shown keen interest in his candidacy only to suddenly cool with no apparent reason, and after several promising positions had fallen through, Crispin made a call to Bishop Stroup in Paris and confirmed what he had suspected: a certain clergyman, highly placed in the Los Angeles diocese, had been blocking Crispin's candidacy. It did not come as a surprise to learn that the man was a friend of Tom Noonan's. Noonan's long arm of moral authority had reached all the way across the ocean to strangle whatever life remained in Crispin's career as a priest.

The interviews were always a struggle for Crispin because he was inevitably obliged to be candid and forthcoming about the scandal with Julia and the misappropriated church funds. He grew tired of defending himself and reasserting his innocence time after time. He was fiercely protective of Julia, and inevitably someone would raise intimate questions, and he would once again proclaim the chaste nature of their love, then leave the interview in a stifled rage because it hadn't been a lie before but now it was.

Crispin had never been the kind of man to shift the blame to others for his own misfortune, but neither was he blind to the mean intentions of self-serving men who would sabotage the welfare of others in order to serve their own ambitions. He felt betrayed by his own kind.

There was an Episcopal church nearby which he attended

weekly, but it only underscored his own sense of loss, for he was a priest, and he had no parish. He missed performing Holy Eucharist and all the ritual surrounding it – the weight of the cross, the silver chalice cool to the touch, richly worked vestments in vivid hues of greens and purples according to the seasons, the crack of the thin wafer echoing through the silence of the great cathedral, and that awareness of being part of a miraculous transformation. No one kneeled before him now with expectant eyes lifted to his, waiting for him to deliver grace, and no one trusted him with their conscience or their soul.

Even though he was living among tribes of displaced people like himself, Crispin didn't reach out to any of them. There was misery all around him – Santa Monica was a retreat for the homeless as well as the affluent – but he felt he had nothing special to offer them. When he passed them on the street, he would stuff dollar bills into their hands and then walk on.

At first he took up aviation insurance again, just to make a little income while waiting for a calling. But right away it felt good to be back in the secular world where no one was judging him. He was very good at it. He was tenacious and struck just the right note with people, and they trusted him which was critical. His reputation grew by word of mouth, and his client base expanded quickly. At first it was just a temporary measure, but then the commissions started to come in, and it was a relief to be able to reimburse Phoebe's parents and pay off some of the debt that had smothered him for so long.

Crispin was firmly resolved to conceal his unhappiness from his daughters, and when they came to visit he took them rollerblading along Venice beach, or to the zoo, or on a whale-watching excursion, or for a weekend on Catalina Island. But there were weekends when they just wanted to stay in, and they would rent videos and light a fire in the fireplace even though it was in the seventies outside, and Crispin would sit with Lola curled up on his lap and her head on his chest, and no one would say much throughout the evening. Sometimes Lola would just wrap her arms around him and quietly cry as if she held a mirror to her father's heart.

Despite Crispin's attempts at stoicism, the girls could see their father was not the same man he used to be; he'd lost something invisible and vital, like he'd lost the fire in his belly. Megan and Caitlin, who had very little in common, were united in their desire to see their father happy. They often talked about it when they were alone, and they began to forge a new closeness, and they almost never argued when they visited him.

Sometimes the four of them would start reminiscing about Paris, remembering things they had liked or disliked. Lola liked the fact that waiters would bring water for your dog and he could sleep under your table in a restaurant. Megan missed seeing buckets of flowers on the pavement in front of the florists, and how they were so lovely and smelled so fresh in the rain. Crispin admitted he was struck by how impatient Americans seemed, and Caitlin reminded him of how he used to get so frustrated in Paris because the owner of the dry-cleaner's always chatted so long with all his customers. Eventually Crispin had figured out that merchants enjoyed getting to know their clients, and that this relationship was important, so he learned to wait in line because impatience was rude.

On special occasions, Crispin would take them out to the girls' favourite restaurant – The Ivy, a bistro where movie stars in dark glasses lunched elbow to elbow on the terrace. It was great entertainment for the girls but nervewracking for Crispin, because there was always the chance that he might run into Julia at a place like that. He knew she was in Los Angeles now – Maddy had kept him informed – but Maddy had never said exactly where she was living and Crispin had never asked. Whenever they went to The Ivy, Crispin would hurriedly down a Scotch before their meal came, just to calm his nerves, but then someone with Julia's walk or her colour of hair would pass by his table, or a certain familiar laugh would cut through the chatter, and his heart would skip a beat. The girls noticed moments like this because their father had always been such a good listener, and there were times when, for no apparent reason, he would just disconnect from them.

One thing the girls had never anticipated was that other women might find their father appealing. But seeing the four of them out together was the kind of thing that touched a nerve in mature single women – a very attractive father (no wedding ring) and his three young daughters in a subdued and exclusive little world of their own. Oblivious to all others, they rattled on simultaneously to one another on a myriad of unrelated topics while they nibbled on bread, sipped Cokes and played games like hangman or tick-tack-toe with the youngest (who spoke in French) while waiting to be served. Even though he was not out there to get noticed, and this was a town where getting noticed was a fiercely competitive game, Crispin generated something special that made him stand apart from other men. Women seated at tables next to them would turn and smile engagingly at him and his children, and often they would try to catch his eye. It was not uncommon for the girls to come back from the ladies' room to find a woman at an adjoining table had struck up a conversation with their father. Sometimes the women even left their phone numbers. Their father was always polite about it; he would take the napkin or the business card that was offered, but when they got home he would always fish the number out of his pocket and screw it up and toss it in the bin. The girls teased him about it and asked him why he didn't ever call any of them. He'd smile and give one of them a hug and say he didn't really want any other women in his life. But even Lola knew this wasn't true.

It was late on a Thursday afternoon in March and Crispin had just walked in the door when Megan called. He had spent most of the day dealing with a fatal accident involving one of the Gulfstreams he insured, and he was glad to hear his daughter's voice. Megan was so excited that Crispin had to make her repeat herself several times. Even then he could only understand enough to know that she was talking about Julia.

'Dad,' Megan said, nearly breathless. 'It's this really big deal and it's formal.'

'What's formal?'

'The party, and we get to ride in a limousine . . .'

'What party?'

'For her movie! Julia's movie!' Megan was talking in hieroglyphics and losing patience with Crispin's inability to decipher.

'You mean the Brontë film she made last year?'

'Yes! She invited us!'

'You mean she's invited you to the première of her film?'

'Not just me, all of us!'

'All who?'

'Dad!' she cried. 'You are soooo frustrating! I told you!'

'You mean you and your sisters?'

'Yes!' she shrieked.

'Well, I didn't know if you meant me, or your mother . . .'

'She said she wanted to make up for not inviting us to the set. It's okay, isn't it?'

'How does your mom feel about it?'

'She's not home.'

'You mean you haven't talked to her about it yet?'

'Look, you want to talk to Caitlin? She's here.'

'Yeah, pass me to Caitlin.'

Caitlin's mind worked a little more like Crispin's, less of

the shotgun effect, more of the blanks filled in.

He could hear excited chatter in the background, and then Caitlin came on the line.

'Dad?'

'Hi, sweetie.'

'It'll be okay, won't it?'

'Of course.'

'You think Mom will go for it?'

'Why wouldn't she?'

'Well, you know, it's Julia . . .'

'Your mother has no reason to bear any grudges against Julia. We're all pretty clear about that now, aren't we?'

'Yeah,' Caitlin answered. 'At least I am.' There was a shade of resentment in her voice. Caitlin and her mother did not get along very well now that Crispin wasn't around.

'The only thing that might annoy her is that she didn't get invited herself,' Crispin teased.

'But she is invited. So are you.'

'We are?'

'Yeah, but us girls get to go with Julia in the limousine.'

'"We" girls. Not "us".'

'Whatever.'

'It all sounds pretty cool to me.'

'Dad, don't talk like that. I hate it when you try to talk young.'

'What? Cool isn't cool vernacular?'

'Here's Megan.'

The telephone was passed back again, and Megan said, 'I'll have Mom call you when she gets back.'

She hung up.

Crispin didn't have anything at home to eat except some stale pretzels. He had planned on running to the store that evening but he put it off to wait for Phoebe's call. By eight-thirty she still hadn't called, but he wasn't about to ring her and look eager, so he finished the pretzels with a bottle of Corona and watched CNN until the phone rang.

'Problem is, there are just five tickets,' Phoebe said.

'You talked to Julia?' Crispin asked.

'Yeah. I called her back.'

Crispin was too stunned for a moment to reply. Phoebe said, 'She was very gracious. She wrote us a thank you note, you know.'

'A thank you note?'

'For letting her stay at the house in Normandy. I thought it was pretty nice of her.'

'You didn't tell me you'd heard from her.'

'Well, anyway, she said since we didn't ever get a chance to visit her on the set when they were making the movie, maybe we'd like to attend the première. Apparently it's a big formal thing. She said the studio's really pushing the film. They think they might get some Oscar nominations.'

'Hey, that's great.'

There was a pause, underlining the awkwardness they both tried to fly around all the time. Then Phoebe said, 'But with just five tickets . . .'

'We don't have to sit together, Phoebe. You can go with the girls.'

'But the girls get to ride with Julia. And apparently she's got special seats for them in the row right behind her.'

'You mean it's like a reserved seating thing?'

'Yeah. The other two seats are together.'

There was silence, then Crispin said, 'You have somebody you'd like to take?'

She took a moment to reply, and then said gently, 'Well, yes, I do.'

'Then take my ticket.'

He would have liked to see her face just then. 'Are you sure?'

'I'm sure. And do me a favour. Check out Heath McEwan's hands.'

It took a second for it to sink in, and then she laughed. It was sweet, bell-like laughter that he hadn't heard in a long time and he wondered if she had been as miserable as all that for the last years of their marriage.

'You're so good to me, Cris,' she said.

He almost replied with something conciliatory, and then he caught himself and said, 'Yeah, well, just pay me back some day, Phoebe. Go out of your way to do something generous for me.'

It stunned her, because he had never really talked to her like that before.

'I will, Cris,' she said, and she hung up.

32

Crispin Wakefield truly liked women, and if at times the feminine nature vexed him, more often than not, it awed him. Other men might lament the absence of a son, but not Crispin. He was a romantic at heart, and he loved the messy, baffling poetics of females. This much he had in common with the French male, whom he had often admired choosing bras and bedsheets with his wife, both uncoerced and unself-conscious, operating on the principle that home furnishings and his wife's underwear were as much for his pleasure as hers. Crispin knew men who could barely conceal their contempt for anything feminine, and many others who were bored or indifferent. In Crispin's opinion, these men were a little freakish, strangely stunted in their humanity. And sharing a home with four females had only reinforced his appreciation of women. He rather enjoyed shopping with his daughters, but shopping had been Phoebe's sacred cow, and money had always been an issue, so that Crispin had generally been relegated to the role of tightwad and grump.

So it was that the invitation to Julia's première gave him the opportunity to appear to his daughters in a new light. Without Phoebe around to run the show, he involved himself in their lives in a way that both amazed and delighted them. As soon as they arrived on Saturday morning, Crispin hauled them off to Melrose Avenue to shop for the event. They tried on dresses and ordered hamburgers and milkshakes at an outdoor terrace, and in the Beverly Centre he watched them spray perfumes on one another and test eyeliners and eyeshadows on their wrists, and open box after box of shoes. There were inevitable disputes and they often grew impatient with one another, but there was also a new cohesiveness that all of them felt. Phoebe had always assumed a certain pre-eminence in her daughters' lives by reason of gender, and pleasures such as this were her prerogative. But Crispin proved her wrong that afternoon. He enjoyed himself thoroughly, and that weekend the girls found much to appreciate in their father, not just because he had opened his wallet, but because they were seeing him without the restraining, possessive presence of their mother.

Since the première was in Los Angeles and fell on a Saturday night, it was understood that the girls would be picked up at Crispin's place. Crispin brought in a hairdresser to style their hair, and a cosmetics lady from Nordstrom's to do their make-up, and he sat around that afternoon with the television tuned to a basketball game and tried to stay clear of their bedrooms. The girls were so excited that they refused to eat the sandwiches he had made for them, so he broke down and ordered pizza which they did eat, although the hairdresser ate most of it. All afternoon there were squeals and squabbles and singing to bass-heavy music, and the constant roar of the hairdryer, and the smell of bubble bath and hairspray and perfumes, and he loved every minute of it.

He took pictures of them, and watched from the balcony as they appeared on the stairs below, taking the steps cautiously, a little wobbly in their high heels with beaded bags dangling from their wrists as they made their way to the waiting limousine.

He was hoping to catch a glimpse of Julia, but the chauffeur closed the door and the limousine pulled away, leaving Crispin feeling very empty and thinking how stupid he had been to give his ticket away to Phoebe.

He went around the apartment tidying up, and he had an armload of wet towels when the telephone rang. It was Caitlin.

'Hey,' she said, sounding very adult. He could hear excited chatter in the background.

'You three all looked so gorgeous walking out of here.'

'Thanks for everything, Dad,' she said.

'Hey, don't thank me. This is Julia's doing.'

'Not entirely,' she said, and it felt like everything in his chest froze up on him. It was Julia's voice.

'Hi there,' he answered. He had to clear his throat, and he hoped she didn't notice.

'These girls look so beautiful. I may need a bodyguard for them.'

'Hey, a great big thanks,' he said. 'I hope you know how much this means to them.'

'It's my pleasure, I promise you.'

'I'm sorry I'm not getting to see your film tonight.'

'Yes. So am I.' He sensed she wanted to say more, but there were too many ears listening.

'I understand there's a party afterwards,' Crispin said.

'Yes, but I'll have them home whenever you say. What's their curfew?'

'You can have them as long as you want.'

'You sure?'

'Absolutely.'

'Then they can stay with us for as long as they can keep their eyes open.'

Excited cheers erupted in the background.

The woman who arrived at the entrance to the Mann Chinese Theatre that evening to give brief interviews to the press and pose for photographs alongside her director and leading man, had all the appearances of perfection – the dress, the hair, the style, the smile. No one would guess by looking at her how difficult it had been for Julia to get here tonight. Michael Langham remained at her side, reassuring her throughout the event, and she was doing beautifully until just around midnight, at the post-screening party, when she began to experience a familiar smothering sensation. Then, all of a sudden, her heartbeat surged. She excused herself and hurried outside to the limousine parked in the lot behind the restaurant where the party was being held. The chauffeur waited outside to give her a little privacy as she huddled in the back, trying to control her breathing so she wouldn't pass out. Finally, the rapid pounding ceased, and, hands still shaking, she opened a bottle of water from the bar and poured a little into her hand to cool her face. The attack left her trembling and a little sick in her stomach, and she pressed a button to open the sunroof. It was cool and misty, and she sat breathing the night air while the nausea passed. She was trying to summon up the courage to return to the party when she heard the chauffeur speaking to someone and she looked out and saw it was Caitlin.

Julia opened the door and called to her, and Caitlin turned towards her. 'It's okay,' Julia said. 'Come on. Get in.'

Caitlin hurried up to the car and climbed in next to her and shut the door. Cat had tried to look sophisticated and glamorous like Megan, but her blue velvet dress — chosen for its slimming effect — seemed dull beside Megan's teal chiffon. But her eyes were dancing this evening, and she was having the time of her life.

'How's it going?' Julia asked. Her voice was weak and a little shaky, and she hoped Cat wouldn't notice. 'Having a good time?'

'Oh yes,' Caitlin enthused. 'It's just all gone by so fast.' She turned a big smile on Julia. 'I just came out to tell you that Mom's leaving, and she wanted to know if you wanted her to take us.'

'Are you ready to go home?'

'Not really,' she replied.

'Then you don't have to go. I'll have the driver take you back whenever you're ready.'

'You sure?'

'Absolutely.'

It was very unlike Cat to do what she did just then, for she was a reserved child; she threw her arms around Julia and hugged her.

'Thank you so much for tonight,' she muttered into Julia's shoulder.

'Oh honey,' Julia said, returning the hug, 'It's so good to see all of you again.'

'I sort of missed you,' she said shyly.

'You did?'

Cat nodded. 'It was cool, being your friend.'

'I liked being your friend, too.'

'You did?'

'Yes, I did.'

'You sort of like the same things I do.'

'Did you like the film?'

'Oh yes. Very much,' she answered. She sat back and looked up at Julia with a shy smile. 'It made me think I might want to be a writer when I grow up.'

'Really?'

Cat nodded again.

'I bet you'd be very talented.'

'Why?'

'For a start, because you're very sensitive. Your father's like that.'

'You don't see Dad anymore, do you?'

'No,' Julia replied. Then, after a pause, 'How is he?'

Cat shrugged. 'He's okay, I guess.'

Julia waited, and finally Cat said, 'He's changed a lot.'

'How?'

Cat shrugged. 'I think he really misses being a priest.'

'I'm sure he does. It was very unfair, what happened to him. He didn't deserve any of it.' Julia looked down at Cat's hand resting in her own. 'It's too bad he didn't come this evening. I would have liked to see him again.'

Cat couldn't help but notice the way Julia's voice grew a shade softer, and the way Julia avoided her eyes.

'He wanted to come,' Cat replied.

'That was very good of him, to give up his ticket to your mother.'

'Yeah.'

'Maybe we could have lunch sometime. All of us together. You think you could handle that?'

'With Dad, you mean?'

'Yes.'

'That'd be cool.'

'You wouldn't be uncomfortable?'

'Not me.'

'How about Megan? And Lola?'

Cat shrugged. 'I think they'd be okay with it. They like you.'

'Then we'll do it.'

'I wish we could all go back to then.'

'To when?'

'To when we were in Paris. Before everything went wrong.'

The girls returned home a little after midnight. Lola, who had fallen asleep in the car, was carried upstairs by the chauffeur and delivered to Crispin, who carried her off to bed while Megan and Caitlin staggered to their room, leaving a trail of shoes and handbags on the carpet. Crispin had Lola propped on the edge of her bed, and was stuffing an arm into her pyjamas when Cat came in to kiss him goodnight.

'Had a good time, huh?'

'Oh yeah,' she said, and she watched while Crispin pulled back the covers and rolled Lola into bed.

'What is it?' he asked, sensing there was something on her mind.

'Oh, I'll tell you in the morning.'

'What? Your mom's new boyfriend?' Phoebe had finally told him, that she was dating a surgeon introduced to her by her tennis instructor.

'No. It's about Julia.'

Crispin switched on the Dalmatian nightlight beside Lola's bed, then turned off the table lamp. 'How's she doing?' he said in a whisper, hoping his voice sounded normal.

'Do you like her?'

'Of course I do.'

'I mean, like a girlfriend. Could you like her like that?'

'Honey, Julia thinks of me like a brother. A friend. Nothing more,' he replied, closing the bedroom door. Cat followed him around the living room as he tidied up.

'I think it's more than that,' she said.

Crispin straightened, shoes in each hand. 'Oh?'

'That's just the feeling I got, from the way she talks about you.'

'Well, I think you're misreading it. Everybody always did.'

'Maybe things have changed.'

'I don't think so. I'm pretty sure I know how Julia feels about me.'

'What about you? How do you feel about her?'

He stood there for a long time, his heart pounding, and then he finally said, 'Do you want the honest truth, honey?'

'Yeah. I do.'

'I think if ever I gave my heart away to anyone again, it would be to Julia.'

'I think that'd be pretty cool,' Cat smiled.

'Do you, now?' Crispin replied lightly, but tears were burning his eyes.

'You know, in some ways, I think Megan really likes it better now that you and Mom are getting divorced.'

'What makes you say that?'

'Because she doesn't have to pretend like she hates you.'

'Megan doesn't hate me. She's just acts like that to please your mother.'

'It's all just so Mom'll buy her things,' Cat said sourly.

'Well, I think sometimes Megan gets a little scared. She's afraid her mom will make her choose between her and me. But that's not going to happen.'

'I'd like it if Julia came around. I think Julia'd be good for you.' She gave him a kiss on the cheek. 'Goodnight, Daddy,' she said, and she turned and went off to bed.

On Monday Crispin got a call from a secretary saying Ms Kramer deeply regretted that he hadn't been able to make it to the première, and that she was calling to invite him to a private screening of her film on Thursday evening on the Warner Brothers lot in Burbank.

'Just a few intimate friends,' the secretary said.

Crispin didn't have high expectations of the evening. He didn't think he'd have a chance to speak to Julia alone. On Thursday evening he drove into the Burbank lot and gave his name to the security guard at the entrance. A receptionist directed him to the screening room, but when he arrived the theatre was empty. He found a seat and waited impatiently, checking his watch, convinced he had the wrong place or the wrong time, but a few minutes later a man entered and unlocked the projection booth, and then Julia arrived.

Crispin got to his feet and she saw him and came down the aisle towards him. She slipped into his row and hurried up to him, hand on her chest, a little out of breath.

'Hi,' she said. 'Sorry, I'm late.' Her eyes betrayed a certain wariness, but there was warmth in her voice and her smile.

'Hello, Julia,' he said softly.

It had been a year, and neither of them knew how to begin nor what to expect. For the moment, there was no superficial chatter, only a silence both awkward and sweet.

'Gosh,' she said, cutting through the nervousness with a grin. 'I don't think I've ever been tongue-tied with you.'

Crispin laughed, and it broke a little of the ice, although he was wary too. 'Yeah. Pretty strange for us, isn't it?' He shifted his eyes towards the back. 'Who else are you expecting?'

'Crispin,' she said gently, laying her hand on his arm. 'I need to tell you something before anything else is said between us. And I just hope that . . .'

'What?'

She took a deep breath to steady herself. 'I lied to you. What I said to you that morning in your house in Normandy, when you came to my room, when you were leaving. Do you remember what I said?'

'I remember.'

'It wasn't true.'

He hesitated. He wanted to make sure he understood her correctly. 'What part wasn't true?'

'About being just friends. I said that my feelings for you were strictly those of a friend. Nothing more. But I lied. I feel so much more, Crispin,' she confessed, her eyes locked onto his with a pleading intensity. 'So much more.'

It took a moment for it to sink in, and then a boyish grin slowly spread over his face, and he looked a little like an unsuspecting kid who'd just been asked to the prom by the girl of his dreams.

'You're kidding me,' he teased.

'No,' she insisted. 'It was all an act.'

Crispin took a deep cleansing breath. He was feeling a little giddy.

She went on, 'I don't have any idea what your situation is now, if you're dating someone, or what, but . . .'

He silenced her with a kiss.

This time, Julia returned the kiss.

'There,' she murmured. 'That's what I really wanted to do last year, but I couldn't. I couldn't let that happen.'

'I know.'

'You didn't tell me about Phoebe. You led me to believe everything was fine.'

'I thought it was best.'

'I understand,' she said, pressing her fingers to his lips. 'You don't need to explain. I understand.'

He leaned forward to kiss her again.

'Crispin,' she whispered, slipping her hands around his neck, 'we can work it out, can't we? With the girls, I mean.'

'I think so,' he smiled, and kissed her eye and then her ear. 'I hope no one else shows up,' he whispered.

'They won't,' she answered with a teasing smile.

'I thought this was for a small group of intimate friends.'

'It is,' she replied. 'You and me.'

He threw back his head and laughed.

'Oh, Cris,' she said as he enfolded her in his arms. 'It's been so hard keeping away from you all this time. But there was just so much confusion in my life, and I wanted to be sure I was in love with you for the right reasons.'

'And are you?' he asked, kissing the top of her head.

'Most definitely.' She sighed deeply. 'But are you sure you want me?'

'I'm sure.'

'But I come with so much baggage.'

'I know, Jules. I was there when you packed it.'

'I guess you were.'

They were interrupted just then by the projectionist who came out from the booth to ask if Ms Kramer was ready to begin. Julia looked up at Crispin.

'Anytime,' he mumbled, his face so close she could feel the word on his lips.

'You know,' she said, slipping an arm around his waist and pulling him closer. 'Maybe we should reschedule this.'

'You mean the screening?'

'Yes,' she said.

'Would you rather do something else?' he whispered, sliding his hand down her hip.

'I'd rather do more of this,' she whispered in his ear.

'Well, if it's just the two of us . . .' he suggested with a smile.

'It is.'

Crispin signalled to the projectionist. 'You can start anytime,' he shouted.

The projectionist disappeared back into the booth and the lights dropped.

'Sit,' Julia ordered. 'I'll be right back.'

'Where are you going?' He was holding on to her, but she slipped out of his grasp.

'Stay there,' she called to him as she hurried up the aisle to the booth.

The studio logos flashed by on the screen, and then the music came up, and Crispin looked over to see Julia coming towards him down the row of seats.

'Come here,' he said to her, pulling her across his lap. 'The closer, the better.'

Julia settled onto him and wrapped her arms around his neck. 'I don't really think I need to see this film,' she said with her mouth against his ear. 'You can watch it. I'd much rather look at you.'

'I think I might have a hard time paying attention.'

'You know, there are a couple of scenes in here where I was imagining Heath was you . . .'

'Now that's a cute little twist,' he muttered. She was doing things to his ear that took his breath away. 'Can I ask him to leave?' Crispin asked, with a nod towards the projection booth.

'He's already gone,' she replied softly, and she raised herself slightly and tugged on her zipper. 'I told him not to come back until the end,' she said as she squirmed out of her jeans.

'How long is that?' Crispin asked, as she straddled him.

'Exactly two hours and twelve minutes.'

'That's not long enough,' he murmured while he unbuttoned her blouse.

Eyes closed, she whispered, 'How long do you need?'

33

It was a little awkward at first, being lovers and being free. They were a little self-conscious, furtively glancing over their shoulders, but eventually they relaxed and behaved like others did. They walked hand in hand down the street, and kissed in parking lots and looked very much in love. They were always reserved around the girls, but the girls could see they were in love, and they accepted it, not because it was easy, but because they needed their father to be happy again.

The sexual fulfilment came only at the end of a long affair of the heart and mind and soul; they were a remarkable fit, Crispin and Julia, and a formidable couple. When Crispin revealed to Julia all that had happened and the role that Tom Noonan had played in spreading the rumours that prompted his resignation and ruined his career, Julia's indignation was colossal. More than anyone, she knew the truth of the matter, and she felt Crispin's disgrace deeply.

Julia believed in Crispin the way he needed a woman to believe in him, and she saw in him what he valued most about himself. She refused to let him give up the life they both believed he had been called to lead. Eventually, armed with a letter of protest signed by hundreds of parishioners of St John's, and a dossier of testimonies, Crispin went directly to the Bishop of the Los Angeles diocese and stated his case. An enquiry into the matter brought to light unethical procedures practiced by certain powerful clergy, and in the end, Tom

Noonan's friend in the diocese was dismissed, and Tom himself received an official reprimand for his conduct in blocking Crispin's candidacy.

It took a while, but eventually he was called, and interviewed, and within a month he had offers from two very prestigious churches, both of which he refused. But then there came an opening with a church in the Hollywood Hills, a struggling parish that served widely disparate needs – young families on welfare and young professionals, a number of homeless and elderly and unemployed, and the fact that Julia encouraged him to go for the interview was an indication of how well she understood him.

As part of the interview process, it was customary for him to give a Sunday sermon as a visiting priest. Crispin arrived early, and Julia slipped into a pew with Caitlin to wait for the service to begin. But the waiting made her nervous and so she went searching for Crispin and found him in the vestment room, putting on his purple stole.

Her hands were shaking when she reached to adjust his collar, and he snatched one of them and kissed it.

'Why are you so nervous?' he asked. 'I'm the one giving the sermon.'

'I'm sorry,' she said, and he could see she was taking it all so earnestly. 'I just want this so badly for you.'

She was radiant, despite her nerves, dressed in a crisp spring dress with her hair chopped short. She had put on a little weight, and he had never seen her look so happy.

She plucked a piece of lint off his robe. 'Turn around,' she said. 'Let me see you.'

He spun slowly around, and she looked at him proudly, then clasped her hands together. 'Oh, Crispin,' she said, and tears came to her eyes and she fanned at them, and then both of them laughed.

'Honey,' he said, 'if it's right, then it'll happen.'

'Do you like the church? Would you be happy here? Because if you're not, then don't take the job. You'll get other offers.'

'You sound like you have doubts.'

'Not at all,' she protested.

'I like it here,' he answered. 'I think it's just what I need. It's a good fit.'

'I think so too.'

'We're in this together. This is going to be your life too. You need to be honest with me.'

'I am.'

He kissed her on the cheek. 'Go. Get yourself a seat.'

'Cat's saving me a place.'

'You're on the end, I hope.'

'Yes.'

'If you feel an attack coming on, you just slide out of there. Don't worry about what people will think.'

'Crispin,' she said with a look that stilled him, 'even if I had a heart attack right there in the pew, I wouldn't so much as squirm.' She kissed him again. 'I'll be fine. We'll both be fine.'

'I have you to thank for this,' he said.

'I love you, Crispin Wakefield.'

'I love you too, the soon-to-be Mrs Wakefield.'

'Oh,' she exclaimed. 'I do so like the sound of that.'

They stood there in the narrow cloakroom holding hands and beaming at one another as the organ prelude concluded with a blast of trumpets.

She kissed him on the cheek. 'Go,' she said. 'I'll put your things away.'

He swept out, looking all priestly and wonderful. As much as she loved him, in all the ways that she loved him – when he was being funny, or making love to her, or playing with his girls – she loved him best like this.

The processional hymn began, and Julia hurried to hang

his jacket in the locker reserved for visiting priests. As she was closing the door, she noticed something sticking out of his pocket.

She knew what it was; Crispin carried it around with him like people carry pictures of their children and spouses and dogs. She pulled it out and took a look at it again. It had been handled a lot and was a little dog-eared.

It was a postcard that she had sent him from Haworth just after his visit. The greeting was short and unsentimental, but he hadn't kept it for the words. He kept it for the photograph.

The image was that of heathery moorland bathed in mist-filtered light, and in the distance, at the highest point of the hills receding into a hazy blue horizon, there stood a gnarly wind-bent tree beside the stone ruins of an old Yorkshire farmhouse. It was a striking image, because of the vast emptiness all around and the solidarity of those two surviving creations, one natural and one man-made. They represented everything that is common and ordinary in life. A weathered tree and a crumbling stone house. And it seemed as if, over time, they had fused together in a state of perfect symbiosis.

Julia knew exactly why he kept it.